Hunting FOR LIGHT

Tripp Blunschi

For Karen, Best Wishes

Tripp Blunschi

Blue Castle Books
P.O. Box 421
Roopville, GA 30170

ISBN: 978-0-9898148-2-9
v1.0

Contents

For my family,

Kimberly, Holden, and Sydney

*You **are** my light.*

Notice to Mariners

Notice is hereby given that at sundown on Friday, the 1st day of July next, the new light-house and beacon on the north point of Hunting Island, S.C., will be lighted, and will be kept burning during that night and every night thereafter from sunset to sunrise.

The Lighthouse Board
March 8th, 1859

CHAPTER ONE

THE QUESTION SURPRISED HER. Rachel Willers felt as if she had slipped over the edge of the Grand Canyon, and the sudden feeling of falling made her sick to her stomach. It was a feeling well known to her, and one she knew would come frequently—just not at the front gate of the campground, one minute after she arrived.

"Just me," Rachel said.

The white haired woman at the gate looked up from her clipboard. "Just you?"

"Well, not exactly just me. I have Riley to keep me company." The yellow lab sitting in the passenger seat of the brand new Fleetwood motorhome barked.

"What's a pretty young girl like you doing camping all by herself?" the woman asked in a proper southern drawl.

That was a much more difficult question to answer. Rachel had asked herself the same question over and over the last two years and had never been able to answer it. She wasn't sure she ever could. And young? At thirty-seven she felt much older than that, and this trip probably wasn't going to help. In fact, it shouldn't have happened for at least another twenty years or so.

For a moment she was angry with John. Angry he wasn't here. Angry that he put her in this position. But then she realized how unfair that was. It wasn't his fault. It wasn't that sweet woman's fault either, and Rachel decided not to answer her. The woman didn't push for one, and Rachel was grateful.

"Have you been to Hunting Island before?" the woman asked.

She had been. Several years ago when she and John first started camping, they heard about this beautiful campground on the coast of South Carolina. They'd been a couple of times since, but she decided to keep her answer simple. She nodded.

"You're going to be in site fifty-four." The woman handed Rachel a parking pass and an information booklet. "Between you and me, and the biggest darn raccoons you'll ever see in your life, it's the best site we have here on the island. If you'll pull straight in and angle the front of your motorhome so the windshield is facing the beach, you'll have the whole right side to yourself. Complete privacy, and you couldn't ask for a better view of the ocean."

"That sounds wonderful!" And it really did. The last two years had been more than stressful. Besides, not having to back the forty-six foot Fleetwood into her site was welcome news. The salesperson at the dealership had been kind enough to give her a few driving lessons, and even though the Fleetwood had a backup camera, it just made her nervous.

"My name is Beverly Duncan. Me and my husband Charles are the camp hosts. We're in site fifty-five. That's right behind you, so if there's anything you need, just stop by, okay?"

"Thank you so much."

"No problem." Beverly looked down at the paperwork, flipping the first page back and forth. "And Mrs. Willers—"

"Oh, Mrs. Duncan, please call me Rachel." Hearing his last name, even though it had been hers for the last seventeen years, was just too painful.

"Okay Rachel, and you can call me Beverly." She took two steps back and stretched her neck, peering down the side of the Fleetwood to the Jeep Rachel was towing. "But really, if you need anything...anything at all, you just let me know."

"Thank you, Beverly." Beverly sounded so sincere. She reminded Rachel of her own grandmother: permed white hair, a tad overweight, and what seemed like a pretty good intuition. A true southern lady.

"All right, and if you have any trouble with the hook-ups, just let me know. I'll send Charles right over."

"Okay. Thanks again." Rachel pressed the gas pedal, and the big diesel engine started to lurch the Fleetwood forward.

"And Rachel…if you need help unhooking your Jeep, I can send Charles over to help."

"Oh, that's okay, I think I can—"

"Charles!" Beverly's voice had no problem being heard over the Fleetwood's engine. Years of practice, Rachel thought. "Charles!"

A man sitting in the shade next to the camp store folded the top corner of his morning paper just enough to peek over the top of it.

"Can you help Rachel unhook her Jeep? She's in fifty-four."

He folded up his paper and took off his glasses, slipping them inside the front pocket of his shirt.

"And after that, make sure she's facing the right way, would you?"

Charles lifted his lanky body off the bench and stepped into a gas powered golf cart used for maintaining the camp.

"And Charles?"

Charles glanced back with an irritated look on his face.

"Help her with the hook-ups, too." The only acknowledgement Beverly received was the sound of the golf cart cranking up.

Charles was a big help getting the Jeep unhooked and the Fleetwood situated. Rachel and John had been no strangers to camping, but he had been the one who took care of hooking up the electricity, water and sewer, and leveling and stabilizing the camper. It was her responsibility to get the inside ready, making it cozy for the two of them. But Rachel and John's dream had always been to camp in style, and that's why she bought the brand new, state-of-the-art, Class A motorhome; a far cry from the inexpensive travel trailer they had used in the past. Though the dealership had been more than helpful, and she'd read the manual over several times, it was nice to have some assistance.

Beverly was right, site fifty-four was beautiful. The front of the motorhome faced directly towards the ocean, which meant the door and awning opened up to the south. There were no other campsites in that direction, only the open view of the beach that curved slightly to the right, back towards the protected wildlife refuge. There was plenty of room for her and Riley to play, with a nice sized patch of St. Augustine grass that covered the area, almost like a front yard. A walkway ran from her site through the small protected dunes to get to the beach. It wasn't her own walkway, but from where it was situated, there would be no reason for anyone else to use it.

After a quick walk to let Riley stretch his legs, she took some time making her home as comfortable as possible. Following her and John's camping tradition, she'd bought some fresh cut flowers in Beaufort and put them in a vase, placing them on the dinette table in front of the window. She set out a water and food bowl for Riley. In the bedroom she placed a couple of small pictures of her and John on the nightstand. She checked and rechecked her drawers to make sure her clothes were like she wanted, and in the bathroom, she set out the few things she needed. All in all, there wasn't a whole lot to prepare.

That was the whole point of having a nice, big motorhome; everything was already done. The only requirement was to open the slide-outs and enjoy. And this Fleetwood had many items to enjoy with a number of standard luxury amenities: convection oven, big screen television, satellite dish, sound system, washer and dryer. She spared no expense, upgrading to marble flooring, leather trim, and opting for the warm honey cabinetry. She paid almost three thousand dollars extra to have a pull out grill kitchenette installed on the exterior. It really was a remarkable piece of camping equipment.

It had everything.

Everything except John.

The last couple of months had been easier because she kept busy with planning. She sold most of the furniture, donated much of her clothing, and sold the travel trailer and truck. Except for her home, almost everything she owned was either here with her and Riley or in her brother's basement back in Atlanta. When the house sells, which could take months in the current economy, she'd be free of that as well.

She decided not to make any plans for the first week to see how everything went. But now that she was actually here, sitting in the recliner without anything else to set up, she looked over the beautiful interior, with all of its fancy furnishings and gadgets, and realized how empty it felt without John. True, the first day wasn't over yet, and the Fleetwood's diesel engine hadn't even cooled completely, but she was beginning to think she made a terrible mistake.

Anticipating she'd feel this way, she made a vow to herself to at least give it the summer before making any big decisions. It was going to be hard, and God knows she wanted John to be here with her, to live out their dreams together. But that wasn't the hand they'd been dealt, and even though she knew that, even though she knew she needed to move on with her life, she wasn't sure she could without him.

She decided there would be plenty of time for visiting the beach, and honestly, she really didn't want to, so forgoing that, she heated up a chicken Florentine frozen dinner and poured herself a glass of cabernet sauvignon.

She and John had always enjoyed a bottle of wine when they camped in the past, and out of habit she set two wine glasses on the table. She'd eaten most of her meal before she realized the mistake, and just like before, when Beverly Duncan had simply asked how many people were in her party, a nauseous pang swamped her stomach. Fixated on the wine glass, she sat motionless for a moment as the reality of the situation began to sink in. Her jaw began to tremble and tears streamed down her face, dripping onto the cardboard box of the frozen dinner.

She couldn't bring herself to sleep in the bed that night. With Riley on the floor beside her, she sat curled up in the tan, leather-trimmed recliner, listening to the sound of the waves gently rolling up onto the shore. She watched the warm, salty air rustle the fresh cut flowers next to John's empty glass. Rachel Willers cried most of that evening, and somehow, sometime before dawn, she fell asleep.

CHAPTER TWO

RILEY NUDGED THE RECLINER. He placed his snout next to Rachel's feet and looked up at her with his big black eyes, but she didn't move. He gently pawed the chair, shaking it ever so slightly to try and wake her. After several attempts with no reaction, he added a whimper to the mix.

At first, Rachel wasn't quite sure where she was. She recognized Riley's whine, and it comforted her to know he was there, but her senses seemed foreign and strange. She heard the sound of waves crashing and a couple of children arguing over whose turn it was to use the shovel. Her eyes opened, and through her clearing vision, she noticed the fresh cut flowers and John's wine glass sitting on the dinette table. Though her next thoughts were laced with the pain of waking without John for the first night, she was glad it was behind her. Riley barked to let her know to give him some attention as well.

"Okay boy, hang on." It was tough prying herself out of the recliner, and her body ached as she stood. Still wearing the clothes she had on from last night, she put on her sunglasses, then leashed Riley up and stepped outside into the bright sun.

"Afternoon!" a woman's voice called. Rachel looked up and saw Beverly sitting in a camp chair under the awning of a huge tan and brown Winnebago straight out of the seventies. It was situated right behind Rachel's Fleetwood. Potted plants and white, decorative latticework surrounded the base of it. Beverly had a book in her hand, but Rachel couldn't catch the name of it. She could tell by the cover that it was a romance novel.

"Afternoon," Rachel replied, in a groggy voice. She looked at her watch. Eleven-forty. She shook her head in disbelief.

"I see Charles got you all squared away yesterday?"

"Yes, he did. He was such a big help. Thanks again."

"That's what we're here for, honey. Anything you need, just holler. How was your first night?"

It was a nightmare.

"It went fine. You were right about the site. It's truly beautiful."

"Well, I'm glad you like it."

Rachel smiled and started to walk away, but Beverly apparently wasn't done yet.

"I saw on your registration that you were going to be staying with us for the summer?"

Rachel was prepared for that question, so she spit it out just like she'd rehearsed in her head. "That's right. I'm a writer. I thought I'd come here for some inspiration and write by the ocean." That was a lie. She wanted to be a writer, but wasn't one yet. She came because that was the plan. It had always been the plan.

Beverly gasped. "Really? Would I have read any of your work?"

She was ready for that question too. "No, I've mostly written for corporations: marketing ads, correspondence, newsletters…things like that. But I've decided to take the plunge and try my hand at writing a novel. Hopefully I'll get a first draft completed before the end of summer." The novel part was true. The corporation part was also true if typing e-mails counted.

"That sounds like such fun. I've always wanted to be a screenwriter, myself. There's something so alluring about the silver screen—the golden era of film. Hepburn, Grant, Bogart, Astaire and Rogers. So romantic." Rachel recalled the cover of the novel Beverly was reading. From the looks of it, it was a *different* type of romantic. "I'm also an avid reader," Beverly continued, "so if you need someone to proofread your book, I'd be happy to help."

"Thanks Beverly. I just might take you up on that."

Rachel turned around and walked away, halfway expecting Beverly to say something else, but she didn't. One thing Rachel was right about: Beverly seemed to be just like her grandmother. Well, except for the romantic part…or at least she hoped.

7

Rachel walked Riley all over the campground. It was composed of seven loops, each making its way through various campsites. Most of the loops were shaded under live oaks and pine trees, and some, like hers, meandered along the edge of the beach with fabulous views of the ocean.

There was something reassuring about most of the campgrounds she had visited, from children bicycling along the loops and trials, to the elderly that stayed inside playing cards in their expensive motorhomes. At night, the scent of campfires and charcoal mixed with the smell of mosquito repellant. Most of the campsites were lit with a varying assortment of lighted ropes or tiki torches. Rachel loved the nostalgic feel of the atmosphere. It was honest and endearing. Campers were a great big family, and though there were exceptions, most everyone was always in the mood for a quick introduction, conversation, or a good laugh.

She and John had always looked forward to their next camping trip, the next new park they hadn't visited, the next neighborly family. It was nice knowing, even after a bad day's work or some unfortunate circumstance, that a trip was planned in the not too distant future where they could spend each moment together for a few days, away from it all.

One by one, she walked past the three sites she and John had stayed at before. The first was located on one of the few primitive sites reserved for tent camping. That's where it all started—their first camping trip together. The site was situated in a secluded area next to a pond, a hundred feet or so away from any other sites. She remembered opening their brand new tent. She could still smell the scent of the new polyester fabric, how they fumbled with it for what seemed like hours to get it to stand correctly, and how it came down on top of them the first night while they were making love. The next morning, they discovered they'd been devoured by mosquitos because John had left one of the flaps unzipped.

The next season, they decided to buy a small pop-up camper they pulled behind their car. John was scared to death about backing it into a site in front of people, so they made sure to reserve a pull through site. As she walked past it, she remembered how far away it was from the beach, so they decided to camp closer next time. Owning the pop-up was really where camping turned into a way of life for them, and they wore it out the next few years exploring The South and their new love of camping.

It took them a few years to return to Hunting Island, and as Rachel walked past the last site, she remembered what a perfect trip it had been. The site was located on the beach, on the other end from where her new Fleetwood sat now. Because their financial situation had improved, they decided to buy a used travel trailer and new truck to pull it with. The weather was perfect, and the travel trailer gave them the privacy they needed after long walks on the beach.

That trip to Hunting Island had been the last of the camping season, and unbeknownst to them, the last of their lives, where their dream of living out their golden years in that fashion would end. That was two and a half years ago, and it was only a few weeks after that, before one of the coldest winters that Atlanta had seen in years, that John was diagnosed with cancer.

Once Rachel returned to the Fleetwood, she made a call she should've made last night.

"Hey Cynthia, it's me," Rachel said.

"So, you're alive, right? I can call the police back? Tell them you're okay?"

"Yes, you can call them back. I'm sorry for not calling you last night. I guess I just lost track of time."

"Yeah, well next time I'm sending in the Coast Guard. You really had me worried."

"I know. I'm sorry."

"So, how was the drive?" Cynthia asked. "Were you scared?"

Rachel *was* scared. Not on the highways so much, but on the side streets where she was concerned she'd get trapped if she had to back the Fleetwood up. "Nah, it wasn't a problem at all. I had lessons from the dealership, remember?"

"Well, I would've been shittin' kittens. No way in hell I could make that drive. So, how are you?"

Rachel cleared her throat. "Oh, I'm good. I didn't have any trouble getting everything hooked up or—"

"Oh, no! You're not getting off that easy. You know that's not what I mean. I mean how are *you?*"

"I'm good Cynthia."

Silence.

Rachel looked at the empty wine glass still sitting on the table. "Okay, it was a pretty tough night. But I knew it would be. I mean, even though he never saw this motorhome or anything that's in it, I just got this feeling he was here with me. For a while it felt good, you know? But as the hours went by, I started to feel so empty. I'm beginning to think you were right. Maybe this was a stupid idea."

"Well, I'm always right, but you're in it now. You've already spent all that money. You need to make the best of it."

Rachel knew she was right about that. John's life insurance had been more than enough to keep her going for a while, but if this motorhome idea didn't work out, she'd lose her butt on the resale value. The idea of blowing that money made her sick to her stomach.

"Any good looking guys?" Cynthia asked.

That churned Rachel's stomach even more. "Yeah, Cynthia, as if I were looking at guys. When are you going to stop with that?"

"When you *start* with that! You can't go around your whole life alone. I mean, you'll never be *alone* alone, you'll always have me…but you know what I mean."

"Maybe after the summer, after I work on this crazy idea that I could write a novel. Maybe then."

"You're lying."

Again, dead silence. You can't trick a good friend.

"It's been over two years, Rachel."

"We've been over this Cynthia. Two years is nothing, we had almost two decades together. I can't just *turn it on* all of the sudden because you want me to."

"That's not what I mean."

"I know it's not what you mean, but I have to do this on my terms. That's why I'm here. I just got here yesterday, and a man is the absolute furthest thing from my mind right now. This motorhome, this trip, the rest of our goddamned lives were supposed to be about us."

"Okay, look I'm sorry Rachel. You know I just want you to be happy."

"I know you do, and I *want* to be happy. I think one day I can be, but I really think I have to go through this first."

"Okay. Just promise me you won't stay cooped up in that motorhome all the time. Get out and enjoy the beach, have a few cocktails, go skinny dipping in the ocean on a moonlit night."

"I'll call you in a couple of days Cyn."

"I'll call the Coast Guard. I wasn't kidding."

After Rachel fed Riley and grabbed a bite to eat, a turkey sandwich and carrot sticks, she went back to the bedroom and found her bathing suit. As far as clothing goes, it was one of the few new items that she'd bought. It was a simple, black one piece that fit her well—not that anyone was going to see it, because she also bought a black and white, striped cover-up.

She slipped on the bathing suit and looked at herself in the mirror. She turned from side to side studying her body. Considering everything she'd been through, she was fairly satisfied with how she looked. Her breasts looked natural for her size, and if she had any complaints about them, it was that they were on the smallish side. Never having children of her own, she wondered how much that contributed to their current shape. She stood on her tiptoes and her calves still had good definition. She'd always been proud of her legs. If she ever wore another pair of high heels, something she seriously doubted, she was confident that at least her legs would look good.

Her face was another matter. She looked in the mirror at her blue eyes with disapproval. Ever since the weight loss, they just never seemed to recover. Her eyes seemed sunken and dark. Cynthia had told her she was crazy, that she looked great, and once she got serious about looking for someone, they were going to be all over her.

Rachel had been about fifteen pounds overweight and had already started a diet before John was diagnosed. But there's nothing like a good tragedy to help a girl shed some pounds, and once John died, she really began to lose too much. More and more pounds came off for the next six months until she looked just this side of anorexic.

She had to give Cynthia credit for that one. She kept on her to start eating more, and after a lot of persistence, it worked. It took Rachel almost a year before she felt like she was somewhat healthy again.

But as she looked at her face in the mirror, she was skeptical, and doubted anyone would notice her. Quite frankly, she couldn't care less. Cynthia's wishes about her finding someone were just going to have to wait—maybe permanently.

Rachel brushed back her hair and noticed it was a bit tangled, probably due to the increased humidity. She thought about grabbing a quick shower, but then shrugged it off and pulled her hair back in a ponytail. She was going to the beach anyway and figured she could take a shower once she returned. After putting on her cover-up, she threw on a straw hat and a pair of wide, black sunglasses to hide her atrociously sunken eyes, and headed for the beach.

Although it was low tide, which considerably extended the size of the beach, there were plenty of people enjoying the sand and sun, but not in a resort kind of way. She'd been to Panama City and Daytona when she was younger, and more recently, Myrtle Beach. Those places were slammed with vacationers living in condos, and the beaches were always packed. While she enjoyed it in her younger days and certainly understood the draw, Hunting Island only had so many sites, so even if everyone came out all at once, there would still be plenty of beach to enjoy.

After setting her bag down, she unfolded her chair and stabbed a beach umbrella deep into the sand. She brought a Kindle reader with her, and planned to catch up on a few novels she'd been meaning to read before starting to write one herself. But as she took it out, she caught herself looking over the beach, realizing why she and John had liked it so much.

The beach still had that camp feel to it. She always thought it was because there weren't nearly as many young adults or older teens around like there were at resort beaches. By the time most kids turned sixteen, the last thing they wanted to do was hang out with their parents at some camp. The beach here reminded her of what she imagined beaches would've been like in the 1950s.

To her right, a boy and his father were attempting to fly a kite into the wind that was much too strong for it. It lifted up for a moment, looking like it was going to make it, but then, after a couple of quick figure eight turns, it crashed into the ground. The father laughed when his son stomped his little foot in the sand. They tried again and again, but didn't have any luck, and the little boy grew angrier by the minute. Rachel noticed a woman sitting in a beach chair in front of them, surely the boy's mother. She covered her mouth with her hand, laughing through her fingers with each failure.

To Rachel's left was a pool of water, perhaps only two feet deep. Kids with snorkeling gear and nets were searching for crabs or other unfortunate sea creatures that got trapped by the outgoing tide. Ever since her first visit, the large pool of water had always been there, filling up with seawater at every high tide, then filling up with playful children at low tide.

In front of her, a boy and a girl were building a sand castle. The brother, obviously the architect, instructed his younger sister to fetch water for the moat. Every time his sister came back with a pail full of water—a pail that was almost bigger than she was—her brother poured it in the moat, watching it dissolve away into the sand. Then he'd say, "We need more water, Bella." Rachel could tell the little girl was getting frustrated, but wanting to see the moat also, she did as she was told and gave her brother more water. Soon, fed up with her brother's instructions, she jerked the pail out of his hand one last time and stomped off towards the ocean. Rachel almost laughed out loud when Bella returned and dumped the water right on top of her brother's head, completely destroying one of the castle towers. Bella ran away as fast as she could, but her brother quickly caught up with her. Their parents had to separate them, both oblivious to what had happened.

Rachel first noticed the older couple as they stood and talked to a fisherman who was trying his luck on the south end of the beach. Both of them wore white beach attire and looked to be in their late sixties or early seventies; it was getting harder to tell these days. The husband, a little overweight and apparently a fisherman himself, was engaged in some discussion about the type of bait he was using. The thin wife held her husband's hand and attempted to look interested.

She nodded her head occasionally and pulled silver strands of hair away from her face that the wind had caught from underneath her hat.

As the conversation came to a close, the couple waved goodbye and continued their leisurely walk over the wet sand, letting the small waves lap over their bare feet. When they reached a point directly in front of Rachel, they stopped and turned to face the water. The wife pulled herself a little closer and placed her head on his shoulder. The husband put his arm around her and gently kissed her forehead as they watched two blue herons dive into the ocean, hunting for fish.

You've got to be kidding me.

Rachel pulled up the end of her cover-up and wiped her eyes. No sooner had she put her sunglasses back on, she heard a familiar voice.

"You mind if I pull up a seat next to you?" Beverly asked.

"Oh, yes…I mean no…not at all." Rachel slid over a bit, giving Beverly some of the shade from her umbrella. She swallowed, trying to ease her throat that had swollen after watching the sweet older couple.

"I hope I'm not intruding, just tell me and I'll go." Beverly plopped herself down in her chair.

Rachel thought that Beverly was being a little forward, but honestly, she was glad to have the distraction. "No, you're fine. I could use a little company to tell you the truth."

"Well, that's what I figured." Beverly placed her hand on top of Rachel's for a moment. Rachel noticed the nice, diamond tennis bracelet she was wearing. "I can always tell when someone needs a little conversation."

Already aware of the similarities between Beverly and her own grandmother, Rachel mentally prepared herself for what was coming.

"It sure is a pretty day out here, isn't it?" Beverly said. "Charles and I have been coming here for ages. We were so thrilled when they let us be camp hosts. This is our second time."

"Second time?"

"Yep. They don't let you stay forever. Every so often, the park will swap out camp hosts. We've been doing it for almost twenty years at various campgrounds."

Rachel realized that was only a little more than the amount of time she and John had been married. "That's a long time," she said. But she knew it really wasn't. Blink, and it's gone.

"Charles was a Colonel in the Air Force, and once he retired we wanted to travel. We bought a motorhome and spent a few years traveling across the country. As you can imagine, it became quite expensive, and though Charles' retirement is nothing to sneeze at, we decided to try the whole camp-host-thing to cut our expenses."

Rachel thought about Beverly's expensive looking tennis bracelet. Definitely nothing to sneeze at. "And you've been doing it ever since?" Rachel asked.

"Yep. We get to camp for free, and some places even pay us a little something."

"And you still like it, I take it?"

"Uh-huh. Plus, it keeps us busy so we don't sit around and stare at each other. Don't get me wrong," Beverly placed her hand on top of Rachel's again, "I love Charles, and I don't know what I'd do without him, but honey, I can only stare at him for so long before I just want to smack him one." Beverly lightly slapped Rachel's hand.

Rachel laughed and almost snorted. "But Charles seems so sweet!"

"Oh, he's sweet all right. Sometimes too sweet and I have to smack him one again." Beverly shifted in her chair and looked around, making sure there weren't any children close by. "Sometimes though, when he's getting a little too sweet on me, I give in and let him smack me around some, if you know what I mean."

Rachel gasped. "Beverly!"

"What?" Beverly shrugged, apparently enjoying Rachel's embarrassment. "You think us old goats don't get it on?"

Rachel gasped again, placing her hand over her mouth.

"Didn't you see the book I'm reading?" Beverly held up the romance novel. *Under the Frozen Tundra*. "Let me tell you honey," she pointed the book towards her lap and leaned in closer to Rachel, "there ain't nothing frozen in *my* tundra."

"Beverly! Oh, my God!"

"That's what Charles says!"

"Beverly!"

"What?"

Beverly and Rachel's conversation carried on for the next few hours with Beverly doing most of the talking. Rachel found out Beverly and Charles were originally from Beaufort—high school sweethearts—and that they were stationed at five different Air Force Bases, finishing up at Langley. They had two children, seven grandkids, and she used to have a miniature white poodle named Sputnik.

Rachel learned everything she ever wanted to know about the Officers Wives Club, or 'OWC' for short, or to be more politically correct, the 'OSC' for Officers *Spouses* Club, and why any man who happened to be married to a female officer would care to spend his time gossiping with a bunch of stuck-up women. She also learned a few more details about Beverly's sex life along with the sex lives of seven other women. Rachel was certain they'd be devastated to know what Beverly had divulged, especially when it came to the few affairs she mentioned. But then again, they were probably doing the same thing. For Beverly, Rachel thought, there was nothing more fun than opening up to a perfect stranger.

As Rachel walked back to the Fleetwood, she wondered if Beverly could be a put off to some people since she was so over the top. Rachel, however, liked her right away. She was charming, bubbly, and certainly vivacious. It was obvious to her that Beverly and Charles had shared a true love story, the kind she always imagined having with John. But she knew that was a little unfair. Okay…a lot unfair. Rachel and John had a love story like that—it just didn't end with *ever after*.

Yesterday had been rough, that much was true. The drive from Atlanta to Hunting Island was a long six hours. The closer she got, the more anxious she'd become, and she spent nearly the whole time wondering if she'd made the right decision. She was still unsure of that and figured it would be several weeks before she had a better answer to the question.

But the talk with Beverly had helped, and she realized she didn't feel as lost or as unsure as she did before. She wasn't sure why, it was just conversation, but there was no question that she felt a little better. It was the first inkling that she *had* made the right choice, and maybe this was the beginning of a new life.

Still, something in her soul kept nagging at her, like a low-grade stomachache, never knowing if and when she'd throw up. She was quite certain she knew the source of her pain, which was easy enough to figure out. What she didn't know was how to cure it, or even if it was curable.

One thing was certain: there is nothing like friendship to help people get through tough times. Cynthia was the best friend a girl could ever have, and she doubted whether she could've made it through without her. But Cynthia wasn't here. Rachel hoped she'd found a friend in Beverly Duncan.

When Rachel returned to the Fleetwood, she found Riley curled up on the couch, fast asleep. He didn't even raise his yellow eyebrows when the door opened. *Poor guy*, she thought. The trip must've taken a lot out of him too. Riley changed as well after John died, although it was always difficult to pinpoint how. He had less energy, and true, some of it was age, but she felt something else had changed about him. She wondered if he still remembered John. It was a long time ago for a dog, but she hoped he did.

After taking him for a quick walk, she noticed that feeling again in the pit of her stomach. She tried to convince herself it was only hunger, but with the scent of campfires and freshly lit charcoal drifting in the air, and the view of the darkening sky over the ocean, she realized it was because evening was approaching. Evenings with John were always special.

John had meticulously planned their meals, and more often than not, it wasn't your typical camping fare of hamburgers, pork chops, or barbecue. Instead, he'd prepare filet mignon, chicken cordon bleu, or a seafood trio of lobster tails, steamed mussels, and lightly grilled Ahi tuna. Even when money was tight, he still found ways to create memorable dishes for their special trips, like shrimp scampi, or inexpensive pasta dishes. Forever the hopeless romantic, he used to tell Rachel that a woman as magnificent as she deserved a meal of equal splendor.

As much as she loved those candlelit dinners, what Rachel looked forward to most came after, when the two of them would stroll along a camp trail or the moonlit sea shore, hand in hand, just talking.

She hoped she could handle her emotions better than last night, but she really didn't expect to. The best thing to do was face her fears head on. It might take a few days, or even a few weeks, but wasn't this the reason she was here? Wasn't it, that deep down, she knew she'd have to face them…alone?

Dinner was another frozen meal. She could cook a few things—like ramen noodles or a grilled cheese sandwich—but right now, frozen was easy. She had bought a whole array of outdoor cooking equipment, and hopefully later on she'd get to use some of it.

The empty wine glass from last night still sat next to the flowers on the table. She didn't have the heart to put it up. That was John's wine glass, and there it was going to stay. She forced herself to look at it as she ate, painful as it was, hoping it would help. But it only made her feel worse. She teared up as she forced her food down, knowing she needed strength for what lay ahead. After the few bites she managed to eat, she cleared off the table, leaving the empty wine glass and fresh cut flowers where they were.

She looked at Riley with resignation. "Okay boy, are you ready for this?"

Riley barked.

"I'm glad you are. I don't think I am."

Riley barked once more.

"Okay then. I suppose we don't have a choice."

Rachel slipped off her sandals before reaching the sand and placed them at the end of the walkway. Her heart pounded quick in her chest, and she found herself almost breathless. Willing herself to calm down, she closed her eyes and took in deep breaths, concentrating on Riley's leash wrapped around her hand. Soon, she regained control of her breathing and opened her eyes.

She saw the first hint of twilight on the horizon, and the moon, climbing from the northeast, had taken on the orange glow from the setting sun behind her. The ocean breeze, still warm but cooler than it had been earlier in the day, had died down considerably.

There was a certain familiar scent to the ocean at night. It smelled sweeter and more organic. One family had already lit a campfire on the beach, so perhaps that had something to do with it. But whatever the cause, Rachel recognized it instantly and it seemed to soothe her. With Riley by her side, she took the first steps towards the water— steps she knew would become more painful the more she took.

Soon, the bottom of her feet touched the hard, wet sand left over from the waves fading back into the ocean, and she turned south, continuing her walk along the shore. She felt the warm waves rush over her feet as they sank into the sand. At first, she thought this was going to be easier than she would've guessed. It's just walking, she convinced herself. No big deal.

She traveled a few hundred yards and even passed a young couple holding hands. Riley chugged along next to her, and she began to feel more and more confident. She really thought she was doing okay.

That's when she saw the lighthouse, the glass lantern room at the top still holding on to a few rays of sunlight. Memories of another time rushed into her mind, like she was there again.

It had been her and John's last evening during their first trip to Hunting Island, and they spent much of the night sitting in front of their tent, talking. Realizing how late it was, they took one last walk on the beach before turning in. The stars were bright and the moon was full as they strolled south along the beach, completely alone.

"Did you have a good time this weekend?" John asked.

Rachel nodded. "I didn't think I was going to like it at first, but I really did. I enjoyed myself."

"Me too. I know we don't have the money now, but once we retire, I could see us doing this full time."

"That's a ways off John."

"Yeah, I know. But if we plan it, we can start building up our gear now, eventually getting everything we need."

"But one thing though," Rachel said, "if we're going to be camping more often, I think you need to work on your tent building skills." She chuckled. "We don't need it falling down on us anymore."

"Hey, I doubt that had anything to do with tent building skills." He thought for a moment. "Baby making skills, maybe."

Rachel gasped playfully then bumped him.

John laughed. "Yeah, just think of the story we can share with our grandkids one day."

"We can never tell them about that? We can't tell *anybody* about that."

"Who knows Rachel, wouldn't it be cool to tell our daughter that's how she was conceived?"

Rachel's voice went soft. "That would be a neat trick, wouldn't it?"

"Yeah, but it could happen."

"You know what Dr. Roberts said. You were there."

"I know. But he didn't rule it out completely. There's still a chance."

"What if it doesn't happen, John? What then?"

John stopped walking, and turned towards her. He took both of her hands, and interlocked his fingers with hers. The lighthouse towered behind him, illuminated by the full moon. "And if it doesn't happen, then I will spend the rest of my days on this earth completely fulfilled, knowing that I was able to spend them with you."

"Are you sure, John?" Rachel looked up into his brown eyes.

"I've never been so sure about anything my entire life. I love you with all of my heart. I know you know that. Kids would be great, don't get me wrong. But our journey is about us. I wouldn't miss it for anything." He pulled her close and gently kissed her.

Rachel led him towards the lighthouse, and by the light of the moon she found a patch of grass underneath a live oak that bordered the beach, and they made love.

The wind picked up and blew across Rachel's face, and now she found herself sitting on a bench in front of the lighthouse with Riley lying by her feet. Completely dark outside, the orange moon had turned a pale gray as it moved behind the thickening clouds.

She pulled her hands tight into her stomach, one on top of the other, and with tears streaming down her face, she cried, "I'm sorry John. I'm so sorry."

That night, after Rachel found her way back to the Fleetwood and fell asleep, she had a dream. She was lying in a metal hospital bed inside the bottom of the lighthouse. The bed felt like it was floating, and the humid air fell from the darkness above, wafting over her body. She placed her hand over her stomach. It felt round and hard.

It moved.

"Push Rachel!" John stood next to her, his eyes focused between her thighs.

"Oh, my God! I'm pregnant!"

"Push!"

"I'm really pregnant, John!" She looked up at him as tears streamed down her face. "We're finally pregnant!"

Thunder clacked in the distance, and the lightning that followed revealed the wet, rusted metal of the lighthouse walls. The warm air began to swirl around her body.

"Push Rachel!" John yelled.

Rachel gripped the edges of the bed and pushed. The baby revolted and thrust itself back up against her stomach, fighting to stay inside.

"Harder, Rachel."

She pushed harder. Her stomach muscles ached and her hips began to burn.

"That's not enough. Harder. Push harder!"

She did, but the baby wouldn't budge, nestling itself near the top of Rachel's womb.

"I can't do it John." Rachel said. "I can't do it."

John put his hand on her forehead and he stroked her hair. "It's okay Rachel. Take a second. You can do it." He took her hand, lightly squeezing it. "I know you can do it. We won't be able to live happily ever after if you don't." His face stiffened and his voice sounded stern. "You're gonna push. You're gonna push as if the world depended on it…as if we depend on it. Do you understand?"

She nodded. Again, the thunder boomed and lightning lit up the lighthouse. Rain began to fall from the blackness above.

Rachel took several small breaths, and then drew in as much of the humid air as she could stand. She reached back to the metal headboard and gripped it with all of her might, and pushed as if their relationship depended on it. She focused all of her energy on her hips. She held her breath as she pushed, feeling her legs going numb. The baby resisted at first, trying to stay in the comfort of Rachel's womb, but it finally began to move forward.

"I see the head!" John's eyes grew large. "Push Rachel. Push!"

It rained harder, and the thunder so close it jarred the metal bed. The lightning flashed, lighting up the inside of the lighthouse once more.

"Push!" John yelled.

Then suddenly, the rain stopped. The thunder and lightning passed. The wind died down.

John held their baby girl against his chest and he cried. She looked just like him, so beautiful with a headful of dark brown hair. The baby gazed up into her father's eyes, cooing.

John seemed so happy, like on their wedding night. He looked at Rachel. There was no need to speak; his tearful eyes said it all.

Thank you, Rachel.

The baby began to cry, just softly at first, but then the thunder clacked in the distance and a steady rain returned. Their baby girl started to cry louder. The lightning flashed, reflecting the fear in John's eyes.

"What do I do?" John asked.

"I…I don't know?" Rachel sat up in the metal bed. The thunder boomed and jolted the lighthouse once more.

"Rachel, help me. Please help me!" The rain intensified and smacked at John's face. He tried to shelter his baby girl, but couldn't. The rain roared, and the wind wailed all around her.

Lightning struck the bed, then a flood of water funneled in from the darkness above, sweeping them all away.

Rachel sat up in the bed inside the Fleetwood and cried inconsolably into her hands. The rain pelted the brand new motorhome, and rocked it as the wind howled in from the sea. For a solid hour, the thunder clacked and the lightning bolted across the ocean sky like a web of synapses firing uncontrollably. The next hour, the rain let up and the thunder grew distant as the storm headed inland. By the third hour, the wind died down and all was calm. The storm was over. The sobbing was not. For Rachel Willers, the storm was just beginning.

CHAPTER THREE

SHE WOKE BEFORE DAWN. Rachel had been a morning person for as long as she could remember, but the fact that she was up at five-thirty in the morning had less to do with being an early riser and everything to do with being unable to sleep after that terrible dream.

Dressed in blue running shorts and a black tank top, Rachel plugged her headphones into her iPod and set it to shuffle through her collection of 80's and 90's pop music. She stretched her legs for a bit, and then she and Riley hit the beach.

Jogging had become an important part of her routine. After John died, the depression had been almost too much to handle. Her health declined rapidly, and she felt exhausted all the time. And quite frankly, she didn't care. For several months, as her desire to live plummeted, so did her weight. Feeling like she had nothing left to live for, she considered suicide as a way out.

Cynthia had been the one that really saved her life. She begged Rachel to eat more, and to appease Cynthia, she did. Gradually, she began to feel better and her energy level lifted. As part of that process—and constant persistence from Cynthia—she started exercising.

The real benefit came when she realized she could channel all of her anger, all of her sadness and pain, and focus it to drive those emotions from her mind. Instead of letting her feelings get the best of her, she decided to take them out on a pair of running shoes. Of course, that had only taken her so far, and she still had many demons to face, but at least it allowed her some peace.

She and Riley started their jog, heading north towards the tip of the island. The sand was still moist from last night's rain and the morning high tide was just starting to recede. The combination made for a nice, hard surface for her to jog on. The sun threatened to crack the horizon, and its orange glow beamed through the thin cirrus clouds left over from the storm, then stretched upwards towards the dark blue sky.

As they approached the tip of the island, where the ocean met the waterway that separated Hunting Island from Lady's Island, Rachel saw the distant silhouette of a fisherman casting a line. There was something engaging in his movements; the way the rod, some twelve feet in length, began its arc from the sand behind him, and then accelerated towards the sea, casting the hook beyond the breaking surf. The sun's rays danced on the line as he rhythmically pulled up on the rod, then reeled in the slack as it dipped.

The fisherman prepared for another cast as she approached. The sunlight pitched a warm yellow hue over the front of his body, and she could make out his features more clearly. He looked handsome, perhaps not better looking than John, but attractive in a more blue-collar kind of way. His light brown hair appeared thick and just touched the back of his shirt. The stubble on his face seemed to suit the angular shape of his jaw.

Even for a woman like Rachel, not actively seeking anyone, she could hardly ignore the alluring scene. She half-sensed that she was staring at him, and if he had turned to see her, particularly with the way the light was shining on her face, he would've known it. Luckily the sea had his full attention, and she was in no danger of being spotted. But every time she thought to look away, something else compelling about him caught her gaze.

He wore a light gray tee-shirt, and his muscles printed into it as the wind pressed it across his chest. The outline of his forearms and biceps flexed in the shadows when he slung the rod over his slim body. Knowing that she had nice calves herself, she was curious about his and found them to be well defined, matching the rest of his physique.

On a deeper level, he looked confident and strong—a hard worker. He seemed to be the kind of man that would do what he said he was going to do. But what did she know?

The fisherman didn't notice Rachel as she and Riley ran by, and she didn't turn around to see if he had once they passed. Why? For one thing, she wasn't interested, and for another, he could be married. But even so, she had to admit he was nice to look at. He'd be just the type of man Cynthia would try to hook her up with.

What is it with Cynthia?

Rachel wondered why Cynthia was pushing so hard to set her up with someone. Sure, she'd been right about life—that eating was somewhat of a requirement—but why so pushy about replacing John? As far as Rachel was concerned, there could be no replacement. She knew Cynthia was just trying to help, but both of her parents and all four of her grandparents were still alive. She'd never lost anyone close, so what the hell did she know about losing the most important person to have ever existed in someone's life?

Maybe Cynthia had been too smothering. Maybe it was partly her fault that Rachel was here, having nightmares and crying all the damn time. But she knew better. It was certainly unfair to blame Cynthia for Rachel's own shortcomings.

As Rachel and Riley jogged on, she tried flipping it around. What if Cynthia *did* know what she was talking about? Maybe she *should* be looking for someone. She was only thirty-seven, and really…did she think she'd spend the rest of her life alone? She didn't think so, or at least she hoped not. But love? She knew she'd never love anyone like she loved John. There would never be a replacement, and the best she could hope for was someone that would be happy just being her companion.

She and Riley reached the tip of the island and ran out of sand. By the time they made their way back, the fisherman had gone, perhaps trying his luck in a new spot.

After a quick shower and breakfast, Rachel turned on the television, flipping through the channels looking for anything good. All she found were soap operas and an infomercial about a cheese slicer.

Well, two cheese slicers…no…three cheese slicers and a peeler, all for $19.95 plus shipping and handling of $24.50.

She pondered the significance of the dream she had last night. This wasn't the first time she'd had nightmares about John, but none had been so vivid. Sometimes, they were of her and John lost in the woods and they couldn't find their way out. Other times, they'd be walking along in the city or at the park, holding hands when suddenly she'd fall into a gaping hole that opened up in the ground beneath her. John would reach for her, but not fast enough. She'd fall away, watching him become smaller and smaller until she was swallowed up by complete darkness. She never had a dream about him with a baby.

Deciding there wasn't anything good on television, she went to her bedroom and opened up her closet. On the floor to the right, sat a cardboard box. She stared at it for a second. Her eyes moistened, and she could feel the pain rising up in her chest. She quickly ignored it, and looked around for her blue and black backpack.

She took the backpack to the dinette and pulled out her laptop and turned it on. As Rachel waited for it to boot up, she glanced at John's wine glass. She wondered what the two of them would be doing right now if he were here. Getting ready to go to the beach? Just sitting and talking? Birthing babies and getting swept away in a flood of water?

Her computer beeped, indicating it was up and running. She launched her word processor and selected the *Novel Template*. A fresh project opened up, already formatted in proper manuscript form for submission to publishers. All she needed to do was write a few thousand words and voila!

The cursor flashed in front of the title on the page. It read *The Name of Your Novel* by *Your Name Here*. She deleted the name portion and typed *Rachel Willers*. Simple. Then, she deleted the template text for the title of the novel.

For five minutes she stared at the screen. There were twenty-six letters to choose from on the keyboard and not a single one came to her. The cursor kept flashing at her, like a heartbeat. She looked around the room for inspiration. Surely, there was something worth writing about.

Riley was sitting next to her feet, so she typed *My Beautiful Yellow Dog.* With that done, she began her novel—the one she'd waited her whole life to write.

My dog is the most beautiful dog in the world. His name is Riley. He is yellow and sweet and kind to children. John and I—

"Ugh!" Back to John again? She closed the lid to the laptop and closed her mind to her best seller at the same time.

"Come on Riley, let's get some air."

Riley barked in agreement.

The Fleetwood sported an automatic awning, and Rachel had opened it up the first day she arrived. Charles had pulled the wooden picnic table under it, so if Rachel decided to eat outside, she wouldn't get wet if it rained. She walked past the picnic table to one of the many storage compartments on the Fleetwood and opened it.

Inside, next to some boxes with *Winter* written on the side, she slid out a black guitar case and set it on the picnic table. She looked down at the case for a moment, wondering if she'd even remember how to play it. She opened up the latches and lifted the top open.

Inside the case, untouched since before John died, lay his acoustic guitar that she'd bought for him a couple of years after they were married. When he was a teenager, John used to play in a band, and actually, they were pretty good. They'd even created a couple of decent demos, but as with most garage bands, they split up and he never did anything else with it. They were fairly poor when they were first married, so he sold all of his music gear to help support them. Once they were better off financially, she surprised him with the guitar on Valentine's Day.

Rachel was afraid it was going to need a string change, but as she ran her fingers down the fretboard, it surprised her to find them almost new. John must have changed them sometime before he died, knowing she had never changed them before herself.

At first, she couldn't bring herself to pull the guitar out of the case. John was the last one to do that. Rachel sat down at the picnic table with her hands in her lap, hopelessly staring at the guitar.

This had to stop.

How pathetic to sit here, not wanting to pull out a stupid guitar from its case, because her husband was the last to do so. She convinced herself that if she was going to move forward, she had to take baby steps, and this was one such step. She yanked the guitar out and spun her body around so that her back was up against the picnic table, then she placed it on her knee.

Soon after John received the guitar, he taught her how to play it. She wasn't very good, but he taught her the basic chords: minors, majors, and sevenths—pretty much the necessary chords to strum out simple songs.

She strummed a G-major chord. Surprisingly, it was mostly in tune. She tweaked a couple of tuning keys and strummed the G again. It sounded good to her, organic and clear, ringing true in her ears. Listening to the sound of a recorded guitar was nice, she thought, but it wasn't the same as strumming it herself. Something got lost during the whole recording process.

She hung on to the G chord for a while, listening to the guitar's sweet, sultry tone. Eventually, she added an E-minor chord. Then she added C-major, D-major, and a D-seventh. She got lost in the progression, playing it over and over again, listening to the movement of the chords. She closed her eyes, feeling melancholy, and let her mind float. Her heart began to feel pain and sweet sorrow, barely aware that she was strumming the chords to *Unchained Melody* by The Righteous Brothers. She sang the words in her mind, letting the melody sweep her away to another memory, from another time.

She and John danced.

He held her close, his hands wrapped around her back, and hers around his neck. They swayed back and forth, turning slowly while they danced in his parent's barn. The music sounded tinny, coming from the cheap radio that hung on a nail near one of the horse stalls.

"Let's get married," John said.

"You know we can't. My parents would kill me if I don't finish school."

"I'm not talking about quitting school. I want to marry you. We can still go to college."

Rachel pulled back so she could see his face. His big brown eyes were soft and honest. "We can't, John."

"I don't know why we have to wait." His voice sounded anxious, if not frustrated. "I love you."

"I love you too, but we don't have to be married to love each other."

John pulled her close to his chest again. "I know. I just want to be with you. I want to live with you. I want us to have babies and grow old and—"

"Shhh." She squeezed his body. "Let's not get ahead of ourselves okay? One step at a time. We have our whole lives."

"I love this song," he said. "This is exactly how I feel about you. I *need* your love, Rachel"

She pulled back slightly and put her hands on each side of his face. "You have it."

"That sounds pretty," a young girl's voice said, snapping Rachel out of her daydream.

"Huh?"

"The guitar. It sounds pretty." The girl couldn't have been more than eleven. Her hair was dark brown, almost black, and she had a short boy-cut that looked a little out of place. Rachel wasn't sure she'd ever seen bluer eyes, like bright sapphires. They were framed by long, dark eyelashes, the combination of which seemed hypnotic. Her skin looked pale and her lips naturally red. She appeared thin, but not exceedingly so. She wore khaki shorts and a white top and carried a beach bag.

"Thanks," Rachel said. "Sorry, you surprised me."

"What's it called?"

"Huh?" Rachel was still a little dazed at the moment.

"The song. What's it called?"

"Oh. It's called *Unchained Melody*."

"Do you know the words?" The girl sat down at the picnic table next to Rachel

"Sort of."

"Can you sing them?"

"Oh, I'm not a very good singer at all." Rachel knew she had to change the subject quick, or she was about to be doing her best

Righteous Brother. Nobody deserved to hear that…ever. "What's your name?"

"Ellie. What's yours?"

"Rachel."

"Pretty." Ellie smiled at her. "So…Rachel…can you sing it?"

Shit!

"Um…" She needed a way out, and quick. "Do you play guitar?"

"Me? No. I paint." Ellie lifted her bag up in the air.

"Well, there's no time like the present to learn, eh?"

"Sure!"

Rachel carefully handed the guitar to her. Ellie held it, and it looked completely foreign, like she was holding a cinder block or something in her lap.

"Okay, scooch up on the end of the bench and straighten your back. Now cross your legs and place the guitar over your thigh, like this." Rachel situated the guitar on Ellie's leg. "Now…you *are* right handed aren't you?" Ellie nodded. "Good, now take your right arm and wrap it over the top and place it on the strings over the hole."

The guitar looked huge on Ellie's lap. She looked up at Rachel with a half-smile, her body somewhat contorted and awkward looking trying to hold it. "Is it supposed to feel this weird?"

"I know, don't worry. You'll get used to it. Everyone does."

"Well, I don't know about that." Ellie started rubbing her right hands across the strings, and the guitar sounded with muted thuds.

Rachel took hold of Ellie's right hand and positioned it. "Strum with your thumb. Up and down, up and down." The guitar still sounded muted, but a little better. "Now, here's the hard part. Take your left hand and wrap it around the neck, but keep your thumb pressed against the back of it." Ellie had to tilt the guitar back and up, and twist her whole body to see her left hand.

Rachel showed her how to make a G-major chord. For the next twenty or thirty minutes, they worked together, trying to get the chord to ring out. Finally, something musical started to resonate from the guitar.

"There you go," Rachel said. "Not bad, Ellie."

"Ouch, my fingers hurt."

"You'll get used to that too. I haven't played in a couple of years, and I was only out for a few minutes before you showed up, and my fingers hurt a little."

Ellie handed the guitar back to Rachel and stood up. "What's your dog's name?"

"Riley. He's my sweetheart, aren't you boy." Rachel knelt down to Riley, who was lying next to her feet. "That's a good boy." She looked up at Ellie while she rubbed him all over. "You know...he's the best dog ever. As in the whole world. In the history of the world, too!"

Ellie laughed. "Can I pet him?"

"Sure you can. Thanks for asking."

Ellie knelt down on her knees next to Riley and rubbed his head. "He's sweet. How old is he?"

"Seven."

"Well," she stood up, "I should go. Can I stop by some other time? Maybe you can show me some more of those..." Ellie looked up to the sky, thinking.

"Chords?" Rachel said.

"Yeah, chords. The ones to that song you were playing."

"Sure, I'd love to."

Ellie took about ten steps towards the beach, then turned around. "Rachel?"

"Yeah?"

"Thanks." Ellie smiled from ear to ear, her cheeks plumping up under her blue eyes.

"You're welcome, Ellie."

Ellie waved goodbye, and as she made her way towards the beach, Rachel couldn't help but wonder what it would've been like to have a daughter her age, just on the verge of growing up with a ton of questions and a world of dreams ahead of her. She knew as well as anyone, if not more so, that not all the answers were fair, and not all dreams come true. But just the same, she wished she could've been a mother for a girl like Ellie, to help guide the way, and to be there for her when things didn't work out.

Whoever was guiding Ellie's way seemed like they were doing a good job. She was polite, charming, and very sweet. A few times while she was strumming the guitar and had finally gotten the hang of it a little, Rachel saw her close her eyes and feel the music. Not just listen, but really feel it in her heart. There was something very genuine about Ellie, and she seemed mature for her age.

But there was something else Rachel couldn't quite put her finger on. Maybe she looked familiar, or perhaps reminded her of someone. Maybe herself?

Or maybe…Rachel wanted to be like Ellie. An innocent young girl without a worry in the world, unaware of the sadness that comes at the expense of love.

Either way, she looked forward to giving sweet Ellie a few more guitar lessons.

The rest of the afternoon went well for Rachel. She had lunch, then sat on the beach for a few hours and actually got in some reading. She watched children playing and couples holding hands, and considering how the trip had gone up to this point, it felt good that she was having somewhat of a normal day. For the first time since coming to Hunting Island, she relaxed a little. She admitted she felt okay yesterday talking with Beverly, but she wasn't sure she'd call that relaxing. Exhausting, more like it. It wasn't like she even had a choice in the matter, either.

For dinner, she ate her last frozen meal. Then, she spent the rest of the evening in her recliner and read some more of the novel she started on the beach. Seeing how she didn't get any sleep last night, she turned in early.

Before she drifted off, she thought about Ellie and how sweet she'd been. Ellie was going to make some lucky fella a happy man someday—if there was a good enough man that deserved such a sweet girl. To Rachel's knowledge, there had only ever been one man *that* good, and he was dead.

CHAPTER FOUR

HER LEGS BETRAYED HER. Rachel wasn't used to jogging on the sand, and the soreness in her calves reminded her of that fact as she rolled out of bed. Shuffling over to the bathroom, she washed her face and brushed her teeth, then put on a pair of red running shorts and another black tank top. She recalled from yesterday morning, the sunlight had shined in her eyes after the sun had come up. She put on one of those old style baseball caps she'd bought, and pulled her hair through the opening in the back.

Before she went out, she looked in the mirror and felt happier about what she saw. Maybe her eyes weren't so sunken in after all. She pinched her cheeks to bring out a little color. Today was going to be a good day.

The morning wasn't quite as picturesque as it had been the day before. Though still beautiful, there were no clouds to interact with the sun's rays, and the hue looked more yellowish than the orange of yesterday.

As she and Riley started their run, Rachel's legs immediately revolted, but after a few hundred feet, they loosened up a bit and she began to hit her stride. She ran a little more upright today, a little more confident. The exercise felt good, and she liked the way her chest felt as it expanded and contracted, stretching with each breath. Her lungs had grown in capacity over the last couple months, and she could run longer without discomfort.

As Rachel ran, she found herself looking for the fisherman from yesterday. He had looked so determined and sure of his ability, she was curious if he would appear that way again today. But as she approached the spot she saw him last, there wasn't a trace. *Well, of course not*, she thought. The shore was huge. Why would he come back to the exact same spot as yesterday? Surely he found a better spot, or moved on to a different island.

She continued on, heading towards the northern tip of the island, and her mind thought of Ellie. She didn't know why, but for some reason, she really looked forward to seeing her again. Maybe spending time with Ellie would do her some good. Rachel didn't even know her last name, or where her parents were, or really that much about her at all. She only knew that she liked her.

The sun had indeed been brighter than yesterday, so she pulled the brim of her hat down to block the light. Above her, four egrets flew in formation, heading north, the same direction she ran. The oncoming wind started to pick up, so the birds didn't look like they were flying all that fast. She watched them fly ahead when she noticed a fisherman on the shore.

As she approached, he looked like the same man from yesterday. Not so much because she could see his features, but the way he casted his line seemed very similar. When she got closer she could tell that it was him.

The man had just placed the rod on the sand behind him and was getting ready to sling the rod forward when he glanced at her for an instant. But the very next instant, he stopped his cast and looked back again, watching her as she ran by.

Shit, did he just do a double-take?

Rachel looked at him also, almost staring, and they locked eyes for a second or two. Rachel smiled, and so did the fisherman. He tracked her as she ran by.

Oh, he was good looking.

For a second, she felt like a schoolgirl passing by a boy that she knew liked her. Too bad she wasn't interested. Too bad Cynthia wasn't here to stop them for a chat. Not wanting to take things any further—knowing she couldn't take things any further—she took her eyes off him and looked straight ahead. She wasn't looking at anything in particular, she just knew she shouldn't look at him anymore.

And that was unfortunate too, because her foot caught on a piece of driftwood and she tripped, launching her body forward into the sand. By the time she knew what happened, there was no chance to catch herself. She pretty much nosedived into a full body face-plant.

"Are you okay?!" The man dropped his rod and darted for her. Riley barked.

Rachel jumped up almost as quickly as she fell. Her hat was crooked and practically smashed into her face, the whole front part of her body covered in sand. Wanting to spare herself any further embarrassment, she jogged away before he could reach her. She turned her head and yelled, "I'm okay." After she took a few more steps, completely red in the face, she turned once more and waved at him. "Thanks!" she said.

That's when the tip of her shoe snagged in the sand and she tripped again! Luckily, she caught herself this time. The fisherman watched her as she jogged away.

Oh, my God! Did that really just happen?

She ran on, wiping the sand off her body. She straightened her hat. Sand fell off the brim. Her legs wobbled and she panted, same as Riley. She dared not look back. Just keep jogging, she told herself.

Rachel followed the bend along the shore until she reached the tip of the island. She stopped running and checked herself to make sure she didn't have any cuts or anything. All was well.

"Riley," she said, still panting. She placed her hands behind her head. "Why didn't you warn me there was a big stick in the sand?" Riley sat down, and his tongue hung out. She reached down and rubbed him around his neck. "You gotta look out for me, okay boy?"

Per usual, Riley barked...and Rachel agreed.

But then Rachel realized she had another problem. It was bad enough parading past a guy only to find herself buried face down in the sand, now she had to turn around and run by him again. There was no way around it. The north end of the island didn't lend itself to any other route back except the way she came. She could run close to the tree line, hoping he didn't see her. No, that would be completely obvious. She'd just have to pass him again.

"Come on Riley."

As they started running, the thought came to her that the fisherman probably knew she'd have to pass by him again. What if he was still there? Did that mean he thought she was cute? *How stupid.* If he was still there, it's because he's fishing in a good spot. He only looked at her for just a couple of seconds.

But what if he wasn't there? Sure, she'd escape additional humiliation, but did it mean he thought she was unattractive? She wasn't interested in him—she wasn't interested in anyone—but it didn't mean she wanted to feel unwanted. She thought about it some more and really didn't think that was the case. He *had* smiled at her, after all. Perhaps he was going to be a gentleman and allow her to save face.

A little late for that, wasn't it?

She laughed. Just a little.

Or…could it be that if he wasn't there, it was only because he moved on to fish somewhere else? What did it matter, anyway? She wasn't interested. She wasn't looking for anyone.

She began to wonder if she was thinking clearly. Maybe she'd hit her head too hard on the sand. She decided not to think about it anymore, and if he was there, he was. If not, so be it. She wasn't interested.

But he was there. A knot in the back of her throat formed, making it that much harder to breathe. Maybe he wouldn't look at her. Maybe he'd just keep casting his rod, caught up in what he was doing.

But what about her? Should she pretend he wasn't there? What if he turned around and saw her, and noticed she wasn't looking? Would he think she wasn't interested? She's not interested, but she didn't want him to feel bad. What if he was having these same thoughts? What if he was confused? Oh, maybe he won't look, and she wouldn't have to worry about it at all.

But he did look. She knew, because she looked at him, too. She glanced down at the ground for a second to make sure there wasn't any driftwood lying around. He noticed what she did and their smiles widened. Then she waved, and he waved back. Good. No need for words. It was already a hopeless situation, no sense in making it worse by opening her big mouth.

As she passed, she wondered if he was still looking at her. Was he looking at her butt? Maybe checking out her calves? She didn't know what part, but she had that feeling he was looking.

Should she turn around and catch him in the act? That might be embarrassing for him. Good. It was his turn, wasn't it? Before she thought about it any further, she looked back to catch him, but the only catching going on was him reeling in a sea bass.

She actually felt relieved. Perhaps tomorrow she'd run south. The lighthouse was there, so she'd have to deal with that, but it might be better than dealing with him again. At least then she could run in peace and not worry about this guy she wasn't even interested in.

Crap. What if he moved to fish on the south end? She'd have to run by him again. But why would he do that? Because he didn't want to see her? And what would he think of her decision to run south? Would he think she wasn't interested? She wasn't, so why was she continuing to think about it?

The way she figured, she had two choices: either start analyzing her thoughts, or shut it down right now. Analyzing her thoughts was out of the question, because she wasn't sure if she was ready to answer, so she decided to not think of it anymore.

He was good looking though.

Rachel showered and ate breakfast, then grabbed her guitar and Kindle, and sat under the awning. She had sort of planned to go into Beaufort this morning to pick up a few more frozen meals and maybe some fresh fruit and vegetables if she felt like cooking. Though she didn't think Ellie would stop by so early, she didn't want to miss her either. Rachel thought that if she were Ellie, she'd be excited to come and learn some more guitar, so there was a chance she'd show up. Besides, Rachel was in a good part of her book and didn't mind reading for a bit. She could drive to town later in the afternoon.

Rachel read for a while, slouching in one of the camp chairs. Every now and then she'd look up to see if Ellie was there and to give Riley a pet. Soon, she found herself lost in her book, and she reached a part where the hero was about to make yet another huge mistake, taking the story into a whole new direction.

"Hi," a girl's voice said.

"Hi Ellie!" Rachel immediately put her Kindle down and looked at Ellie's contagious smile. Her lips were wide and red. And those blue eyes. They were *so* blue.

"Whatcha' doin'?" Ellie put her bag down on the picnic table and took a seat.

"I was just doing a little reading."

"What's it called?"

"*Wish You Were Here*," Rachel said.

"Sounds sad."

"It is a little bit. But I'm hopeful things will work out."

Ellie seemed to ponder that for a second or two.

"Would you like something to drink?" Rachel said. "I have some orange juice." Ellie nodded.

Rachel went inside and poured her and Ellie a glass of juice. When she came back out, Ellie was sitting next to Riley who had rolled over on his back, now in complete doggie bliss, because she was rubbing his belly. "I wish all dogs were as good as Riley."

"Me too. But seeing how he's the best dog in the whole world, I really don't think that's possible."

Ellie looked up at Rachel and smiled. "You must've spent a long time training him."

"No, not really. He was already trained by another family that had him before we did."

"Another family? What happened? Did they die?" Riley rolled over on his stomach and Ellie stroked him from the top of his head to the tip of his tail.

"No, they didn't die. A friend of mine found out that his owners were moving out of the country and wouldn't be able to take Riley with them. My husband and I drove almost two hours to meet him. After we spent some time with him, we knew he was perfect, so we took him home."

"Were the owners sad? I know I would have been." She bent down and rubbed her cheek against Riley's back.

"They were. But after they met us and realized Riley was going to a really good home, it was a little easier for them. I write to them occasionally and send pictures."

"That's nice." Ellie's smile soured and she remained quiet for a moment, rubbing Riley from head to tail again. "I used to write my mom a lot, but she never got to read any of my letters."

Rachel wasn't going to ask, but she sensed that Ellie wanted to talk about it. "Why not?"

"She was in a car accident a few years ago."

A lump the size of Atlanta filled Rachel's throat, and she swallowed so she could respond. "I'm so sorry, Ellie. I shouldn't have asked that."

"It's okay. The doctors said that she probably wouldn't wake up, so I drew some pictures for her and wrote some letters so she'd have something to do once she got to heaven."

Rachel couldn't speak. It was all she could do to hold back her tears. She had her own loss to deal with, but here was this girl that had been through a similar situation, yet she was able to talk about it so easily with almost a complete stranger. Rachel couldn't have done that, and she admired Ellie for it.

"That was nice of you, Ellie." The words came out a little bit fractured. Desperately needing to change the subject and completely afraid that Ellie might have heard her say *husband* in the story about Riley, she focused on the guitar. Rachel wasn't ready to tell *her* story yet. "So, you up for a lesson?"

"Absolutely!" Ellie said. "But my fingers sure are sore this morning. I didn't realize how painful playing the guitar was."

Rachel walked over to the picnic table and pulled the guitar out. "It gets easier I promise, but they're going to hurt for quite a while."

Ellie took a seat at the picnic table, and fixed her posture how Rachel had taught her. They went over everything she'd learned yesterday. Ellie fingered the G-major chord with her left hand, and then shook the pain out of her fingertips. She strummed for a while, reacquainting herself with the up-down motion. Soon, she was doing as well as she'd done yesterday. Each note from the G-major chord began to ring out clearly and her strumming became more rhythmic.

When Rachel thought she was doing well enough, she taught her how to play the E-minor chord. It was a little harder because Ellie had to really stretch her hand over the neck to get her fingers to reach the right frets, but she eventually got it. She strummed and strummed on the E-minor chord, so focused and determined. Her fingers got sore, and she shook out the pain, then fingered the chord and strummed some more. Like yesterday, Ellie closed her eyes as she strummed. The E-minor chord was naturally a sad sounding chord and Rachel could tell that Ellie felt it in her heart. It wasn't just her hands making music, it was her whole body.

As she listened to Ellie's playing, Rachel began to feel a little overwhelmed. Ellie had so much passion, and all she was doing was strumming the guitar. The notes sometimes came out a little muted, but it didn't matter, the feeling of the artist is what mattered, and Ellie's feeling touched Rachel. What's more is that she wasn't at all shy about it, her feelings sprung out from her effortlessly and she didn't seem to care who saw it.

Rachel sat with her eyes closed, listening to sweet Ellie strum the guitar, and she figured out why Ellie seemed so familiar to her. It was because she reminded Rachel of herself, before the cancer, before John died, before the grief. Up until that point in her life, she had everything she ever wanted. Not that there weren't setbacks, there had been, but by and large her life was headed just as she always dreamed it would—like the harmony of notes that came together as one to form a chord, like Ellie's passion, like the fisherman's casts.

The cruel lesson Rachel learned was that not all chords sounded good. Some were dissonant and tasteless, some were meant to provoke, and some were just plain bad. But Ellie's weren't. Even though they weren't perfect, they rang true to Rachel's ears and spoke to her heart. Rachel felt like she could feel her soul, because Ellie laid it out there for anyone to hear. All you had to do was listen.

Ellie stopped strumming and opened her eyes, looking up at Rachel.

"That was really good, Ellie," Rachel said. "I think you have a real talent for it."

"Really?" Ellie's voice squeaked as she said it, and her eyes brightened.

"Yep. I can tell you play from the heart."

"Thanks! It's a lot of fun. Can we do it again tomorrow?"

"Absolutely. I love listening to you play."

Ellie gave the guitar back to Rachel, and just like yesterday, she took her bag and headed for the beach, but not before turning around, smiling, and waving goodbye.

The beach was hot. In fact, there weren't nearly as many people lying out as there had been yesterday. Rachel easily found her a spot and opened up her chair, then twisted the umbrella deep into the sand. Anticipating she might see Beverly today since she didn't see her at all yesterday, Rachel positioned herself so she wouldn't have to shift things around if Beverly came to sit. She flipped on her Kindle, and while waiting for it to come on, she scanned the beach, looking for Ellie.

Two days in a row Ellie went to the beach after her guitar lesson, and two days in a row Rachel hadn't spotted her when she came out to read. She meant to ask who she was with and where her campsite was, but she got so caught up in Ellie's playing that she completely forgot. She thought Ellie might like to take the guitar with her and practice some, but didn't want anyone to think that some strange person just gave her a guitar.

"Is this sand taken?" Beverly said. She wore a bathing suit today, and flip flops.

"No, not at all. I was sort of hoping I'd see you today."

"Yeah, seems like I was running around all day yesterday." Beverly set her chair next to Rachel's and plopped down in it. "I'll tell you, when the store runs out of firewood, even in this heat, the folks around here almost rebel!"

"I bet."

"What have you been up to? Are you getting some writing done?"

"A little," Rachel said, even though she hadn't written a lick. "But, it's so beautiful out and I've got plenty of time. I thought I'd enjoy the beach and catch up on some reading."

"I hear you. Charles is in the camper taking a nap, and I'm almost done with *Under the Tundra*." She flashed the book and all Rachel could think about was Beverly pointing towards her crotch the last time she saw her.

Beverly opened up her book and started reading, and Rachel found that strange. The other day, she talked a mile a minute. Not giving it another thought, Rachel turned her attention to her Kindle and started reading as well.

After about five minutes, Beverly spoke up. "How do you like that Kindle of yours? My nephew keeps telling me I should get one."

"I really love mine. It can carry a couple thousand books on here. If I don't like the one I'm reading, I can find something else."

"Where did you get it?"

"You can order one online."

"Online. Why does everything have to be online these days? I can't even figure out my microwave, much less a computer."

Rachel, no stranger to technology, forgot that not everyone knew how to navigate the internet. How is that possible? "Your nephew can probably get you one."

"That's what he says. But, I'm probably too old to get one of those. I think paper works just fine." Rachel smiled, and Beverly went back to reading. So did Rachel.

Ten minutes passed this time. "So," Beverly said, "how long have you had your camper? It sure looks nice."

"I bought it about three months ago. It really is too much, but I figured if I'm going to be living in it for a while, I might as well get a nice one."

"You're living in it? Aren't you scared driving such a big thing?"

Rachel wasn't sure where this line of questioning was going, so she proceeded cautiously. "It's not so bad. You get used to it. The dealership I bought it from gave me some driving lessons and stuff. I have to admit, it gets a little tricky in the city."

"Well, I only drove ours once and vowed never to again. It's just too big."

It shocked Rachel that Beverly didn't dive into a story. Beverly simply put her nose back into her romance novel and continued to read. But Rachel thought she looked fidgety, and not really sure Beverly was even reading. It made Rachel anxious, but eventually she focused back on her own novel and kept on reading.

Only five minutes passed before Beverly spoke this time. "Hey, you want to get in the water?"

"Oh, I don't know—"

"Come on." Beverly stood up and grabbed her arm. Rachel barely had time to toss the Kindle in her bag before being dragged away. "Wait…you're not going to need that." Beverly pointed to Rachel's cover-up. Rachel took it off and threw it on her seat.

Beverly was on a mission. Rachel wasn't quite sure what that mission was, although she had her suspicions. Whatever it was, Beverly looked awfully determined, and Rachel figured she was the type of lady that pretty much got whatever she was after. As she was being dragged to the water, she told herself that if it came up, she'd just tell her the truth. If Ellie could do it, so could she.

The water felt warm on her feet, much warmer than walking along the shore the other night. As Beverly dragged her further out, the waves crashed on Rachel's thighs. Soon, she had to turn her back to avoid being splashed in the face, but Beverly kept pulling her further and further out. Once they passed the surf, they ended up on a sandbar and Rachel could touch the bottom easily. She could also squat just a bit to keep the water up around her neck. It felt good. It had been a long time.

"I just love the ocean," Beverly said. "Don't you?"

Rachel nodded.

"I remember when Charles and I were first married, and his first assignment was Edward's Air Force base in Los Angeles. We used to love going out to the beach, holding each other in the water at night, just watching the stars."

"At night? Weren't you scared of sharks?"

Beverly threw her head back and laughed. "Lord no, honey. We were young and in love. I don't think we'd let a little old shark come between us. Besides, I'd put a shark up against my Charles any day…at least back then."

"That's sweet, Beverly."

For the next couple of minutes Beverly and Rachel enjoyed the water. On the sandbar, the ocean seemed calm and Rachel relaxed. She dug her feet into the sand and felt her body gently sway with the water.

"Rachel, can I ask you something?" Beverly held her hand up above her eyes, blocking the sun.

"Sure," Rachel said, knowing what was most likely coming.

"I don't mean to sound forward, but I suppose I'm fixin' to." Beverly took a deep breath then said, "Why are you alone out here?"

"Why, I'm not Beverly? I'm out here with you!" Rachel splashed a little water Beverly's way.

"Oh, honey, you know what I mean."

Rachel had prepared for this moment a long time, but now that it was actually here, it seemed a lot harder than she thought it would be. It was difficult to admit to herself that she was never going to see John again, much less admit it to others. But as she contemplated it, she thought of Ellie, who had so effortlessly been able to speak about her mother—and Ellie was only eleven. Here she was, a grown woman having issues with coming to terms about her own husband's death over two years later. If she was ever going to move on with her life, she had to face these types of situations. It's not that she didn't know that, but she wondered if it would get any easier as time went on.

Rachel took in a deep breath and spoke. "My husband died two years ago from cancer."

"Oh, I'm so sorry, honey."

"This trip, the overpriced motorhome...this was supposed to be our dream. Not a lot different from what you and Charles have, I suppose."

Neither of them said anything for a while. The water welled up and receded around them, and Beverly looked in a different direction. Rachel could tell that Beverly probably wasn't saying anything because she was trying to prevent herself from crying.

After a couple of minutes, Beverly faced her. "I've got an idea. Why don't you come over tonight for supper?"

"Oh, I couldn't impose. I've got Riley and—"

"You wouldn't be imposing. Besides, Charles and I get lonely sometimes and it would be nice to have some company."

"I don't know, Beverly."

"What don't you know?" Beverly looked at Rachel like her mother used to. "Rachel, it's only supper. We're only one site back from you."

She had a point. Maybe it would do her some good to socialize a bit. Like Beverly said, it was only supper. "Okay," Rachel said, still a little unsure. "Is there anything I can bring?"

"Wonderful! Nope, Charles is going to barbecue some chicken on the grill. I just picked up some fresh tomatoes and squash at the farmer's market."

"I'm going into Beaufort for a few things this afternoon, so the least I can do is pick up something for desert. I'll also bring a bottle of wine…oh, I'm sorry…I don't even know if you and Charles drink or not."

Beverly gasped and looked insulted. "Rachel, we don't drink anymore."

Rachel felt bad for not thinking about it before she spoke "Sorry about that, I'll bring some—"

"But, we don't drink any less, either!" Beverly swatted her hand down and splashed some water in Rachel's direction.

"Beverly!" Rachel was relieved.

"I'm a gin drinker, honey." Beverly looked sternly into Rachel's eyes. "But I suppose I can lower my standards a notch or two and have a glass of wine." She laughed again. "How's seven o'clock sound?"

"That sounds great."

"Marco!" Beverly held her nose and went under.

When Rachel got back to the Fleetwood, she took another quick shower to wash off the saltwater, and then walked Riley. She wondered which one of the campsites Ellie stayed at. Maybe Ellie would see her walking and come out and say hi. Rachel didn't have that much time to walk all seven loops, hoping that one would be Ellie's, and further, hoping that Ellie might spot her. She made a mental note to ask her tomorrow where her campsite was.

Rachel returned to the Fleetwood without seeing Ellie at all. She fed Riley, and for the first time since she arrived, she cranked up the Jeep and pulled out of the park, heading towards Beaufort.

Rachel pulled the phone from her pocket and connected it to the hands free device built into the Jeep. She pressed redial, since

Cynthia was the last person she called. The phone rang and Cynthia answered on the first ring.

"You're lucky, Rachel."

"What?"

"I was calling the Coast Guard first thing in the morning."

"Yeah, right."

"How's it going?"

"Not bad," Rachel said, "the last couple of days have been really good."

"Yeah? How good?"

"I met someone." Rachel placed her fingers over her mouth.

"Shut up!"

"Yep."

"When?

"Yesterday."

"Oh shut up! You have to tell me everything!"

"Okay, okay," Rachel said. "I was just minding my own business, you know, not feeling all that great. So I stepped outside and just started playing the guitar."

"Yeah? And?"

"And then someone comes up to me and asked to play it?"

Cynthia gasped so hard it almost overpowered the speakers. "No way!"

"Cynthia, I was blown away. The music that came out…it was just amazing. I've never heard such passion from such a—"

"Cute?"

"Very! In all of my thirty-seven years, I don't think I've seen bluer eyes. They are big and beautiful. Oh…and that smile. I've never seen anything like it!"

Cynthia screeched. "Oh Rachel, I'm so happy for you! What have I been trying to tell you? See? I told you!"

"I can't wait for you to meet her. You're going to adore her."

"What?" Cynthia's voice dropped about an octave. "Did you just say *her*?"

Rachel's hand completely covered her mouth, and she stopped breathing. She didn't say anything. For a few seconds the line went completely silent.

"Rachel?"

Rachel's head started bobbing up and down. She laughed so hard on the inside that air started to escape between her fingers.

"Oh, my God Rachel! You're a switch hitter?"

Air spewed out from between Rachel's fingers and she tried her best to not give it away just yet.

"Rachel, honey, I think that's great! I mean, it's not my thing, I tried it once in college, but if it makes you happy then I'm happy."

Rachel laughed so hard she almost ran off the road. A truck going the opposite direction honked at her.

"Why are you laughing? What's so funny?"

"Cynthia, I'm not bisexual."

"You're not? Then what the hell are you talking about?"

"I met an eleven year old girl and I'm giving her a couple of guitar lessons."

The line went silent again.

"That's not funny Rachel!"

"Yes, it is."

"No, it's not!"

"It is too."

"Okay, it's a little funny. At least your sense of humor has come back. Maybe this trip is working out for you after all."

"I think maybe it is. I was serious when I said the last couple of days have gone well."

She told her all about Ellie and Beverly—there was plenty to tell—and about her dinner plans for the evening. Rachel decided not to mention the humiliation from this morning's face-plant. In fact, there was no mention of men at all, and Rachel was glad that Cynthia didn't bring it up.

They ended up chatting for the twenty miles that it took Rachel to drive to Beaufort. As they said their goodbyes, Cynthia mentioned something about coming to visit when Rachel was ready.

After they hung up, Rachel found a bakery and bought the most delicious looking blackberry cobbler. Next, she went to the grocery store, and bought some more frozen dinners, a few snacks, and a couple bottles of red wine. As she started back for Hunting Island, she saw a flower shop, so she stopped in for some flowers to give to Beverly at dinner.

"Good evening, Charles." Rachel nodded to him as she walked up to their campsite. She would have waved but she carried a blackberry cobbler in one hand and some flowers in the other. Charles was scrubbing the crud off the grate from the previous barbecue.

"Evening," Charles said. "Cobbler and flowers, huh? Sorry, but I'm already taken." He winked at her and smiled.

"I guess I'll have to start looking for someone else then."

"Well, a pretty girl like you won't have to look too far." Charles seemed pretty confident about that statement. Rachel wasn't so sure. "Hope you like chicken. Lemon pepper okay?"

"Sounds great."

"Head on in." Charles motioned towards the Winnebago. "I think Beverly's getting some vegetables ready."

The Winnebago was several years older than Rachel's Fleetwood and the inside looked pretty dated. Beverly and Charles seemed to be the kind of people that bought something once and kept it forever. All of their accoutrements looked like they came from one of those antique consignment malls, but Rachel was fairly certain they had bought them new.

"Hi, Rachel!" Beverly was her bubbly self, washing some squash. It looked like a lot of squash for just three people. "How was Beaufort?"

"It was fine. It's such a sweet town. John and I made a habit of stopping by and doing a little shopping when we used to camp here."

Rachel realized she'd said John's name. More than that, it didn't seem to bother her. She was beginning to feel very comfortable around Beverly.

"Oh, I got you these." Rachel handed the flowers to Beverly.

"Well, thanks honey. They're beautiful." Beverly walked over to one of the cabinets over the sink and pulled out a white vase. It had a cute trail of gray mice glued onto the ceramic handle, climbing their way up to the top.

As Rachel looked around the Winnebago, she noticed that mice were everywhere. A few trinket sized ceramic mice sat on the dinette table, and on the counter in front of the window lived a family of brass mice. Beverly had placed stuffed animal mice in the windshield. There was nowhere in sight that a mouse, or a family of mice could not be found.

"Rachel, I wanted to apologize for earlier. I shouldn't have pried into your personal business. Sometimes I let curiosity get the best of me. I picked up that bad habit from mother, God rest her soul."

"Don't worry about it, Beverly. I have to learn to deal with it."

"Well, I'm sorry just the same."

"Can I help you do anything?" Rachel asked.

"You want to cut up some squash?" Beverly took the bowl of washed squash from the sink and placed it on the counter, next to the cutting board. "Knives are to the right of the canister set."

Rachel saw the olive green canister set and the knife block next to it. She pulled out a Ginsu chef's knife. "Diced or rounds?"

"Rounds are fine. I'm just going to steam them with some onions."

The Ginsu knife cut the squash with great ease. Rachel was impressed. It had been a long time since she used a really sharp knife. Being the cook of the family, John had been adamant about quality knives. He spent over a hundred dollars once on a single chef's knife.

As Rachel sliced the squash, she remembered back to the day he brought it home.

"Ouch!" Rachel blurted. Blood dripped on the pieces of white onion that she diced.

"What happened?" John rushed to her, leaving a pot of fresh tomatoes he was blanching. "Are you okay? I told you it was sharp, didn't I?"

"Yes," Rachel said, sort of embarrassed. "I cut my finger. I don't think it's too bad."

John took her hand and looked it over. "Yeah, you sure did. Looks like just a nick though."

She took a sip of her wine as John walked over to the sink and opened up the first aid kit inside the cabinet. He took out a small bandage and wrapped it around the tip of her finger, then brought it to his lips and kissed it. "All better now?"

"Yes. Why, thank you, Rhett Butler," Rachel said in her best Scarlett O'Hara accent. After an exaggerated hair flip, she looked at him with big sexy eyes. "You saved my life! Why, how will I ever repay you?" She put her finger up to her chin, looking up to the ceiling. She suddenly gasped. "I know? I'll just have to kiss you." She pulled him towards her.

John pulled away. "No, I don't think I will kiss you, although you need kissing badly." John smiled at her. Then his forehead wrinkled and his face turned serious. "That's what's wrong with you. You should be kissed, and often, and by someone who knows how."

"Fiddledeedee. You think you know how, do ya?"

"Oh…I think you know."

"Well, then…I guess you'll just have to show me."

John closed his eyes as he moved closer and gently kissed her lips. Rachel wrapped her arms around him. She opened her mouth and they kissed harder, and she could taste the sweet wine they'd been drinking on his tongue. John nibbled her lower lip and pressed his body close to hers. He kissed his way down to her chin, and mouthed her throat. Rachel pulled his head into her neck and ran her hands through his thick hair, as her breathing grew heavy. She opened her eyes for just a second and noticed steam coming from the pot of tomatoes.

"John, you're boiling over!"

"I know baby!" he said, still pressing his mouth into her neck.

"No! The tomatoes!"

"Potatoes!" An echoed voice said.

"Potatoes?"

"Yes," Beverly said, "would you mind peeling them?"

"Oh…*potatoes*. Certainly." Rachel caught her breath and cleared the daydream from her mind. The bag of potatoes was already beside her and Beverly had placed a peeler on the cutting board. Rachel gave Beverly the squash that she cut up and started peeling away.

Beverly reached up into one of the cabinets above the dinette, and pulled down some avocado colored plates. "So Rachel…are you seeing anybody?"

"No, but I haven't been looking either. I'm not sure I can. It's just too soon."

"Oh," Beverly said. She put the plates down on the counter then scratched her ear. "But you wouldn't rule it out completely would you?"

Rachel put a couple of the peeled potatoes into a bowl filled with water. She grabbed another, really going to town on it. "I guess I wouldn't rule anything out. My friend Cynthia keeps trying to get me to start dating. It's just way too soon for me."

"Really?" Beverly looked outside at Charles. He flipped a couple of pieces of chicken, and flame and smoke shot out from the grill.

"Yeah," Rachel said, "I know she means well, and I'm sure there's a part of me that might even agree with her. But sometimes, she just gets pushy." Rachel put her peeler on the cutting board and turned to face Beverly. "I'll be ready when I'm ready. Do you know what I'm saying?"

"Oh, yes…I think." Beverly looked fidgety again, but Rachel didn't notice. "Rachel, would you mind taking these plates out to the table?"

"Sure thing, Bev." Rachel felt good around Beverly. She was beginning to think that Beverly was going to be a key component in helping her get through this. "You know, I'm really glad you asked me over for supper. I think this is exactly what I needed."

Rachel took the plates from the counter and opened the door.

"Rachel?" Beverly's voice sounded nervous.

Rachel turned to look back. "Yeah?"

"I'm sure your friend was really just trying to help."

Rachel smiled. "I know."

Rachel didn't notice that Beverly had given her five plates instead of three, but she became profoundly aware of the weight of them when she spun around and saw two people sitting at the picnic table. One of them she recognized right away as Ellie. The other was the fisherman from this morning's humiliating face-plant.

And he just pulled off his second double-take of the day.

CHAPTER FIVE

THEY WERE BOTH FROZEN, their eyes locked on one another. Neither of them knew what to say or do. Both looked just as shocked and surprised as the other. The plates in Rachel's hand seemed like they weighed a hundred pounds, and she felt the blood pulse in her ears as her heart pounded. She might have dropped the plates altogether if Beverly hadn't spoken up.

"Rachel, this is my nephew, Marc Sanders. And this is his sweet daughter Ellie."

Nephew? The one with the Kindle?

"Daddy, this is the lady I was telling you about."

And Ellie is his daughter?!

Rachel knew she needed to move, to walk over to the table and set the plates down, but she seemed paralyzed. She tried to force her legs forward, but they wouldn't budge. She felt like the whole world could hear her heart beating inside her chest.

Beverly took the plates from Rachel's hands, looking back at Marc. "Marc, do you two know each other?" She walked over to the picnic table.

Marc's gaze went unbroken, and it appeared as though he didn't hear her.

"Marc?" Beverly asked, once more. She stopped and everyone waited for him to answer.

Like breaking out of a trance, he looked over at Beverly. "Oh, uh…no," he stammered. "I mean…yes." He shook his head. "What I mean is, we saw each other on the beach this morning." He fixed his gaze on Rachel again. "You were watching the egrets flying in formation." A soft smile emerged on his face.

Rachel's knees grew weak and she could feel them start to wobble. She felt sick and lightheaded, afraid she was getting ready to pass out—another humiliating moment she didn't think she could handle.

"Excuse me," Rachel said as calmly as she could. "I need to pee."

She attempted to move her legs once more, and somehow they did. She turned and walked to the Fleetwood. She could feel four sets of eyes watching her walk away, following her every move. Her hands began to tremble. Her heart was beating so fast she halfway expected it to leap out of her chest and beat uncontrollably on the grass below. She was sure that her knees were going to buckle and that she was going to fall helplessly to the ground, humiliated once again.

But she didn't. She made it to her motorhome and went inside. Riley barked as she passed by. Her face lost all of its color and her lips tingled. She found the door to the bathroom and opened it. She turned on the light and looked at herself in the mirror.

Her vision started to tunnel and the Fleetwood swayed. A gaping, black hole seemed to form underneath her, and she could see the darkness rising up to pull her in. The bathroom started spinning and her whole body started to tingle. She tried to take a breath but couldn't.

Breathe Rachel, Breathe!

The air finally rushed into her chest and she heaved. Color rapidly came back to her face, and her vision cleared. She took deep, gasping breaths and the Fleetwood slowly stopped spinning. She reached for the bed and started to lie down, but then caught herself. She needed to sit. Lying down would only make it worse.

Riley jumped on the bed and nudged her arm. She began to pet him and it soothed her, and soon she felt better. She focused on her breathing again, and it became controlled and rhythmic. The blood began to circulate normally through her body and her heart rate slowed. Rachel still felt sick to her stomach, but at least the risk of passing out subsided. She petted Riley some more, and he put his head in her lap.

Rachel slid her hand under Riley's jaw and lifted his head up and looked at him. "I need to pee?" She had a disgusted look on her face as she sighed, dropping his head back down to her lap. She stroked his fur over the full length of his body, and for mutual benefit.

What now? Should she just stay in the camper, and hide out from them? Should she try to make up some excuse, how she wasn't feeling well? Perhaps she could blame it on Riley. She could tell them that Riley had eaten something that upset his stomach, that he was throwing up, or maybe she had to rush him to the vet.

Oh, don't be stupid.

No, she'd have to go back over there and face him. It was apparent, after all, the he, Marc Sanders, seemed just as surprised to see her, as she was to see him. That being the case, then Beverly might have been scheming. Or maybe it was all innocent and just a coincidence. She was such a nice lady. But what was the last thing she had said? *"She was sure my friend was just trying to help?"* Yeah, she was definitely scheming. But Rachel wasn't too upset at her. Somehow, she knew Beverly was just trying to help.

To keep from lying to all of them, she went ahead and used the restroom, then fixed her hair a bit and put on a bit of blush and some neutral colored lipstick.

As Rachel walked back to their campsite, she thought about what she'd say or do. She decided that considering what just happened, she probably needed to appear confident and a little more in control.

When she got there, Beverly had already set the table and set out the squash, mashed potatoes, and some fresh tomatoes. Even the flowers that Rachel brought over were in the center. Charles continued to flip the chicken on the grill, and was talking to Marc about something.

Ellie ran up to Rachel. "Are you okay?"

"I'm fine, Ellie." Rachel smiled. "Especially now that I'm talking to you." Ellie gave her an unexpected hug. It made Rachel feel better, and she wished it were just the two of them back under her awning, playing the guitar.

"I want to show you something," Ellie said. "I'll be right back." She bolted around the end of the camper.

"Rachel," Beverly called out, stepping out of the camper, "why don't you have a seat over there." She pointed to the place setting directly across from where Marc sat earlier.

Rachel sighed. "Don't you need some help with—"

"Nope," Beverly interrupted. "I got everything out already." Beverly took her seat at the picnic table then cupped her hand over her mouth like a megaphone, and shouted, "Just waiting on the chicken, boys!"

Marc looked back over his shoulder at her and laughed. "Just a couple more minutes, Aunt Bev."

"Isn't he something else?" Beverly whispered in Rachel's direction.

"I don't know," Rachel whispered back. "But next time, how about a little warning?"

"Well, if I had warned you, would you have come?"

Rachel thought about it, and knew it was a valid point. "I don't know," Rachel said. "I just know that I'm pretty stressed out at the moment…oh, speaking of which, I forgot to bring the wine, let me go get it."

"Don't worry about it." Beverly moved quicker than a cat. "I have some inside."

"I thought you said you were a gin drinker?"

"I am, but I always keep a couple bottles of wine for emergencies. I think this qualifies."

Like Rachel's site, Charles and Beverly's Winnebago opened up to the wildlife refuge and seemed fairly private. Charles had lit eight tiki torches that framed the area like a patio, and the picnic table sat right in the middle. Beverly had hung a set of multicolored globes from her awning. As the sun began to set, the combination of flickering torches and the globes gently rocking in the breeze, cast a familiar and once comforting scene.

Under normal circumstances, it was the type of setting that brought Rachel much pleasure. But as Marc and Charles were engaged in family conversation over the grill, and Beverly, inside looking for the cork screw, cursing, Rachel sat alone with the somber thought that she'd never spend another night as grand as this with John.

Marc looked over at Rachel, and it only took him about five seconds to extricate himself from Charles. When Rachel saw him coming towards her out of the corner of her eye, she really just wanted to hide.

The reason she came here in the first place was to live out her and *John's* dream. But she had looked at Marc on the beach, didn't she? What's worse, was that she *wanted* to look at him. Did she want more? She couldn't deny to herself that she had thought about it, if only for an instant. Wasn't that the same as cheating? Maybe that was the reason for her confusion, and maybe confusion was camouflaging her guilt. Still, she had no choice but to deal with Marc, because he was almost to her.

She looked up and smiled at him, and just as he was about to speak, they were interrupted by an out of breath Ellie who came flying around the end of the motorhome.

"Rachel, I made this for you today," Ellie said, panting.

Rachel gasped when she saw the painting, and she put the tips of her fingers up to her mouth. It was a beautiful watercolor in pastels of a woman underneath the awning of a motorhome strumming a guitar. Her eyes were closed. Behind her, ocean waves were breaking on the beach, and a pair of seabirds were suspended in the blue sky. Ellie signed her name at the bottom.

"Oh, Ellie," Rachel said, almost at a loss for words. "It's just so beautiful." Her eyes began to fill up with tears, and she fanned her face with her hand to keep them from streaming.

"Ellie, that's really good," Marc said.

Ellie looked up at her dad and smiled, then faced Rachel again. "It's the first time I saw you."

Rachel reached out to her and pulled her close for a hug. "That was so sweet of you. I really don't know what to say." She released Ellie and then looked at it again. The painting seemed to capture exactly how Rachel felt at that moment, almost as if Ellie read her mind and painted her emotions.

"Marc!" Charles hollered. "Come grab this chicken." At that same instant, Beverly came out of the motorhome with the bottle of wine, waving the corkscrew up in the air, victorious.

Rachel looked up at Ellie, who was clearly proud of her painting. "Thank you," Rachel said.

"You're welcome. I hope it's okay that I painted you like that." Ellie looked down at the ground with sort of a frown. "I could tell you were sad about something."

"Not at all. It's really great," Rachel said. Ellie's smile came back right away. "Beverly, take a look at what Ellie painted for me!"

"Oh my Lord." Beverly took the painting from Rachel. "That's so good."

"Thank you." Ellie took a bow.

"You've always had such a talent." Beverly looked over the painting some more.

"Would you do me a favor, Ellie?" Rachel said. "Would you mind taking it over to my camper and put it on the table inside? I don't want anything to happen to it. Riley's inside. I'm sure he could use some petting."

"Sure!" Ellie took the painting from Beverly and took off as fast as when she left to go get it. Marc walked up and placed a platter of chicken down in the center of the table.

"Your daughter is amazing," Rachel said. "Did you know that? I betcha didn't."

Marc laughed. "Yeah, she's a pretty special girl."

"I have never seen such passion before in such a young child."

"She gets it from her mother," Marc said. He went quiet for a few seconds, and he seemed to be in another place. A smile from long ago materialized on his face. Rachel recognized it instantly, and she remembered what Ellie had said about her mom being in a coma.

"Well," Beverly said, and well timed, "let's eat! Charles? Charles!"

"I'm coming! Give me a second, will ya?" Charles pulled the lid down on the grill, holding a platter topped with the last of the chicken.

Rachel was in no mood to eat. As they passed the food around, filling up the plates with chicken, fresh tomatoes, squash, and potatoes, she felt like an outsider intruding on a family get-together. However, the glass of wine that Beverly poured was a welcome site, and she took a sip, quickly feeling the alcohol work its magic as it entered the blood stream of her already frazzled body. Beverly poured Marc a glass and set the bottle down between the two of them.

As they ate, Rachel snuck a couple of peeks up at Marc. When she first saw him on the beach, she thought his hair was brown. Looking at him now, it seemed lighter than that, but not something that could really be called blonde. The slightest bit of gray formed on the sides. His eyes were hazel, shifting in color from a golden brown in the center out to streaks of blue green at the edges. His skin was tan, and not the kind you get from laying out at the beach, but the thick kind that was earned from working outdoors every day. Four or five lines cut into his forehead when he smiled, though not in a negative way. He looked much different from John, who was clean-cut and very professional looking. Marc looked a bit rough around the edges, but in a way that suited him. Rachel found his appearance to be appealing.

She noticed he wore a thin, silver wedding band, and wondered if he saw hers. She hoped so.

"Marc," Beverly said, "Rachel's writing a novel."

Marc looked up at Rachel, a bit of a surprise on his face. "Really?"

"Well…" Rachel had a bite of chicken in her mouth, and she washed it down with some wine. She was sort of embarrassed by the question and the attention. "I'm attempting to write one. It's something I've always wanted to do."

"And she's staying here for the summer," Beverly said.

Ellie's eyes lit up. "The whole summer?"

Marc quickly jumped in. "And I'm sure she doesn't want to spend it giving you guitar lessons."

"I don't mind," Rachel said. "It's a nice break."

Marc looked at his daughter. "Okay, but don't take up all of her time. I know how you can get."

"Oh, I won't. I promise."

Rachel took another sip of wine and looked up at Marc. "How long are you guys here for?"

"We don't live too far away. A little west of Beaufort. Since school is out and Aunt Bev and Uncle Charles are working here again, we thought we'd spend a month or so. Maybe up until July 4th." He glanced over at Charles and winked. "Plus, the family discount is great!" Charles acknowledged by raising his glass of sweet tea.

"A month?" Rachel said. "That's a nice vacation."

"It's not really a vacation, it's one of the perks of being self-employed."

"Marc is a photographer," Beverly said.

"Photography." Rachel nodded, trying to keep the conversation off of her. "What kind?"

"Stock mainly. I like it because I can set my own hours, shoot what I want, and best of all, I don't have to deal with clients."

Rachel was familiar with stock photography. Part of her job had been to create marketing material, which frequently required the use of stock photos. She'd spent hundreds of hours searching online stock photo agencies for just the right shot.

"Don't let him fool you Rachel," Beverly said. "Some of his pictures have been in *Time Magazine*, and—"

"Aunt Bev?" Marc seemed embarrassed by it, and really wanted to change the topic.

"Well, they have been. I still have a copy." Beverly stood up to go get it.

"How about another time?" Charles said, nodding in her direction. "Finish your supper, honey."

Begrudgingly, Beverly sat back down and almost huffed.

"Uncle Charles, how's your sister?" Marc asked. The question was well timed because it started up a family discussion, a break Rachel was thankful to get—anything to keep the discussion off of her.

Charles started talking about his sister Mary and how she was taking too many prescription drugs, and then started dating the pharmacist after she dumped the prescribing doctor. Charles and Beverly gossiped some more about that side of the family, and Marc did a good job of asking questions to make sure they stayed there.

Though she was invited to stay after dinner, Beverly practically insisting, Rachel told everyone that she had a long day, and said goodnight. Two major embarrassments in a single day was about all a girl could handle.

Rachel woke up to a predicament the next morning. She'd have to decide what to do about Marc, because at this point, she knew she'd have to talk to him again. Before last night's dinner, she could've just waved if she saw him, or better yet, she didn't have to do anything at all. But that was no longer an option. Eventually she'd see him again, either on the beach fishing or on the campground. Plus, the fact that he was Ellie's father almost guaranteed it.

As soon as she and Riley hit the sand and started their jog, she realized there'd be no time to think about it. On the shore, she saw a man looking out over the horizon, waiting on the sunrise. It was Marc, and he wasn't fishing.

She'd have to wing it.

Once Marc heard the sound of footsteps behind him, he turned around and smiled at Rachel. "I was hoping you'd be out this morning. I wasn't sure if you would be."

"We come out for a run most mornings. Don't we boy?" She reached down and cupped Riley's face with both hands and rubbed his snout with her thumbs.

"That's a nice lookin' fella you have there. How old is he?"

"About seven." She stroked his back a couple of times then stood back up. "Do you have any pets?"

"Me and Ellie? No. We had a golden retriever years ago, but we had to give her away." Marc dropped his head a bit and studied Riley who was looking up at him. Marc gave him a quick pet on the head.

"I wanted to apologize for last night," Marc said. "Aunt Bev can overstep her bounds sometimes."

"It's okay. I probably wouldn't have reacted like I did, had I not completely embarrassed myself in front of you yesterday morning."

"That was you?" He cocked his head a little and smiled.

"Ha ha," she said. "Hard to believe, but yes, that was me. I felt like such an idiot."

"I understand. You landed pretty hard. You didn't hurt anything did you?"

She sighed. "No, nothing but my self-confidence."

Marc looked nervously down both ends of the shore. "I know you're out here to run. But, ah…" He looked down at his feet, then up to her. "Would you like to take a walk with me?"

Rachel nodded. She wasn't sure if it was a conscious decision or not.

Marc motioned south, towards the lighthouse, and they started walking. The sun had come up and they watched it as they walked. Rachel thought back to the last time she and John walked on this beach—the last time they walked on any beach together.

"Thanks for showing Ellie how to play the guitar," Marc said.

"I don't mind at all. She's such a sweet girl."

"She is, but sometimes she can get a little carried away. Just let me know if she starts bugging you. I know you're here to work, not babysit."

"Well, I'm here for pleasure too." As soon as the words came out, she wished she could've taken them back.

"Do you have any kids?" he asked.

Rachel felt a sharp stab of pain in her stomach, and hoped it didn't show in her expression. "No," she said, but didn't elaborate. She couldn't. Marc must have sensed her uneasiness because he didn't bring it up again.

Right when they reached the lighthouse Marc stopped and faced her. She could see the lighthouse behind him. Why, of all places did he have to pick this exact spot to stop?

"Rachel, I don't really know how to say this, so I'm just going to say it. I've been thinking about it all night, and maybe it's selfish of me because I don't really know your situation, and you don't really know anything about me apart from whatever Aunt Bev told you, if she told you anything…or everything…I have no idea. But I saw that you were wearing a wedding ring, and you probably saw that I was wearing one too, and Beverly wouldn't have pulled her little stunt last night if she didn't know something. Ellie already knows you, and she was talking about you before I knew it was you…and after I saw you yesterday morning on the beach, and then again at dinner…well…" He looked up at the sky over her shoulder. "I'm rambling, aren't I? I guess I don't really know how to say it."

Rachel smiled at him. The lighthouse was far from her mind, as she tried to put together what he attempted to say. She seemed to know exactly how he felt. Confused.

"I guess what I'm trying to say is…and I don't mean to make it sound like anything has to come of it, because it doesn't." He looked up over her shoulder again and smirked, because he caught himself at the beginning of another ramble.

He sighed and looked straight at her. "Would you mind having dinner with me and Ellie tonight?"

Rachel hadn't been asked on a date since she was a teenager, and she had long since forgotten what that sensation felt like. She'd only dated one other boy in high school, nothing serious until John asked her out, at which point they became inseparable. John was, and always would be, the love of her life. There was no contesting that.

But here came Marc Sanders, twenty-something years later, and apparently he seemed as nervous as she was. Maybe he was right. Beverly wouldn't have pulled her little stunt last night if she didn't know something. Marc had known what it was like to lose someone, same as Rachel. She saw it in his face last night when he spoke about Ellie being like her mother. If anyone could really understand what she had gone through—still going through—it would be him.

Rachel nodded. "I think I'd like that."

"Great." Marc looked so relieved. "Do you like beef?"

"Yes. Oh, and I have a bottle of wine I was supposed to bring last night, but I forgot."

"Sounds good. Seven-thirty okay?"

"Yep."

"Our camper is on loop D. Site thirty-seven. It's in the back, but all by itself. Quiet."

At six-thirty, Rachel stepped out of the shower and wrapped a towel around her. She cleared the fog from the mirror and contemplated how to style her hair. Gathering it up in her hands, she pulled it back, holding it in a ponytail. Marc had already seen her like that three times before: once while she was running, once at dinner with Beverly, and once walking on the beach. So, she decided on a messy up-do: relaxed and understated, yet still attractive.

After she fixed her hair, she put on a pair of khaki shorts and a white, wide strapped tank that wasn't too tight. She noticed her skin definitely getting some sun, so she put on a little mascara and some lip-gloss. *Not bad*, she thought.

She had a few minutes before heading out, so she sat in the recliner to get in a little reading. She read a couple of pages, but didn't seem to remember what she read. She flipped back to where she started and began again, but after rereading the first paragraph three times, she realized that it just wasn't going to happen. Something nagged at her. As soon as she turned off the Kindle and set it down, she noticed John's wine glass on the table. For a couple of minutes, she just looked it.

"I could use a little help here, John," she said to the glass. Riley, who was lying on the floor beside her, raised his ears to listen in. "I'm really confused. I just don't know what to do. I know I'm supposed to move on. I know we talked about this, but it's not that easy." The breeze came in through the windows and rustled the fresh cut flowers. A tear streaked down her face and she looked away.

After a few moments, knowing that she needed to leave soon, she got up and fixed the mascara that had run, and looked at herself in the mirror. "Rachel," she said to the reflection, "it's only dinner. It's not that hard. Just go over there and have a good time." The whites of her eyes had turned pink from crying. "Ugh," she grunted at the mirror then walked out, flipping off the light.

She marched to the table, snatched up the bottle of wine and picked up the guitar case. "I'll be back in a while Riley." He barked as she opened the door to leave.

As Rachel walked along loop D, she felt herself getting anxious. Earlier, when Marc had asked her if beef was okay, it sounded great. Thinking about it now, maybe she should've suggested something else. While she loved beef, it could be hard on her stomach, and this certainly qualified as a situation that already had her stomach in knots.

Site thirty-seven came into view, and it was situated on a big, hairpin turn. She half-thought about walking right by it. If she sped up a bit, she'd be around the corner and home free in about thirty seconds. But just as she started to quicken her pace, Marc opened the door to his camper and stepped out.

"Hey there!" he said. He held a bowl in each hand.

"Hi." Rachel stood at the edge of the road, the guitar and wine bottle dangling from her hands.

Marc stared at her for a second, before apparently catching himself doing it. He set the bowls down on the picnic table and quickly walked up to her, taking the guitar and wine bottle.

"Come on," he said, motioning with his head towards his camper. "Not as nice as your Fleetwood, I know."

She was no expert, but it looked like an old aluminum Airstream travel trailer. Most of it was polished, but towards the back, the aluminum still looked dull.

"No, I like it. Still working on it?"

Marc set the guitar and wine bottle down on the picnic table. "Yep. It was my grandparents. A 1966 Ambassador. It sat out behind their house for years after they were too old to use it. They used to take me camping all the time. It was really in bad shape when I got it. I work on it when I have time."

"I think it's charming," Rachel said. "Plus, it's a family heirloom with a lot of memories. That's priceless. I have no memories in mine."

"Well, give it some time," he said. There was something genuine in the way he looked at her. Something familiar.

The door to the Airstream swung open and Ellie ran out. She gave Rachel a big hug like she'd always known her.

"Hey, I brought you something." Rachel motioned towards the guitar case. Ellie's eyes widened and she hugged her again. "You can keep it over here for a while. That way, you can practice whenever you want."

"Daddy, you want to hear me play some?"

"Sure, sweetheart."

Ellie opened the case and gingerly took out the guitar and placed it on her lap, taking care not to bang it up against the picnic table. She fingered a G-major chord and started strumming with her eyes closed.

"That's really good," Marc said. Ellie fumbled to the E-minor chord and continued to strum. Next, she played the C-major chord and then the D-major chord. The transition between chords was a challenge, and where she had to open her eyes, but as soon as she fingered the next chord, she closed her eyes again and kept strumming.

Marc looked over at Rachel and mouthed silently, "Thank you." Rachel smiled, but Marc had already turned his gaze back towards his daughter, smiling as she played.

After a couple of minutes, Ellie hit one final chord and let every little bit of it ring out before she opened her blue eyes. She looked up at her father, whose smile really could not get any bigger.

"Bravo!" Marc clapped like he was at the opening night to a Broadway musical. "I'm stunned that you've learned so much, so fast."

Ellie looked at him and tilted her head to the side, blushing. "It's so much fun. I love it." She looked up at Rachel. "Can you teach me some more chords?"

"Work on the transition between the ones you already know, and tomorrow we'll learn some more. How's that sound?"

"Great!" Ellie started playing again and Marc and Rachel watched her for a moment.

Glancing down at his watch, Marc grabbed the bowls from the table. "I know you brought some wine, but dinner's probably a little over an hour away. You want to grab a couple of beers from the fridge? " He motioned towards the door.

The interior of the Ambassador was straight out of the sixties, complete with light blue upholstery. To her right sat the dining table, where Ellie was working on some additional paintings. The kitchen was to her left.

She opened up the refrigerator, and saw beef tenderloin marinating in a bowl. Next to it were some Coronas, so she took out two of them. She saw some limes on the counter opposite of the refrigerator, and then hunted for a knife. After finding one in the drawer next to the sink, she cut two wedges and pushed them through the bottle. One started to overflow, so she took a large swallow to avoid it dripping on the linoleum.

Back outside, she saw Marc standing next to a white folding table where he had placed the bowls. On top sat several items: a couple of cast iron Dutch ovens, cooking utensils, a variety of spices, wild mushrooms, some butter, an onion, pine nuts, and cooking twine. Next to it stood a black, metal table. On top of it sat one of those chimney charcoal starters, the kind that didn't require lighter fluid. It was full of red-hot charcoal.

"I see you're a real Chef Boyardee." Rachel said, handing him his beer.

He acknowledged her smile with one of his own then took a couple of swallows. "My mother never missed a rerun of *The French Chef with Julia Child*. When I was growing up, my dad was away a lot, so mom made me help her with dinner. I liked it. It was something I always looked forward to after school. I guess it stuck."

"I saw the beef tenderloin marinating in the fridge. Looks like I'm in for something yummy."

"I hope so," he said, nervously. "It's one of my favorite meals."

"What's this table for?" Rachel pointed to the metal table where the charcoal was burning. "I've never seen anything like it."

"It's called a Dutch oven table. That's how we're going to cook dinner."

"We?" Rachel said. "I don't think you want me to cook anything."

"Oh yeah? Cooking's not your thing, huh?"

"Let's just say, my mother probably didn't even know who Julia Child was."

Marc laughed. "The metal table holds the charcoal. We'll take some of the hot coals and place them right on top, in a circle. Then we'll put the Dutch oven over them. After that, we take some more coals and put them directly on the lid. Viola. The food gets heated from both sides."

"So, it's like an oven." Rachel thumped her forehead with the heel of hand. "Dutch oven...duh."

Marc laughed, again. "Yeah, just like an oven. And then we can stack another oven on top. The coals on the lid of the bottom one will heat the bottom of the oven on top."

"Ahhh, very cool. Or hot in this case...I guess." Rachel took another sip of her beer, thinking about how stupid she sounded.

"You want to cut up this onion?" Marc said. Beer was still in her mouth when he pointed towards one of the knives on the table. She instantly recognized it as the same kind that John used to have; the same one that she'd cut herself with. Suddenly, she felt as if she shouldn't be here, like she was stealing or keeping a secret she knew she shouldn't keep.

Marc's calm voice interrupted her thoughts. "Or I can, if you don't want to."

"No, it's okay. I can do it. It's just that I haven't seen a knife like this in a while."

Marc looked surprised. "You don't cook, but you know about cutlery?"

"No," Rachel said. "My husband did all the cooking. He had a knife just like that."

"I see." Marc paused, sensing her uneasiness. "Rachel, we don't have to—"

"No, I think we should." Nervously, she picked up the knife, the feel and weight of it seemed familiar. "It's just dinner, right?"

"That's right." Marc smiled warmly.

Rachel picked up the red onion and cut it in half, letting the knife do all the work. As she started to peel it, Marc picked up another knife and began dicing the chanterelle mushrooms.

The table was rather small, forcing them to stand close to one another—so close that she could almost feel the heat coming from his arm while they worked the vegetables. Marc brushed up against her when he reached over the table to get a bowl for the mushrooms.

"Sorry about that," he said.

Rachel smiled, as she finished dicing the onion. Another bowl sat on the other side of Marc, so she reached across him to get it. She sort of bumped him a little.

"Oh, I'm sorry," she said, grinning. Marc smiled back, a goofy looking one.

Once the vegetables were prepared, he took the grill tongs and pulled out a dozen or so hot briquettes and placed them directly on the metal table. Then he took one of the Dutch ovens and placed it on top of the briquettes. He put in a couple pats of butter, then added the mushrooms, onions, and some pine nuts.

"Now we take a seat," Marc said. "The briquettes sauté a lot slower than you're probably used to."

"Hey, unless it's done in three minutes and forty-five seconds, then I'd have to agree with you."

Marc laughed. "It's one of the reasons I like charcoal. I don't like to be in a hurry. More time to sit and drink beer." Marc picked up his bottle from the table and motioned with it to some camp chairs that he'd set up earlier.

"Daddy?" Ellie yelled from the picnic table. She'd already put the guitar back in its case, and stood next to a few kids close to her age. "Is it okay if I walk around the loop with them?"

"Sure, but don't be gone too long, okay?"

Rachel and Marc watched the three kids walk away. "Well," Marc said, "now that we're all alone, is there anything at all you've been dying to ask me?"

"Let's see." She took a sip of her Corona. There was only about a quarter of it left in the bottle. "Well, there is this *one* thing. Was yesterday the first time you saw me? You know, when I fell flat on my face?"

"That's the one question you've been dying to ask me? If I saw you before yesterday?"

"Yeah. Actually, the day before that, I saw you fishing and ran right past you, obviously with a little more grace." Marc smiled. She continued, "I was wondering if you saw me."

"Hmm," he curled his finger and thumb around his chin.

"Well?"

"Maybe," Marc said quickly. He flipped up his nearly empty bottle and took a quick sip.

"Maybe?" Rachel's eyebrow rose.

"That's right. Maybe. It might have been you. Hard to say. I did see a woman, but the woman I saw had already passed by. I only saw her from behind. Nice legs though, I do remember that."

"Ooh, nice legs, huh?"

"Yep. She was running with her yellow lab, but like I said, it might not of been you. It was hard to tell. Dark out, you know. But yeah. Really nice legs."

Rachel smiled at him as she gulped down the last of her beer and set it down on the table. "Can I get us a couple more?"

"Sounds good."

She stood up and took about ten steps towards the Airstream, then stopped. She turned her head around and looked back at Marc. "Well?"

"Ah, yes. I suppose it was you."

She shot him a quirky smile before she continued on to the Airstream.

When she walked out with two more Coronas, she saw Marc hovering over the Dutch oven stirring the vegetables.

"That smells so good," she said, walking up. "I could just eat that." She handed him his beer and he took another long pull off of it.

"Time for the meat," he said. "Would you take the vegetables out while I go get it?"

"Sure."

"There's a bowl over there with some bread crumbs. Just mix it all together."

After Marc returned with the meat, he put more briquettes under the oven then placed the beef tenderloin in to sear. Once seared on all sides, he took it out, and like a surgeon, cut a lengthwise pocket down the center of it, using his fingers to widen it out a bit.

"Wow," Rachel said. "I feel like I'm in cooking school or something."

Marc smiled, and his face turned a little flush. "All right, spoon as much of the filling inside as you can."

Rachel drank some of her beer, and then took the spoon. "Although I'm hesitant, I guess it's only fair that you get to ask me a question."

"Okay, let me think about it a second." Marc took the lid off a second Dutch oven, revealing some yeast rolls that had been rising. Satisfied with their height, he replaced the lid. Rachel finished up the filling, then he tied up the tenderloin with some cooking twine. After he finished, he placed it in the Dutch oven and covered it, then added about twelve briquettes to the lid in a checkerboard pattern.

As they walked back to the chairs, he said, "All right, I got my question." He paused before he asked, taking his seat. "What happened between you and your husband?"

Rachel's stomach felt like it dropped about twelve floors. She sat motionless for a second, knowing she had to hold it together, especially in front of Marc. She felt the cold beer in her hand and lifted it, taking a few long gulps, feeling the carbonation cool her throat and then her stomach.

"I'm sorry," he said. "I shouldn't have asked."

"No, it's a fair question. It just caught me a little off guard, that's all. I should have been expecting it."

"Still, you don't have to answer it. I don't want to make this evening difficult. Maybe some other time."

As much as Rachel wanted to avoid the question, to never have to answer it again for the rest of her life, she knew she had to, just like when Beverly had asked. Small steps lead to big steps and big steps lead to recovery.

"Thanks, but I think I need to answer it now." She took a deep breath, then spun her wedding band around with the fingers of her right hand.

"John died of cancer," she said.

"Oh God, I'm sorry Rachel," Marc looked embarrassed. "I thought maybe you guys divorced or something. I'm so sorry. I didn't know."

Rachel nodded. She felt her throat tighten, but continued. "We found out two and a half years ago. He started complaining about a pain in his stomach, so I urged him to go see a doctor. After a couple of weeks and dozens of tests, they told us it was cancer, but the good news was that we'd caught it in time." Tears welled up in her eyes and she looked up, trying to prevent them from streaming. She took her fingers and dabbed the corners.

"But for whatever reason, chemo had little effect. Radiation didn't work. We even signed up for clinical trials, alternative medicines, and tried all sorts of herbs. Nothing seemed to slow it down. Seven months later…" Despite her best efforts, tears poured down her face. "We were married for seventeen years."

"I'm so sorry, Rachel." Marc said.

Rachel looked away from him and dried her tears with her hand. She picked up her beer and took a sip, finding it hard to swallow. She couldn't seem to face Marc. She didn't want him to see her like this. Rachel felt his hand on her shoulder, but only for a second, as if he wanted to soothe her but then thought it was inappropriate.

The next few moments were quiet, and Rachel wished she would've kept walking earlier when she reached site thirty-seven. She thought about getting up now and walking home. Marc would surely understand. But, she knew she'd stay, if only because she didn't want to appear rude. Plus, Marc had obviously gone to a lot of trouble for dinner. John would have appreciated that. In a strange way, that comforted her.

"I don't know if Ellie mentioned it to you or not," Marc said, "but about four years ago, my wife was in a car accident."

Rachel nodded. "She did. I'm sorry." She wiped any remaining tears from her eyes and turned towards him. "Ellie said she was in a coma for a while and that she used to write to her."

"That's right. She wrote to her *every day*." Marc's eyes were aimed towards the airstream, but Rachel sensed he really wasn't looking at anything. "For the longest time, I was so angry. Angry at her. Angry at the world." He paused, glancing over at the Dutch oven before looking at the ground in front of him. "Angry at myself."

Rachel nodded. "I know *exactly* how you feel."

After she spoke those words, Marc looked up from the ground and into Rachel's eyes. Something flashed in her mind, and for an instant she felt as though she was looking into John's eyes.

They heard Ellie's voice coming from beyond the bend in the road. Rachel turned and looked for her, but couldn't see her yet.

"Anyway," Marc said, "I don't know what I would've done without Ellie. Ever since she was born, she's always been my guiding light."

Ellie and a boy finally came into view. Rachel noticed the boy was one of the kids that Ellie had left with. His hair was dark and styled like Justin Bieber. When they approached the campsite, Ellie said something to him, then waved goodbye. The boy and his dog continued up the loop road as Ellie skipped to one of the camp chairs next to Rachel and plopped down in it.

"Is it almost time to eat?" Ellie asked. "I'm starving!"

Marc nodded. "Almost. Let me go check."

"What's your friend's name?" Rachel said, after Marc left.

"Jonathan."

"He's pretty cute, huh?"

Ellie blushed and rolled her yes. "I don't know." She smiled and swung her feet over the grass.

"Ah, you think he's cute don't you?" Rachel teased.

"I guess so."

"Did you just meet him today?"

Ellie nodded.

"Do you know how long he's staying?"

"Until Sunday. He lives in Georgia."

Rachel gasped. "That's where I'm from."

"Really?"

"Yep."

"Ellie!" Marc yelled.

"Yes, daddy?"

"Would you please set the table?"

Rachel touched Ellie's hand before she got up. "Keep me posted, okay?"

Ellie blushed again, but this time she giggled too. "I will."

Rachel watched Ellie as she ran off to the Airstream. Though she downplayed it, Rachel could tell Ellie seemed excited about Jonathan. It made her think back to when she first met John. She remembered what it felt like to have butterflies in her stomach, and how she used to wait all night to get a phone call from him just so she could hear his voice.

She glanced over at Marc, cooking away. Here she was, perhaps not with the same feelings she had for John all those years ago, but she had felt *something* when she looked at him that she couldn't quite put her finger on. And though she had only known him for two days, she was interested to know more.

She stood up and walked over to him. "Need any help?" Marc took the meat out, and it sizzled and smelled incredible. She hoped it tasted as good as it looked, but she was pretty sure it would.

"I think I got it," he said. "I'm gonna make a gravy out of the drippings, and I think we'll be ready. You could open the wine if you want to."

"Sure."

By the time she found the corkscrew and glasses in the Airstream, Ellie had set the table. Marc placed the platter of meat down next to the yeast rolls. As Rachel sat down, she saw that Marc had brought another smaller platter with him.

"Asparagus too?" She looked at him curiously. "I must have missed that. I could get used to this." *Again*, she wanted say.

Marc cut the meat into one inch thick slices, then served it. It was cooked medium rare except for the ends that were more medium— perfect for Ellie. Marc and Ellie both waited, watching Rachel as she took the first bite.

"Oh, my God!" Rachel said, before even swallowing. "This is so good."

Ellie and Marc gave each other a high five across the table. Ellie said, "See, I told you she'd like it."

"Well, I knew she would too," Marc bragged.

"Uh-uh!" Ellie shook her head. "No way. That's not what you said earlier daddy!" Ellie swiveled towards Rachel. "That's not what he said."

"What?" Marc shoveled a piece of meat into his mouth. "What did I say?"

Ellie looked up to her father. "Nope! You said you were worried if she was gonna like it or not." She spun towards Rachel and said, "You see, he was worried about it all day. In fact, he almost changed his mind," then to Marc, "Didn't you?" finally back to Rachel, "He almost cooked hot dogs." Ellie cut her meat and popped it in her mouth. "But, I convinced him otherwise."

Rachel grinned as she cut her asparagus. "Oh, that's so sweet Marc. You were worried about me?" She glanced up at him, with a playful little puppy dog look on her face.

"I wasn't *worried*," Marc said. "I just wanted to make sure you liked your food. That's all."

"Uh-uh." Ellie looked to Rachel and nodded. "He was worried."

Rachel took a bite of the asparagus, then peeked up at Marc. She smiled because he was peeking at her too.

After dinner—honestly, it was every bit as good as John's cooking—Marc and Ellie started a campfire. The three of them sat in camp chairs and played twenty questions, except it didn't matter if no one guessed the question after twenty times. Ellie roasted marshmallows. Marc stoked the fire. Rachel got up a couple of times to refill their wine glasses. More than once, a massive raccoon walked right past Rachel, scaring her half to death. Ellie laughed as Marc chased it off, acting pretty scared of it himself.

After what seemed like the twentieth round of twenty questions—Marc had guessed Ellie's subject of *Time*—Rachel glanced down at her watch. "Guys, I need to be going."

"Oh, don't go," Ellie pleaded.

"Yeah, stay a little while longer, Rachel," Marc added. Rachel knew he was teasing, because she'd been yawning for the past twenty minutes or so.

"I'd like to, but Riley needs to be walked, and honestly, after all that good food…and all those *marshmallows you kept feeding me…*" Rachel leaned over towards Ellie and pinched her arm.

Ellie giggled. "Oh, all right."

"But you're gonna come over tomorrow for another guitar lesson, right?"

Ellie nodded.

Marc stood up. "Ellie, why don't you go on in and take a shower, okay Sweetie? I'm gonna walk Rachel home."

Ellie nodded, and then gave Rachel a super tight hug and a quick kiss on the cheek before running into the Airstream.

Marc and Rachel walked casually along the loop road, talking about dinner, the huge raccoons, and of course, Ellie. They walked by some of the older kids running around with headlamps on. Occasionally, they'd play their red beams of light along the windows of the some of the campers, like little aliens, in an attempt to frighten whoever was inside.

As the two of them approached Rachel's site, the conversation quieted. Marc stopped short of the Fleetwood, staying on the loop road instead of walking her to the door. Rachel thought that was a nice gesture; no need to put any undue pressure on an already fantastic evening.

Marc faced her. "I want you to know that I had a great time tonight."

"I did too, Marc. Your food was great. Your daughter is amazing." *And so are you*, she wanted to say, but it didn't feel right.

Marc smiled tenderly at her. Under any other circumstances, circumstances where they'd been younger and had never known pain as they had, Rachel thought he might have kissed her. The thought alone was pleasing enough.

"Hey, I've got an idea," Marc said. "You want to go fishing with me tomorrow?"

"Me? Fish? I've never caught a fish in my life. I tried once when I was kid, but all I ever caught was a cold."

"It's easy. Anyone can do it. Besides, I don't know if I can go to bed tonight without a yes. I'd really like to see you tomorrow."

It didn't take her long to think about it. She wanted to see him too. She nodded.

"Great. I take it you're a morning girl, right?" He looked at her funny.

"How'd you guess?"

Marc smiled. "So, I'll see you here at five in the morning then." He backed away, smiling at her as he did so.

Rachel opened the door to the Fleetwood and stepped in, thinking how glad she was she didn't walk past site thirty-seven on loop D.

The knocking came softly. Rachel's mind, still drifting along in a dream, didn't seem to acknowledge it, but then the knocks grew louder and woke her. She sat up in the bed, rubbing the sleep from her eyes, unsure of what was happening. She looked over at her clock. 5:02.

Shit! It's Marc!

"I'm coming," she called out.

She threw on her housecoat and shuffled towards the door. As she passed the dinette, the knocks grew louder.

"Coming!" she yelled. "I can't believe this," she whispered to herself. She approached the door, watching it jolt with every whomp. When she opened it, no one was there.

"Hello?" She called. "Marc?"

She stepped out and looked left, then right. The fog was thick, and she could barely see past the lighted area under the awning.

"Hello!" she called out again, waiting for a reply. The only sound she heard were the waves crashing against the shore in the distance. She walked to the edge of her vision, still under the awning, and she called out again. "Hello! Anyone there?" For a moment she stood motionless, listening.

Thinking it might've been Beverly or Charles, she ventured out towards their Winnebago, but couldn't find it. She looked for the loop road, but there was no road. Except for the dim lights coming from the Fleetwood, it was completely dark.

Frightened, she ran back to the Fleetwood and stepped inside. She looked out through the door once more. "Hello!" she yelled. "Someone knocked on my door." Again, she listened, but all she heard was the pounding of her own heart. Rachel went to close the door, and suddenly, she heard a voice—a voice she knew well.

"Rachel." The voice floated in the thick fog.

"John!" She ran out under the awning. "Where are you?" She swiveled her head, searching for him. "John!"

"The lighthouse." His words sounded lethargic and slow. "Find the lighthouse, Rachel."

"John! I can't see anything! Where are you?"

She walked towards his voice, past the edge of the awning and into the darkness. She reached out into the fog, searching for him. "Please John! Where are you?" She tripped over a small tree that had fallen over, and almost caught herself with her hands before hitting the ground. She pushed herself up and stood.

"Follow me Rachel." The voice seemed more distant, coming from the ocean.

"John, wait!" she cried. She turned and ran, desperately trying to find him. She glanced back over her shoulder towards the

Fleetwood, its lights beginning to fade away into the fog. Just as she spun her head back around, she slammed into a tree and fell. She got up and sidestepped it. As she picked up speed, a low hanging branch grazed her shoulder, another scraped her forehead. She slowed, extending her arms, feeling her way through the woods into the black night. She glanced back once more towards the Fleetwood, but all she could see was total darkness.

"John, where are you? Please!" She started crying. "I'm scared John!" Another limb smacked her in the face. The underbrush sliced into her legs with every step. She moved as fast as she could towards the ocean, stepping on sharp rocks and pinecones, colliding with more tress and branches.

Finally, she felt the sand beneath her feet, and she darted towards the ocean. "John! I'm here! Where are you?" When she reached the sea, the saltwater splashed and stung her legs where the underbrush had cut into her.

She ran south towards the lighthouse along the shore, sobbing, continuing to scream his name, only to hear the reverberation of her own voice and the crashing of invisible waves against the shore. But she continued on in complete darkness, searching for the lighthouse...never finding it.

CHAPTER SIX

THE KNOCKING CAME SOFTLY. Rachel's mind, still searching for the lighthouse in a dream, didn't seem to acknowledge it, but then the knocks grew louder and woke her. She sat up in the bed, rubbing the sleep from her eyes, unsure of what was happening. She looked over at her clock. 5:02.

Shit! It's Marc!

"I'm coming," she called out.

She threw on her housecoat and shuffled towards the door.

"Morning," Marc said, as she opened it. He smiled once he realized she'd overslept.

Rachel held a hand up to her head, blocking one side of her face, smiling. "I'm so sorry. The alarm didn't go off."

"It's all right. The fish can wait."

"Come on in," she said. "You want some coffee? I know I do."

Marc put down the fishing gear and walked in.

He was clean-shaven this morning and looked taller than he did outside. Rachel caught herself staring at him. Embarrassed, she dropped her head into her hands. She couldn't believe he saw her like this.

"So, this is it. Very nice," he said, glancing around, nodding. "Now I could be quite comfortable in something like this. I wouldn't even need a house."

"That's the plan." Rachel had set the automatic coffee maker last night, so the coffee was ready. She pulled a couple of cups from the cabinet. "Cream or sugar?"

"Black's fine." He walked to the dinette and sat down. Riley got up from his curled position next to the recliner and walked over to him. Marc scratched him on the head. "How's the reception from the satellite dish? Lot of trees out here you know."

Ain't that the truth!

"Not bad." She poured the coffee and handed him a cup. "I've only turned it on once though. Why don't you try it out while I get ready?" She picked up the remote and slid it on the table...almost hitting John's wine glass.

She walked to her bedroom and closed the door to change. Even though Marc was just flipping through channels on the television, it seemed strange having him in here. She took a couple sips of her coffee, wondering if John would have liked Marc or not. Just thinking about it, combined with the java hitting her empty stomach, made her a little nauseous.

After a few minutes, Marc turned off the television. "I had a good time last night," he said loudly, so that she could hear him. "I'm glad you came."

Rachel opened the bedroom door and walked out. "I did too," she said.

Marc grinned at her when he saw her. The print marks from the sheet could still be seen on her face.

"Well, you ready for some fishing?" he said.

"Ready as I'll ever be."

She left Riley in the Fleetwood and the two of them walked to the shore, the sky just starting to lighten up a bit.

After getting everything situated, Marc took out a couple of shrimp from the cooler. "The important thing to remember is that fish are just like humans when it comes to eating. They like their food fresh." He placed the shrimp on the two hooks that dangled from the swivel, hanging just below the sinker. "You said you fished once before, right?"

"That was a long time ago."

"Was the rod and reel the kind that had the push button on top?"

"I think so."

"Okay, well this is a little different."

He showed her how to flip the bail of the spinning reel, catching the string with her index finger. He cast it a couple of times, sending the line far out over the surf.

"Here, you give it a try." He put the rod into position and handed it to her. "Okay, flip over the bail and grab the string with your finger."

"Like this?"

"Yes, just like that." Marc backed up, giving her room. "Now, in a single motion, sling the rod over your shoulder. A little bit after the rod points straight up, let the line slip off of your finger, okay?"

"All right, here goes." The tip of the rod lay in the sand behind her. She planted her feet and looked forward and backward like she was about to swing a baseball bat. In an awkward motion, she slung the tip of the rod up just like Marc had instructed, but the line slipped off her finger way too soon. As the rod continued forward, the bait and sinker fell behind her. The line that did come out simply spun off the spool and fell to the sand.

"Shit!" Rachel said, stomping her foot.

"That's okay. It happens to everybody," Marc assured her.

He reset the reel, and she tried again. This time, she managed to release the fishing line at the correct moment, but the angle of the cast sent the bait flying way over to her left, falling into the waves about ten feet in front of her.

"Why can't I get it to go straight," Rachel said. "This can't be that hard!"

"Try using your whole body to cast, not just your arms. Once you get used to it, you'll feel the sweet spot."

"Are you sure?"

"Absolutely."

Again, Marc reset the reel. "Okay, put your whole body into it this time. Try to think of the rod as an extension of your body. Follow through." He moved back. "*Be* the rod, Rachel. *Be*...the rod."

"Ha ha, very funny."

She set her hips, looked front to back, and then hurled the rod over her head. She released the line, looking out over the ocean to see where it landed. Three seconds later, the bait and hook hit the sand about two feet in front of her.

"Ugh! I don't think I can do it."

"Sure you can." He walked up close behind her, but stopped short of touching her body. "Can I help you?"

"Well, I hope so. Otherwise, I don't think it's going to happen."

He moved in behind her and stretched his arms around her shoulders and down her arms. She felt Marc's chest against her back, his legs pressing against hers. The sun was just starting to crest over the horizon.

"It's really about moving your body with the rod as one single motion," he said. Rachel felt his warm breath on the back of her neck.

"Okay," she said, trying to keep her breathing normal.

"What we're going to try is a nice and easy cast. Nothing hard. We're looking for a smooth motion."

"Okay."

"On the count of three."

"Okay," she said, for the third time in a row.

"One...two...three!"

Simultaneously, they began the cast and she pushed her body against his, matching his speed. She felt the muscles in his stomach tighten against her back as their bodies began to twist forward. As the rod hurled over them, Marc let his right hand slip off of her grip, and it slid up her arm to her shoulder.

The rod fell directly in front of her. She looked out over the water to watch the bait fly, but didn't see it. She looked at her hand and realized she'd forgotten to release her finger; it was still curled under the line. The bait dangled from the tip of the rod.

"Shit!" she yelled, stomping again. "I forgot to let go."

"That's okay."

"Can we try it again?"

"Sure."

Marc positioned the rod again, and once more, he placed his arms around her. This time, Rachel let herself enjoy his body up against hers. She was acutely aware of the places he touched. Her breathing grew heavy, and Marc's lips seemed to be closer to her neck. The sun was halfway up on the horizon, and she felt its orange rays warm her face.

"Here we go." He shifted his weight slightly, setting his feet firmly into the sand. "One…two—hey, hey!"

"Uh-huh?" she said, like waking from a dream.

"Don't forget to release, okay?"

"Okay."

He started his count again. "One…two…three!"

Rachel closed her eyes, and their bodies once again twisted in unison, pressing against each other as if they were one object. This time, Rachel remembered to release the line from her finger. At the end of the cast, Marc's left hand remained on her grip, and his right stayed on her shoulder for a second or two.

"That was better," he said.

Rachel opened her eyes and followed the fishing line to the water. She had no idea how far the bait went.

"We should probably try it once more," he said. "Just to make sure you got it."

"Okay."

For the third time, he wrapped his arms around her and their bodies meshed together. She could feel his large hands grip more tightly than he had before. Rachel pressed up against him before they even started their motion.

"One…"

Rachel closed her eyes and pulled her head up, almost touching his lips with her neck. The muscles in his thighs began to tighten.

"Two…"

She pressed her hips back into him, and he responded with equal pressure. His arms began to clamp down around her.

"Three!"

As they twisted, the rod slung up, and she felt the entire curve of his body compress over hers. The rod arched upward, and his left hand fell to her stomach, pulling her close. She felt Marc's lips touch her and she pushed her neck into him. His right arm swept around her waist, higher than his left.

Somehow, Rachel managed to release the line and the bait sailed into the ocean, beyond the surf. As she straightened her body, he was still holding her, and for a moment, she let him, feeling his hands press against her abdomen. Then, the rod fell, and she spun out of his arms, nearly tripping over it. She backed away.

"Okay," she said, breathing heavily. "I think I got it now."

"Yeah. Uh…good job." He reached down and picked up the rod. "Here you go."

"No…I think I'm good. You go ahead."

"You sure?"

"Yeah, I'm sure."

Rachel sat down in the sand and watched him as he reset the reel and cast it. The sun sat well up above the horizon now, and the orange glow had shifted to yellow. Her breathing slowly returned to normal, and she thought about what just took place.

It happened so quickly, and she couldn't deny what she felt. Was it a natural sexual desire brought on by instinct, or because of a general distance from it? Marc was a handsome man, true enough, so it would make sense that she'd react the way she did. It had been a long time, after all.

But then another thought entered her mind. Did she actually have sexual feelings for Marc…not because he was just some good looking man that put his arms around her, but rather because of *who* he was; someone she had real feelings for?

Having no luck, Marc reeled in the line and placed the rod on the sand next to the other fishing gear. He plopped down close to Rachel, and for a bit he gazed out over the water. They watched a pair of seabirds dive into the ocean and easily come up with fish. The irony of it seemed fitting.

After a while Marc nudged her shoulder with his. Rachel smirked and nudged him back, making him laugh out loud.

"You okay?" he asked.

"I'm fine. This is all so new to me."

"I know what you mean." Marc picked up some sand from between his legs and let it pour out from his loose fist. "Rachel, I really enjoy spending time with you."

She almost said, *you're just saying that*, but didn't. She didn't because she knew he was telling the truth. She felt the same way.

Marc picked up another handful of sand. "Since my wife died, I didn't think I could ever see myself with anyone again, but when I saw you jogging the other day...I don't know...something just told me that I should at least try. I couldn't believe it when you showed up at Beverly's for dinner."

"I want to be honest with you Marc. I'm not sure how I feel right now. I mean, I enjoy spending time with you too, but I feel like I'm doing something wrong. I really don't know what I'm supposed to do."

"I understand," Marc said. "I don't want anything that we do together to be stressful. I really don't. But at least we've both loved and lost, so that's something we have in common. Honestly, and I don't want to make it sound like I don't find you attractive, because I really do, but maybe that's what draws me towards you; the fact that you know what it feels like to experience loss. Real loss. I just feel like I can relate to you."

"I can see that," she said. And she really did. She hadn't thought about it before, but she didn't think she could share her feelings so easily with someone that hadn't been through a similar situation. With Marc, she didn't feel that much anxiety about it, or at least not as much as she thought she would. Still, she had to admit there was something more going on that she couldn't explain.

Rachel shifted in the sand so she could face him. "I want you know that I can't really promise anything."

"Of course not. We're just spending time together. That's all."

"I know, but I needed to say it. Don't get me wrong, I like it when we're together, but I've gambled a lot coming out here. The last two years almost killed me. I mean, there was a point in my life when I really didn't think I was going to make it. Coming here, I guess, is a way for me to confront a future that John and I were supposed to have. Granted, I think I've made some progress, but I know I have a ways to go. I have to focus on that."

"I understand."

"And who knows? Maybe it won't be a big deal. I mean, so far we're just having dinner, right?"

"Right."

"Well, some fishing too...or whatever you want to call what we were doing. Maybe that will help. Maybe it won't. I don't know. I just can't get caught up in a relationship, or have to worry about someone else's feelings. It's hard enough to worry about my own right now."

"Rachel, I really don't think—"

"What I mean is, I've never had to deal with a situation like this. What if we really start to like each other? That's just going to complicate things. Everything could go great for a while and then I might just fall apart. What then? What if—"

"Rachel," Marc said, getting her attention. She stopped talking and he smiled at her. "We don't have to plan anything."

"I can't help it," she said. "I'm a planner. I like to know what's going to happen."

"Okay, well let's plan. I've got a photo shoot this afternoon. You wanna tag along?"

"A photo shoot?"

"Yep, in Beaufort."

"I won't be in the way or anything?"

"No," he sort of laughed. "You won't be in the way. I'll swing by and pick you up about four o'clock. That okay?"

"Sure. It sounds like fun. I've never been on a real photo shoot."

"Well," he said, smirking, "you're in for a real treat then."

Marc poured out the rest of the sand he'd been holding on to, then stood up and offered his hand to Rachel to help her up.

"I think I like fishing with you," Marc said. "You might need a few more lessons though."

Rachel blushed. "I don't know if I can handle any more of *those* lessons."

Later that morning Rachel sat under the awning of the Fleetwood and read. She'd had enough fun at the beach for one day. But like before, it was difficult to concentrate on the words. Her mind seemed preoccupied with Marc, thinking about the last couple of days she'd spent with him.

After a while, Ellie walked up, but she didn't have the guitar with her. Rachel noticed right away that something wasn't right. Normally, Ellie looked so excited to see her.

"Hey Ellie."

"Hi." She produced a quick little smile and it fell flat as swiftly as it came.

"You didn't bring the guitar today?"

Ellie shook her head.

"How come?"

Ellie shrugged then took a seat at the picnic table. Riley walked up to her, and she gave him an unenthusiastic pet on the head. Riley took what he could get though.

"What's the matter?" Rachel said. Ellie stared at the ground, moving some of the small pebbles around with her feet. "Ellie?" Rachel continued, "Is everything okay?"

Ellie shrugged again and sat there a moment before she spoke. "I guess I just miss my mom," she finally said.

"I'm sorry Ellie. I know that must be really hard."

Ellie nodded. "If I tell you something, will you promise not to tell my dad?"

Rachel wasn't sure if she should agree or not, but this seemed pretty serious. "Okay, I won't."

"When I got out of the shower last night, I saw some blood on the floor." At first, Rachel didn't know what she was talking about because Ellie had said it so quietly. "I think it came from here." Ellie pointed to her lap.

"Oh, you started your period," Rachel said. Not having her mother around to explain things, it probably caught Ellie completely by surprise. "Do you know what that is?" Ellie nodded, then dropped her head and began to cry. Rachel got up and sat next to her, then put her arms around her. Ellie hugged her back. "It's okay," Rachel said, her heart aching. "It happens to every girl."

Ellie's mother would never be around to help her through times like these. Marc probably hadn't even thought about it. Why would he? That's always been a mother's job.

Ellie's crying slowed and eventually turned into sniffling. "It's so stupid. I don't know why God had to make us like this."

"I know. Come on." Rachel took her by the hand and they went inside the Fleetwood, then she led Ellie to the bedroom.

"Have a seat. Are you using anything now?"

"Kleenex."

Rachel walked into the bathroom and came back out with a couple of pads. She explained to Ellie how to use them. "Now, go in the bathroom and put this one on. I'll be back in a couple of minutes. I'll go to the camp store and get you some."

When Rachel came back, Ellie was sitting at the dinette table. "Did you have any trouble with it?" Rachel asked.

Ellie shook her head.

"This should last you quite a while." Rachel set the bag with the pads down on the table. She double bagged them so no one would be able to see what they were when Ellie walked back.

"It feels so weird." Ellie shifted in her seat. "Almost like I'm wearing a stupid diaper or something."

"You'll get used to it. Just always make sure you carry at least one in your purse. Oh, and it might be a good idea to avoid light colored pants or shorts when you're getting ready to start. Believe me, I know from personal experience."

"You do? What happened?"

"I was nine when I started my period. That's pretty young, but not unheard of. I was in fourth grade, in Coach Spalding's class. Not only was he the sole male teacher in the school, but he was also the strictest. Well, there was the chorus teacher. She was pretty mean too, but Coach Spalding was definitely the worst.

"Anyway, I felt sick to my stomach most of the day, and I started hurting so bad that I really thought I should try and go to the bathroom. But Coach Spalding didn't let students go except during break or if it was *an emergency*; everybody knew what that meant.

"I waited, trying to just deal with the cramps until my next class with Mrs. Allen, but the pain got so bad that I didn't want to have an accident. I raised my hand. 'Coach Spalding?'

'Yes, Rachel, what is it?' he said in one of those *please don't bother me* voices.

'May I go to the bathroom?' I asked him.

'No, you may not. You can go at break.'

"Another couple of minutes went by but the pain had worsened, so I raised my hand again. Coach Spalding didn't even give me a chance to ask. He only said, 'No Rachel, you can't go to the bathroom.'

'But it's an emergency!' I said.

"He looked at me for a second, peering over the rim of his glasses. 'Really? An emergency?' he said, like he was testing me. I felt everyone in the classroom looking at me as I nodded.

'All right,' Coach Spalding said. Even then he sounded so mean. 'But hurry up.'

"When I stood up, I felt something wet in my shorts…my khaki colored shorts. I walked past a couple of the desks and heard one of the boys in my class, Jason Wetherby, I'll never forget his name, whisper 'look, she pooped her shorts,' and then I heard nothing but giggles. Another one of the boys, I wasn't sure who, started to make farting sounds. Soon the rest of the class joined them.

'That's enough!' Coach Spalding yelled. I walked up to his desk and took the hall pass.

"When I got to the bathroom, I found blood in my underwear and saw that it had leaked all the way through my shorts. I had no idea what was happening. Crying, I ran as fast as I could to the office and asked to call my mom. When the nice lady at the office asked why, I told her that my guts were coming out and that I thought I was going to die. The school nurse was at least some comfort in reassuring me that I wasn't. When mom picked me up and explained everything to me, I was really upset that she hadn't talked to me about it sooner."

"What did you say to your friends the next day?" Ellie asked.

"I told them that I sat in some ketchup during lunch. My best friend though, Cynthia, I told her the truth, and I found out that her mom had already talked to her about it. When I asked her why she didn't tell me, she told me that her mom said it was up to each mother to talk to their own daughter, and that she wasn't to mention anything to anybody."

Ellie lowered her head. "I wish I had my mom around to talk to."

Rachel's heart hurt, and she wanted to take that pain away from Ellie. She couldn't though, no more than she could take her own pain away. Marc was a great dad, at least from what she'd seen, but there were certain things that only a woman could answer, and a lot that only a mother could.

"Ellie, you can always come talk to me about anything you want to, okay?"

Ellie nodded.

"You'll need to talk to your dad about this. If you want, I can do it for you. You want me to?"

At first Ellie didn't say anything, but finally she nodded again.

"Do you have any questions?"

Ellie pondered it for a second, then looked up at Rachel. "Do you have any kids?"

That's not what Rachel was expecting. She shook her head.

"How come? Dad said that you used to be married but not anymore."

"We tried to have children and couldn't," Rachel said. "A doctor told us there was only a slim chance. It just never happened."

Ellie looked down at the ground, taking in what Rachel said. Then: "Well, since you don't have any, if you ever have some questions about kids, just let me know." She smiled. "I'm pretty much an expert."

Preparing for the photo shoot, Rachel looked at herself in the mirror, applying the last bit of mascara to her eyelashes. She never wore a lot of makeup, but today she took her time applying it. Deciding to wear her hair down, it flowed over her blouse: a blue one she picked out that really pulled out the color in her eyes. She wanted to remain casual, so she put on a pair of white shorts, which did wonderful things for her tan legs.

Marc knocked on the door promptly at four. When Rachel opened it, she saw him looking down at something, perhaps impressed by the automatic steps that extended out of the Fleetwood when the door opened. Marc looked up and seemed stunned.

"What?" Rachel said.

"Wow. You look…amazing."

Rachel smiled. She looked at him in a similar fashion. "Thanks. So do you."

Marc wore a red polo and a pair of khaki shorts. It didn't matter what color his shorts were, his strong legs always looked good. Hell, all of him looked good.

Rachel caught herself staring, and she blushed as she started down the steps. Marc couldn't seem to look away. He almost didn't let her by, moving only at the last possible second. He motioned with his arm to show her the way to his truck.

"Is Ellie coming with us?" Rachel asked.

"No, she's gonna stay with Aunt Bev tonight. My aunt has a certain infatuation with Monopoly. She always has. I can't tell you the number of games we've played together. Most of the time she won. Ellie on the other hand…she gives her a good run for her money." He chuckled. "No pun intended."

Marc opened the passenger door of his truck and helped Rachel inside. He walked around the front and Rachel saw him look at her, then quickly turn away, as if trying not to appear rude. When he got in and cranked the engine, he glanced at her again.

It was hot. Marc flipped on the air conditioning, and pulled out.

"So," Rachel said, "are we going to shoot some hot model or something?"

"Models," he said, emphasizing the plural form of the word. "And yes, I think they're going to be quite hot."

"So, some real knockouts, huh?"

Marc smiled, "If we're lucky."

"When did you get into photography?"

"Sort of a crazy story, really. You remember that book *Bridges of Madison County*?"

"Sure. In the movie, Clint Eastwood played Robert Kincaid, a photographer that falls in love with Meryl Streep. I can't remember her character's name though."

"Francesca Johnson." The way he said it, the words sort of rolled off his tongue.

"That's right. Francesca. I remember liking the book better than the movie."

"Yeah, me too. It's funny how it always works out that way. Anyway, I was well on my way to flunking out of college, and did by the way in case you were wondering, when my mom told me about the book. She called me up and said I had to read it, right then and there. I wasn't going to class anyways, so I picked up a copy and read it during finals."

Rachel gasped. "During finals?"

"You gotta understand," he continued "I was majoring in business, just like my father had. It's one reason I was doing so bad in school. I hated it. After I read that book, I was swept up by the whole idea of becoming a *National Geographic* photographer, just like Robert Kincaid, and the allure of it that was represented in the book. Don't get me wrong, the love story was good, but as a business major with no real desire for business, this was a complete one-eighty from that. I bit, hook, line, and sinker."

"So did it turn out like you thought it would? Like some free spirit roaming from exotic place to exotic place?"

Marc laughed. "Well, I never made it to *National Geographic*, but yeah, in a way it did, I guess. It's just like anything else though. It's a lot of hard work. Not anything how you might think it would be. And the business side of it…well, let's just say I could've used that business degree after all."

As they crossed over the drawbridge on Sea Island Parkway, the tires of his truck began to rumble, impeding their conversation. Rachel glanced over at him a couple of times, the second of which, he glanced at her too. Like catching each other with their hands in the cookie jar, they looked away, both smiling.

Once they reached the other side of the drawbridge, Marc picked up where he left off. "For a few years I traveled to some beautiful places as well as some tragic ones. After I met Carrie, I settled down a bit and focused on stock photos. I had already collected a pretty substantial photo collection, so it was an easy transition. Plus, it enabled me to spend a lot of time with my family once we had Ellie. It was something I could do locally, and every now and then, we'd travel to a few locations that I wanted to shoot. I even did a series on South Carolina bridges a few years back. The state made a calendar out of it."

"Full circle, huh?"

Marc laughed. "Yeah, I suppose so. It was pretty cool. It wasn't too long after that that Carrie died."

Marc's smile faded, and though he continued to drive, Rachel could tell he was on autopilot, thinking of his wife.

"So, where's the most beautiful place you've ever been" she said, trying to bring his mind back to her. "You know…to take pictures."

"I don't know if it's the most beautiful or not, although it is very beautiful, but my favorite place was Machu Picchu in Peru. It's simply awe-inspiring. There's no place like it. I could spend weeks there photographing the place. Some of the photos ended up in the article in *Time Magazine* that Aunt Bev mentioned." He paused for a second. Again, the look on his face mimicked a child that lost his puppy. "Then I met Carrie."

Rachel knew his wife was burning a hole in his memory right then. She knew, because it happened to her so many times before thinking about John. But now, she felt what it was like to be on the other side of it.

Something snapped Marc's mind back to the present. "I want to take Ellie there someday. Hey, maybe the three of us will go." Surprised by his comment, Rachel was just about the say something when Marc said, "You ready for the shoot?"

Rachel hadn't realized that they'd come to a complete stop until Marc put the truck in park. She pulled her sunglasses down over the end of her nose and looked around. "This can't be it."

"Yep." He said, wearing a sinister little grin.

"A little league baseball game?"

"That's right."

"I thought you said we were going to be shooting hot models?"

"Well, it's pretty darn hot out there." Marc looked through the steering wheel to the instrument cluster. "Yep, about ninety degrees it says. Although I may have been wrong about the knockouts. This is farm league so I'm not sure if they can hit it over the fence or not. But like I said, maybe we'll get lucky."

Rachel sighed and rolled her eyes in a playful way. She pushed her sunglasses back up the bridge of her nose, and opened the door, swinging her legs out in sort of a provocative fashion.

Marc turned off the engine and reached in the backseat to grab his backpack full of camera gear. He got out and closed the door, then looked over the hood of the truck, a conniving little smile adorned his face.

"Well played," Rachel said. "I'd be on the lookout if I were you, though." She gazed out over the park.

"Is that right?"

"Uh-huh." She glanced back at him, smiling.

"Well, I look forward to it Mrs. Willers."

"Can I help you carry anything?"

"Nope, I've got everything right here." He slung the backpack over his shoulder and they made their way towards the field.

The ballpark seemed a little run down, but the field looked nice and green. Marc talked to both coaches, the umpires, and what appeared to be every set of parents for each player on both teams. Like all small towns, everybody knew everybody—and everybody's business. Rachel and Marc couldn't walk more than ten feet without being stopped for a short conversation or an update on what was going on. What seemed to be *going on* was Marc had a *strange lady* with him. Rachel overheard a couple of the older, gossiping type women—as if there were any other kind—talking about them. She'd heard the phrase '*it's about time*' or '*good for him*' more than once.

They finally found themselves somewhat alone, next to the fence along the third base foul line. Marc set his backpack down and unzipped it, revealing an array of cameras and lenses, organized neatly in padded sections.

"Sorry about all that back there," he said.

"I lived in Atlanta, remember?" Rachel said. "It's a boomtown right now, but we still have our share of little old ladies. It's still The South."

Marc laughed. "I suppose so. I guess that makes you a southern belle then, doesn't it?"

"Why yes, I suppose it does," she said, in her best southern accent. She followed it up with a curtsy, which apparently some of the gossipers saw, because the chitchat from the bleachers quieted down.

Marc strapped a couple of cameras around his body, and then he stood up and faced her. "That would mean you like grits then, right?"

"I don't think I could call myself a southern lady if I didn't. Besides, I might get hurt in this crowd if I said otherwise."

"True." Marc swiveled his head towards the bleachers as twenty women swiveled theirs back towards the field, simultaneously checking the curls in their hair—whether they had them or not. Rachel could tell Marc enjoyed toying with them.

"How about some dinner after this?" Marc asked. "I know a little place that has the best shrimp and grits on the planet. Or at least south of Charleston anyways."

"Sounds great."

"All right then," Marc said. "It's a date."

A date?

As Marc took the lens cap off and walked to the gate that led inside the fence, Rachel felt a touch queasy. Had last night been a date as well? And if so, did that mean she was now dating?

She walked up to the fence and folded her arms across the top of it and watched Marc as he took pictures. She enjoyed watching him as he shifted his body around to get different shots. He seemed to almost glide from position to position, firing off a series of quick shots of the pitcher or sweeping close to the ground as a base runner slid into third.

Between one of the innings, after Marc had taken a couple of candid shots of the team in the dugout, Rachel saw, from the corner of her eye, that he had the camera trained on her. Pretending she didn't notice, she gazed out over the field trying to look pretty for him. The wind caught her hair and she swung her head to fling the hair out of her face. After a moment, she turned to face him. In that same instant, she heard the camera's shutter click as he snapped a photo of her. Marc pulled the camera down from his face and looked at her. Something fluttered in her stomach. She wasn't sure if the sensation came from Marc, or from the hundred sets of eyes certainly staring at her from the bleachers.

Marc walked up to the fence separating the two of them. "You doing okay?"

"Yeah."

"You're not bored or anything?"

"Oh, no!" she said, almost a little too enthusiastically. "I'm having a good time."

"You know," he said with that little devilish look on his face that she was beginning to be acquainted with, "I wish I could kiss you right now."

Rachel motioned to the bleachers. "Yeah, that would really freak 'em out, wouldn't it?"

"It doesn't have anything to do with them."

Rachel felt her heart skip a beat…or two. She bit her bottom lip and contemplated seizing his face with both of her hands and pulling him towards her. She really wanted to.

"Play ball!" the home plate ump called out. Marc studied her face as he backed away from her. Rachel felt her heartbeat quicken in her chest, and it stayed that way even when Marc finally turned around…*after* the first pitch of the inning had been thrown.

At the end of game, it took several minutes of additional conversation with a host of people that knew Marc before they were able to leave. This time, there seemed to be an even bigger interest in Rachel by the gossipers, and she found herself speaking to several of them. *'How long have you known Marc'* they'd say, to which she'd answer *'not long, we're just friends.'* From others she heard *'Marc is such a wonderful person,'* and *'isn't Ellie just the most precious little thing?'*

When they got back inside Marc's truck, Rachel sighed.

"Sorry about that," he said. "When I asked you to come, it didn't even cross my mind that they'd be all over us. But I should've known."

"You sure do know a lot of people."

"It's a pretty small town," he said, "and I guess there are those that think I'm some sort of celebrity or something. But honestly, I've known most of them my whole life. They're good people, even if they are a bit nosy." Marc cranked the truck and headed for the park's exit.

As they drove to the restaurant, Marc filled Rachel in on a few tidbits about some of the gossipers that she met. Little old ladies weren't the only ones that gossip.

They arrived at the restaurant about seven-thirty. The color of the place looked to be originally sea foam, but weathered from years of coastal humidity and salty wind, it looked closer to a gray than anything. Huge letters that used to be painted white, now cracked and aged, hung across the gable that spelled *The Lighthouse*.

Naturally, the first thing Rachel noticed when she walked in was the owner's apparent fondness for lighthouses. With the exception of a few ceramic sea horses affixed to dark wooden beams that ran lengthwise across the width of the place, images and objects of lighthouses appeared everywhere. Pictures of old lighthouses hung between the large open-air windows. Miniature lighthouses with fishing nets strewn over them stood in each corner; one had a working lamp that rotated inside the dome. The barstools were lighthouses. Lighthouses were inset deep in the yellowing, shellac tabletops. Even the salt and pepper shakers were little lighthouses. All of it made Rachel feel a little uneasy.

Thankfully, the place wasn't too crowded, and Marc chose a spot next to a window that opened up to a fabulous view of the waterway. The sun began to drop, as did the temperature, and a cool, salty breeze blew in from outside, which made Rachel feel a little better.

"You okay?" Marc said. "You look a little pale."

"I'm fine. I think it was just a little hot out today." She took one of the menus that had a picture of a lighthouse on the front, and opened it. She closed it immediately, remembering why they came. "I guess I'll have the famous shrimp and grits."

"Howdy Marc," the waitress said. *Just great.* The waitress knew him too.

"Hey Julie, how are you?" Marc said.

"If I was any better, I'd be you! Who's this?" She looked over at Rachel and smiled.

Rachel returned the gesture. "I'm Rachel," she said before Marc could answer. "I'm just a friend, staying at Hunting Island."

"Oh, okay." Julie nodded her head. She looked uncertain about Rachel's answer. "So, what's it going to be guys?"

"Do you like oysters?" Marc asked.

"Love them," Rachel said.

"Let's get a dozen raw, two shrimp and grits, and…" he looked at Rachel, "two Corona's?"

She nodded.

As the waitress left, Rachel gazed out the window. In the distance, a shrimp boat made its way through the waterway, and she wondered if the shrimp they ordered came from that boat.

Watching it fade from her view, her mind drifted back in time, as she started to daydream, back to a time before the Fleetwood, before cancer.

A time when she was much younger.

"Look!" John said, pointing to the boat that had just left a quaint little fish market situated on the waterway. "I bet we're just in time. Come on." He and Rachel jumped out of their car and he grabbed her hand, pulling her as he practically ran to the door. "What do you want? I'll cook you anything you want! Just name it!"

"How about shark! A hammerhead."

"Okay. What else."

"Some lobster, and some caviar!"

"And?"

"King crab! And maybe even a puffer fish."

They walked in through the screen door, and it slammed shut behind them. A man in a well-worn cap greeted them. "Mornin'. What can I do for you folks?"

John looked up and down the ice filled bins full of different sized shrimp, crawfish, crabs and fish. "Hmmm." He tapped his chin with his finger. "Do you have any hammerhead?"

"No sir." The man looked at John with his head cocked to one side. "We don't have any kind of shark. All we have is right here."

"No puffer fish?"

The man studied John for a second, and then shook his head.

"Okay, then I'll take a pound of the baby lobsters."

"You mean crawfish?"

"Yes. And two pounds of shrimp. You don't happen to have any caviar, do you?"

The man looked at John like he'd lost his mind. "Fish eggs?"

"Yes. Caviar"

"No sir. We don't carry fish eggs."

"Okay, then how about some Old Bay seasoning, potatoes, and corn."

"That, we have."

As the man walked to the other end of the room to pick up the items, John put his arms around Rachel. He pulled her tight into his body, and placed the tip of his nose on hers. "I guess you'll have to settle for a low country boil this time…with little baby lobsters."

Rachel placed her hands on his face. "As long as I'm with you, I'll never have to settle for anything."

"How about some beer?"

"Huh?"

"Your beer?" Marc pointed to the Corona.

"Oh. Yeah." Rachel shook the fog from her mind. She smiled at him and picked it up, pushing the lime down the neck before taking a sip.

"What about you?" Marc said. "Rachel Willers. I'd like to hear more of your story."

It was a true love story.

"It's nothing really," Rachel said. "Certainly nothing as exciting as being a photographer, I'm sure."

"Ah, come on."

She took another sip of beer and shifted forward in her seat and put her elbows on the table. "Well, I grew up west of Atlanta. We lived on about two hundred acres of farmland."

Marc finished swallowing some of his beer. "The farmer's daughter."

She laughed. "Hardly. My dad worked for Lockheed. He was an aeronautical engineer and designed planes for the military, but he had grown up on a farm. He made pretty good money, so he saved up and bought the farm." Rachel chuckled, and then shook her head. "It's funny. He always wanted to be a veterinarian, but grandma said we already had a vet in the family, so he had to be something else."

Marc laughed. "Grandma sounds like a pistol."

"Yeah, she was. She was an amazing lady, and a great grandmother. You would have liked her. She would have fit in perfect at the park today."

"Sounds like it."

"Actually, she was a lot like Beverly."

"Well, then I *know* she would have fit in." They both laughed and Rachel took another sip of her beer, as did he. She enjoyed talking to Marc. He was easy to talk to and seemed genuinely interested in her.

Rachel continued, "I met John my freshman year in high school."

"Ah, high school sweethearts, huh?"

"Yeah, it truly was love at first sight. We had science together and the teacher made everyone sit alphabetically according to their last name. My maiden name is Walker. The lab tables were only big enough for two people, and we shared one of them. He was so goofy, always cutting up in class, even with the teacher. He was a lot of fun. I gave him my phone number and he started calling me."

She took a couple of sips of her beer and barely swallowed before she continued. "Oh, my God, he started calling me every night at nine! Like clockwork. We talked for hours and hours. Ten, eleven, twelve o'clock at night. It got so bad that I had a hard time getting up in the morning, and eventually mom made me stop talking to him so much. So John, he starts writing me letters for me to read at night. Can you believe it? And they were the most beautiful, sweetest words I have ever read."

She suddenly realized that she was rambling, like talking to one of her girlfriends. "Marc, I'm sorry. You don't need to hear about any of this."

"You two hit it off, and he fell head over heels for you. Sounds like a guy madly in love. What's wrong with that?"

"Nothing, I guess. I just should've been a little more thoughtful."

Marc leaned in towards her a little bit. "Look, we both have a past. No need to apologize for that."

Julie came and sat a dozen raw oysters down on the table. Rachel's eyes bulged. "Those…are enormous."

"Pretty nice, huh?" Marc said.

Rachel didn't see any cocktail sauce, but it came with a small cup of prepared horseradish, a bit of ketchup and some lemon wedges to make it on their own. Marc started mixing the ingredients together. "What happened next?"

"John and I started dating, and we were together ever since. Even after we started dating, he still wrote me." She appreciated Marc's consideration, but she decided not to go into further detail about his letters, not so much for his sake, but for hers.

"And college?"

"Well, I wanted to be a writer. I know it sounds stupid, but John's letters inspired me."

"No. It doesn't sound stupid at all."

"He was so good at it. Words just flowed so easily from him."

"Did John become a writer?"

"No, he didn't want to. He said his only interest in writing was to write to me."

Marc took an oyster and placed it on a cracker, topping it off with a little of the cocktail sauce that he made, and handed it to her. "Wow, I don't think I can compete with a guy like that."

Rachel thought about it for a second. She liked Marc, she really did, but he was right. No one could hold a candle to John. Rachel popped the assembled cracker into her mouth, and washed it down with some of her beer.

"Daddy really wanted me to go to business school." Rachel started assembling another. "And John didn't care where he went as long as we were together, so we both went to Georgia. I majored in Marketing, and John in Finance."

"Marketing? That's a long ways off from a writer."

"Not as much as you'd think." In went another oyster. "You see," she said, chewing, "it really involves a lot of creative thinking. It's really about creating value for consumers, and communicating to them in such a way that focuses in on what they need, whether they know it or not." Rachel stopped, sort of abruptly, and then: "You know what, I don't miss corporate life one bit!"

Marc just finished up an oyster himself. "Here, here!" He lifted up his beer and clanked the neck of it against Rachel's. They both finished what was left of their beers, so he ordered a couple more.

"Oh, I almost forgot to tell you," Rachel said. She leaned over the table like she had a secret to tell, and Marc did the same. "Ellie started her period."

Marc swallowed hard. His jaw opened and he turned ghost white pale. He fell against the back of his chair, and stared at the table. He shook his head, a sort of confused look on his face.

"It's okay, Marc. I went to the camp store and got her some pads. I showed her how to use them and everything."

"Pads?" He looked up at her, his eyes glassy. "It didn't even cross my mind. What was I thinking...or not thinking? How could I have been so stupid?" He shook his head again, blinking. "Is...is she okay?"

"Yeah, she's okay."

"Are you sure? Was she in pain or anything?"

"She's fine, Marc. She came to me this morning and we took care of it." Rachel thought about telling him about Ellie missing her mom, but didn't want to upset him further.

Marc fell back into his seat again.

"It's not a big deal," Rachel said. "It happens to every girl sooner or later."

"I know. I just should have been there for her. God, she's grown up so fast. She's a pretty special girl."

"I know. And I've only known her for a couple of days."

For a second, it looked like Marc was about to say something else, but didn't. He lifted his beer up to his mouth and took a long, hard, almost audible swallow, then gazed out the window into the darkening amber sky.

"I can remember holding her as a baby against my chest just like it was yesterday." A slim smile formed on his face and he spoke gently. "One night she was having trouble going to sleep. Carrie was always the type to let her cry. She always felt it was best to let Ellie fall asleep on her own. She was a great mother, just a little stricter than I was.

"Anyway, I finally went in to her room and picked Ellie up. I know I probably shouldn't have, but I did. By this time, she was worked up pretty good. You know how babies can get. So I took her into the den and turned on the radio, hoping I could dance her to sleep. It took almost forty-five minutes, but she finally drifted off." Marc smiled warmly. "*The Very Thought of You* started to play on the radio."

Marc paused, and Rachel knew that he was replaying that moment vividly in his mind. Marc spoke softly. "I kept dancing with her. My arm started to cramp up, but I wanted that moment to last forever; her little head on my shoulder, her eyes closed and her mouth open, slobber drooling out and everything. She just slept."

Marc turned away from the window and looked directly into Rachel's eyes. "You know, she was as safe as she could ever be, right there in my arms. I probably danced with her for another hour before I put her back in her crib."

"Marc, that's so sweet." Rachel blotted the corner of her eyes with her napkin. "Ellie's a very lucky girl."

Marc seemed dazed for a few seconds and Rachel thought about asking him if he was okay. But then he turned up his bottle of beer and downed the remaining half. For some reason, Rachel felt compelled to do the same, like Russian soldiers toasting with shots of vodka before a big battle, except that Rachel grimaced when she finished.

Julie set the plates of shrimp and grits down on the table with a loud clank. "Here we go guys. You need a couple more beers?"

"Yeah," Marc said, quickly. "I know I do."

"Make that two," Rachel said, just as fast.

Like the oysters, the shrimp that sat on the bed of grits looked huge. Ladled on top, a savory brown shrimp stock oozed into the grits, and the whole thing was topped off with some Andouille sausage and green scallions.

Rachel took a bite and looked at Marc, who was already staring at her, waiting on her to comment. "Now, *this* is amazing!"

"I told you. Would I lie?"

"Well, I really don't know. Would you?"

"Of course not," he said, playfully acting like his feelings were hurt. "Would you lie to me?" he shot back.

"Hmmm." She moved her eyes up and to the right, chewing her shrimp, considering his question. "I don't know. I might."

"What?" he said in a high-pitched voice. "What do you mean, *you might?*"

"I just might."

"Well, give me an example," he said, then put an entire shrimp in his mouth.

"Okay." She took another bite as she thought about it. Grits and sauce only this time. "Like if I said I liked your cooking, but really didn't, I might lie and say I did."

Marc's spoon fell out of his hand, and it hit the plate with a clank before bouncing onto the floor. He sat straight up in his chair and stopped chewing. Most of the shrimp was still in his mouth and his left cheek bulged out like there was a golf ball in there. Widening his eyes, and with a voice that only a man with a mouthful of food could produce, he said, "You don't like my cooking?"

"I didn't say that." She dipped her fork into the delicious grits and took another bite, then stared him down, chewing.

Marc shifted the golfball-sized bit of food in his cheek and swallowed the whole thing down in a single gulp. Just then, Julie walked up with another spoon and the two beers that he had ordered. It was a good thing she did too, because Marc swallowed more than he really should have, and his face was turning red. He let out one of those internal coughs, and he picked up his fresh beer as his eyes watered. He drank down a good third of it to help the food go down.

Rachel laughed into her napkin.

"I'm glad you think it's funny," he said, his voice muffled. He smiled then coughed into his own napkin.

Julie slid the clean spoon into his grits. "Here you go big boy." Rachel fell back into her chair and laughed harder into her napkin, this time bringing tears to her eyes.

Marc cleared his throat a couple more times. "Okay, thanks for the help ladies. I'm good."

"You sure?" Julie replied. "I've got a bib and a highchair right over there." She pointed to the lighthouse shaped highchair next to the bar.

"I'm fine. But thanks, Julie. You've been more than helpful, I assure you."

"Okay then. Enjoy the rest of your meal."

"Thanks," Rachel said, giving Julie a little wink.

Marc took yet another sip of beer to soothe his throat, then he said, "See what you made me do?"

"I didn't make you do anything. That was *all* Marc Sanders." She put together a little smile, like she'd caught an innocent child doing something he wasn't supposed to. "Just for the record though, I thought your dinner was delicious."

Marc lifted his palms up in the air; one still had a beer in it. "*Now* she tells me."

"Well, it was. I like a man that's good in the kitchen, because I sure as hell can't cook." Rachel stirred some of the sauce into the grits. "Can you cook this?" she said, then took a bite.

"Sure, I can cook that," he replied, looking playfully offended once again. "Not a problem."

"Even this fantastic sauce?"

He cocked his head to the side. "Would I lie?"

"Oh no, we're not going there again."

They continued with dinner, Marc chewing a little more judiciously. Rachel also noticed Marc drank his third beer, and so had she, the effect of which felt very satisfying. By the time they finished dinner and walked back to his truck, the sky was nearly dark, just a touch of blood orange in the western sky was all that remained.

When Marc pulled his truck up to the Fleetwood, he left the motor running. Rachel opened the door, and then glanced in Marc's general direction, catching his eye for a second before turning away.

"I had a good time tonight," she said. And she meant it. Honestly, she really didn't want it to end.

"I did too," Marc replied.

Rachel felt him looking at her. She glanced up at him again, and their eyes met. For a moment, an uncomfortable silence fell between them. Her stomach fluttered, and though they'd been drinking, she sensed something more than an attraction brought on by alcohol, but something else. Something real.

Her mind flashed back to the ballpark, when he said that he wished he could kiss her: the look in his eyes, the rush of blood to her head, the pounding in her chest. And now, she wanted him to wish it again. She wanted him to turn off the truck, pull her towards him, and kiss her. It could be their little secret. They could go on with the rest of their lives, acting as though it never happened.

The sound of waves crashing on the shore, and the scent of the briny ocean mixing with the unmistakable smell of campfires pleased her. She slid out of the truck, and when her feet contacted the grass, she became aware of the tingling in her toes, and how good the sand would feel beneath them.

"You know," she said, "it's still a little early."

Marc smiled. "I suppose it is."

She looked towards the ocean, and to the stars that were just beginning to twinkle. "It looks like it's going to be a beautiful night. You wanna take a walk on the beach?"

Marc acknowledged by turning off the engine.

"Let me just check on Riley real quick, okay?"

Rachel stepped inside the Fleetwood, and she consciously decided not to think about anything. She didn't look at John's wine glass, the fresh cut flowers on the table, or John's picture in the bedroom. Riley seemed content lying on the couch. Quickly, she refreshed his water bowl then exchanged her blue blouse for a white tank top. She bunched her hair up and secured it with a black hair bow.

When she walked out, she saw Marc sitting up against the picnic table with his arms folded. He was looking out towards the woods, apparently unaware she'd come out, caught up in a daydream. He had an expression on his face, the same one he wore earlier when he spoke about Carrie.

"Ready?" Rachel said, but Marc didn't hear her. "Hey you," she said, a bit louder.

Marc's head snapped around like he'd been startled. He stood up, and rubbed his palms on his shorts. "Yeah, I'm ready."

They walked along the sidewalk that led to the beach. As they got closer to the sand, Rachel felt uneasy. It seemed wrong, but right at the same time. The memory of her and John walking along the shore flashed in her mind, and she needed a diversion to keep it from surfacing.

"What were you thinking about back there?" Rachel said, thinking the question might've sounded slightly rude.

"Oh...I was thinking about what a good time we had tonight." He smiled, but Rachel found it somewhat contrived. That was fair. It must be hard on him too. It's not like she's the only one haunted by their past.

Once they came to the sand, she reached up and used his shoulder for support, slipping off her sandals. He felt warm, and she could feel his muscles hiding underneath his polo. Marc seemed conscious of the fact that she touched him, but nothing indicated that he felt uncomfortable by it.

Marc angled south towards the lighthouse, but Rachel pulled his arm in the opposite direction. "Let's go this way," she said.

They walked along the beach, and the nighttime activities were in full swing. They passed a large group of people sitting in beach chairs circled around a campfire. Some kids were searching for sand crabs with their flashlights and headlamps.

Rachel saw an elderly couple headed their way, walking hand in hand. She exchanged a smile with the woman as they passed by. Rachel recognized her as the silver haired lady that stood patiently by her husband's side while he was talking to a fisherman. It was the same couple that had stopped right in front of her, holding each other as they gazed out into the ocean, watching the blue herons dive for fish.

"Sweet aren't they?" Marc said.

Rachel nodded. She wanted a story that ended like that, and felt pretty sure that's what Marc wanted too. Speaking about it though, would have been like driving a stake into her heart. But then Marc asked a question that did anyway.

"Did you and John have any kids?"

At that exact moment, coming from behind them, they heard one of the girls looking for sand crabs yell out, "Stop it Sam! Stop it!" Sam replied, "Hey, I found it first!" Rachel and Marc looked back for a second, then glanced at each other and laughed. But the question Marc had asked still loomed in her mind, and she knew her laughter was just a front.

She looked down and saw the telltale sign of a sand crab bubbling into the sand as a thin layer of sea foam quickly melted away. She admired the crab's ability to burrow down like that, hiding from the world. But, then she realized how easy it was to reach down and scoop them up.

"When Ellie turned four," Marc said, "Carrie and I talked about having another child. We went back and forth on it, but she worked so much, and it was already a challenge to find quality family time as it was. We knew how much work raising one child was, and we'd heard that raising a second wasn't just double the effort, but more like quadruple. We finally decided against it. But, what we didn't count on was how fast time goes by. When I think back and look at the past eleven years and how fast Ellie has grown, and all we've been through..." He paused and looked out over the ocean, seemingly searching for his next words. "Well, I sometimes wonder if that decision had been a mistake."

It amazed Rachel that he wasn't afraid to put his feelings right out there for everyone to see. He and Ellie were a lot alike in that way. She was certain that's what Carrie had seen in him too, and probably what drew her to him. She had to admit, it was tough to match him feeling for feeling.

As much as she didn't want to talk about what Marc had asked, she realized it was another step she had to take. She thought about John for a second, and wished was here to help her. But like her dream, searching for him in the fog, alone and scared, fighting whatever obstacles her mind conjured up, somehow she knew she had to face it alone.

"We tried for years to have children," Rachel said. At first that's all she could really say. She looked down at the sand, hoping to find another crab bubbling its way under, wishing she could jump in right behind it. She didn't see one. She drew in a deep breath and the salty air stung her lungs. "There was only a slim chance that I could ever get pregnant and it just never happened. And that was the hardest part, you know. Every month there was hope. And every month, despair. I wanted to have children just as much as any woman. I did. But John, though he never really came out and said it, I could tell it really disappointed him. It was his dream to have a bunch of kids running around."

Marc and Rachel could no longer hear the sound of children playing, or the occasional burst of laughter coming from the group of people gathered around the campfire. They had walked beyond the range of the campground, and the only sounds Rachel heard were the waves, and the sound of her own heart breaking.

"I've thought about this a lot," she said, trying to find the courage to say the next few words out loud, something she had never said to anyone, not even to Cynthia. "If I could go back in time and change one thing, if I could either save John from cancer or give him a child…" She swallowed hard, trying to dissolve the swelling mass in her throat. "I would have chosen to give him a child."

She stopped walking and closed her eyes tight. Her tears broke free, and she put her hands up to her face, trying to stop them from streaking. Marc put his arms around her, and pulled her into his body, and she sobbed.

He held her. The harder she cried, the tighter his embrace, and the more she allowed herself to free her feelings. In the darkness of night, his body seemed to absorb her emotions, pulling them from her soul, and accepting a part of them as his own. A minute or so passed and she withdrew from him.

"I'm sorry Marc," she said, feeling guilty for putting that on him.

"Don't be," he replied.

They walked quietly and she felt his hand reach for hers, and for reasons she didn't try to reconcile, she let him, somehow knowing that it was okay. She felt something in her heart. Not pain or sorrow, but a sense of affection, inasmuch as she could allow herself. It felt nice, and peaceful, like the bright stars above them.

Once they reached the tip of the island, they turned around, heading back to camp. "So," Marc said, in a much more cheerful manner, "we've already established that you might lie."

"Hey, that's not fair." Rachel bumped him.

"Well, you said you might." He smiled, but Rachel thought his remark seemed a little strange.

"You know what I meant," she said. "I'd only tell a little white lie to avoid hurting someone's feelings. I wouldn't *really* lie."

"I know. I'm just playing around."

"So, what's the worst lie you've ever told?" Rachel asked, flipping it back to him.

"Me? Lie? No, never."

"Come on Marc, everyone's told a lie."

Marc didn't respond right away. Instead, he looked out over the ocean, as if there was something to see. There wasn't. Then, he looked at the sand in front him; perhaps he too was looking for a crab hole to hide in. Suddenly, she regretted her question.

"I did lie one time," he finally said, letting go of Rachel's hand. "To Ellie no less. You know how I told you about Carrie's car accident?"

Rachel nodded. "You mean she wasn't?"

"She was. Everything I told you was true. After it happened I explained to Ellie about the accident. It happened in the middle of the night and Ellie wanted to know why her mom was out so late, and maybe if she hadn't been, none of it would have happened. I told her that she was just working. That was my lie, and I blamed Carrie for it." He looked out over the ocean again, like he was afraid Rachel might see his faults.

"Supposedly, it was just a one-time thing," he continued. "She and a co-worker of hers were working on a case over dinner. They had a few too many and one thing led to another. They both knew they had made a mistake and that's where it ended, but Carrie convinced him they shouldn't mention it to anyone, figuring it was best that way. She was right about that. Looking back on it now, I wish to God I hadn't found out. Anyway, her co-worker, well he couldn't keep the secret. Apparently he told his wife, but he still struggled with the mistake. The only way to get past it was to come clean with me.

"Afterwards, me and Carrie had huge arguments about it. One night it really got out of hand—I let it get out of hand. I kept questioning her about it, wondering about other nights she worked late, pressing her to confess to something she may or may not have done. She left the house at two-thirty in the morning, angry with me, insisting that I just couldn't let it go.

"That was the last time I talked to her. Some drunk, five times over the legal limit, ran a red light. He walked away with ten stitches on his forehead."

Marc's voice changed; culpable and even a little angered. "A stupid argument that really didn't matter. I couldn't let it go. All I had to do was forgive her, to love her, to prove to her that we could overcome it. But I failed, Rachel. I failed her. And I failed Ellie. It's really my fault that she'll never see her mother again, that she wrote letters her mother will never get to read."

Rachel took Marc's hand, and for a second she didn't think he even knew. "Marc," she said softly, "it's not your fault." She stopped and looked up at him, seeing the guilt in his eyes. "I will never lie to you."

When the campground came into view, she noticed that they had slowed their pace considerably. She really didn't want their walk to end, and maybe he didn't either. Nonetheless, Rachel found herself standing under the awning, nervous and scared at the same time.

"Can I ask you a question, Marc?"

"Sure. You can ask me anything."

"You have to agree this was a pretty emotional evening, right?"

"I know." He said, looking almost embarrassed. "It's not what I intended, Rachel."

"Do you remember what you said to me at the park today?"

Marc's eyes brightened, and he nodded.

"If I let you kiss me, I know I won't be able to stop, and we both know what will happen. I really like you, but I'm not sure I can handle any more emotions tonight. Are you okay with that?"

Marc looked deeper into Rachel's eyes, not with a look of disappointment, but of truthfulness. "I mean this as much as I've meant anything in my life. I do want to kiss you, but ever since I first saw you, and every time since, I have felt something I didn't think I'd ever feel again. Actually, I'm not sure I've ever felt like this. I don't want to do anything that might ruin it."

She took his hands, and she wanted to pull him to her, she wanted him to kiss her more than anything. She felt it over her whole body, and it took all of her will power not to throw herself at him. Honestly, she was about to give in when he spoke.

"When can I see you again?" he said.

Rachel collected her thoughts, thinking about it for a second.

"Are you busy tomorrow?"

"Hopefully, I'll only be with you. What do you have in mind?"

"You'll have to wait to find out. I'll drive this time. I'll pick you up at three, okay?"

Nodding, he pulled away and their hands stayed fastened together until the last possible second.

As he turned and walked to his truck, she opened the door to the Fleetwood and went inside. She closed the door and leaned her back against it, feeling her heart race. A couple of minutes passed until she heard the sound of his engine crank. As he pulled away, she considered those endearing words he said to her, and she became frightened. Not because of how he felt, but because she suddenly realized she felt the same way.

She went to bed that night, wondering how all of this happened, and more importantly, where it would lead. She fell asleep unable to answer either question...then she reached out into the thick fog, desperately trying to follow John's voice to the lighthouse.

CHAPTER SEVEN

THINGS WERE LOOKING UP. If anyone would have told Rachel that on the Friday after arriving on Hunting Island, that she'd befriend the camp host and her eleven-year-old niece, and be planning a third date with the niece's father—or fourth date if she included the fishing adventure—she'd have laughed in their face. Especially if it was Cynthia. Yet it was true.

In fact, there seemed to be sort of a routine that she could depend on. Being a planner, that pleased her. After Ellie's lesson, she'd spend a little time on the beach, then head into town and pick up some things for her date with Marc. Sure enough, things began with Ellie's lesson, right on schedule. After the lesson, Rachel and Ellie took a walk on the beach.

"Can I ask you a question?" Ellie asked.

"Sure."

"I gotta warn you, it's a pretty serious question. It might be uncomfortable."

"Okay." Rachel thought there was no way it could be more uncomfortable than what happened yesterday with her period.

"What's it like to French kiss a boy?"

She was wrong. "Wow! That *is* a pretty serious question."

"I warned you."

"Why do you ask?" Rachel took about two more steps, then stopped in her tracks and gasped. "Do you want to kiss Jonathan?"

"I'm thinking about it."

"You're only eleven, Ellie. You have your whole life to worry about things like that." Rachel could tell that Ellie was chewing on those words.

"Well, what if I don't?" Ellie finally said.

That was a pretty heavy question for anyone, let alone an eleven year old, and quite frankly, Rachel didn't really know how to respond. Luckily, Ellie let her off the hook. "You know, I'm pretty mature for my age. I'm going to be twelve soon."

"I know you are," Rachel said. They started walking again. "But trust me, things can get complicated pretty quickly."

"How old were you when you kissed a boy?"

Shit!

Rachel thought about lying, but then she recalled the conversation she had with Marc last night, and decided there was no way she'd be able to. "I was eleven," she said, shaking her head.

Ellie gasped, and her mouth opened about as big as it could go. "Oh, really?" she said, drawing out her words.

"Yes," Rachel said, begrudgingly. "I was."

"Well, what was it like? How did it happen?"

"If I tell you, will you promise me that you'll give this kissing thing a lot of thought before you just run out and do it?"

"Oh, I promise."

"All right." Rachel sighed. "My cousin Kelly and I went to the same school and we were both in the seventh grade. Kelly was the kind of girl that pretended to like lots of boys." Rachel snickered. "Come to think of it, she's still that way." She looked at Ellie and tapped her on the wrist. "You know how I told you that things can get complicated?"

Ellie nodded.

"Perfect example. But that's another story. Actually, lots of stories. Anyway, Kelly flirted with boys whether she liked them or not. If she thought they were just so-so cute all the way up to 'H-O-T-FINE' as she liked to put it, she'd flirt with them. She figured the more boys she flirted with, the more choices she'd have when we got to high school. Let me just tell you now, it didn't work out so well."

"Wait, we're talking about *your* first kiss, right?" Ellie asked.

Rachel laughed. "Oh yeah, I'm getting to that."

"Okay, just checking."

"Near the end of the school year, we had a skating party. As usual, Kelly was talking to all the boys, promising each that she'd skate with him during couples skate. There was this one boy, Matthew, that Kelly really liked, but she wouldn't talk to him. Instead, she made *me* talk to him."

"He was the one she wanted to skate with, right?" Ellie asked. "Why didn't she talk to him?"

"She was scared. It's easy to flirt with a boy that you don't really care about it. It's a lot harder if you actually like him. Anyway, I asked Matthew to skate with me because Kelly kept bugging me. So we skated together during couples skate and Kelly was right there beside us the whole time, ditching one boy for another every couple of laps."

"So, you decided to kiss him?"

"No, not really. Well…maybe, but it's not what you think. After couples skate, Kelly asked me if I would kiss Matthew. I told her no, but that wasn't good enough for her, because she kept asking, and I kept telling her no. She wouldn't let up and it went on and on. Eventually I told her I'd think about it, just to get her to shut-up, but to her that meant yes. So, Kelly decided that when it was time to leave, she'd go over and tell Matthew I wanted to talk to him about something, and then she'd lead him to a spot between the lockers. The plan was for me to give him a kiss, and then right after that, she'd kiss him too before he had a chance to open his eyes. Then we'd run outside to where our parents were waiting to pick us up."

"Sounds pretty sneaky to me," Ellie said.

"It was. The next twenty minutes or so, I remember being terrified. I tried to get out of it, but Kelly said that a promise was a promise. Of course, I didn't promise anything, but that didn't matter to her. We had taken our skates off early so we could run when it was all over. Then, when the time finally came, she led me over to the lockers. I was so nervous, I felt like I was going to throw up. Just as I was about to make a run for it, Kelly pushed Matthew forward and he stopped right in front of me.

"So there I was, leaning up against the wall between the lockers, and I had stopped breathing. I can remember my heart beating so hard I thought it was going to pop right out of my chest. I don't exactly know what Kelly told Matthew, but it was obvious that he was there to kiss me too, because he looked like he was about to pass out. For a few seconds we both looked at each other wondering who was going to make the first move, or who was going to run away first. Then Kelly said 'Kiss him, Rachel! Kiss him!' She pushed him towards me and the next thing I knew we were kissing. It lasted only a second, but before it was over I saw Kelly run for the door."

"Are you serious?" Ellie said. "Oh, my God!"

"Yep, she sure did."

"What did she say? Why did she run?"

"She never said anything, and I wasn't about to bring it up. But I know she ran because she was scared. I know I was. To this day, we've never spoken about it to each other."

"What about Matthew? What happened to him?"

"I don't know. I never saw him again. It was the end of the school year and I think his family moved away after that."

"And the kiss?"

"I don't remember. It wasn't anything special, which is my point. Take your time, Ellie. There's no need to rush things. You'll know when it's the right time."

For the next few moments, they walked along the shore and Ellie kept quiet. There are special moments and then there are *special* moments, and when Rachel felt Ellie's hand take hold of hers, for the first time in her life, Rachel felt she knew what it was like to be a mother.

Rachel held it together pretty well for a minute or so, but then her eyes welled up with tears. She turned her head away from Ellie and dabbed them dry.

"Look!" Ellie let go of Rachel's hand and pointed to a couple of seabirds that flew past. "Did you ever wish you had wings?"

"I ah—" Rachel's voice strained, and she cleared her throat. "I suppose I did at one time, I don't really remember."

"If I had wings, you know what I would do? I'd fly all around the world, helping as many people and animals as I could. If I saw some sea turtle eggs in trouble, I'd swoop down and protect them. An old woman having trouble crossing the street? No problem. I'd dive down and fly her across."

She looked up at Rachel for just a second. "I'd raise money too! I mean, have you ever seen a flying girl? No. You haven't. So I figure lots of people would like to see a flying girl, and they'd be willing to pay for it. Then, I'd take that money and I could fly over all the world carrying food and medicine to everyone who needed it."

"You know what?" Ellie said, looking up at Rachel.

"What's that?"

"I've made up my mind. I'm going to do it."

"Do what?"

"Kiss Jonathan."

Later in the day, Rachel drove into town to pick up some things for her date with Marc. As she drove, he entered her every thought. Just crossing over the drawbridge, listening to the rumbling sound of the tires as they ran over the corrugated metal, reminded her of their drive together to the park, and when they returned from dinner.

When she reached Beaufort, she found an old hardware store called *Mallory's* that she remembered from her previous trips. Although she recalled them keeping some nuts and bolts around, as well as some outdoor tools and stuff like that in the back—enough to still be called a hardware store—what she really remembered were the cute picnic baskets, plates, decorative napkins, and an endless array of knickknacks in the front of the store.

Rachel opened the door and the sound of an old bell clanked up against the glass. She saw the same lady that had helped her the last time she was there. Although a bit older and a little more white headed than she remembered, her charm seemed exactly the same.

"Good afternoon!" the lady said. Her name-tag read June Mallory.

"Hello," Rachel said, looking at some of the stained glass trinkets on display at the entrance.

"Can you believe this heat?" June fanned herself, even though the temperature inside was cool enough.

"I know. I don't think it's going to get any cooler, either."

"You know, I tried to get my husband to fix that damned air conditioning in this place for years, God rest his soul." She fanned herself again. "What can I help you find, dear?"

"I'm looking for a picnic basket."

"A picnic? In this heat?" June swatted at Rachel, not really touching her. "Honey, I hope he's worth it."

Rachel laughed. "He is."

"Come on back."

Rachel followed, and she noticed that June glanced back at her a couple times, and seemed to be troubled with something. When they reached the appropriate section, June said, "Here you go. We only have about three different styles in the store, but we can order whatever you like; although, it sounds like you're in need of one today, am I right?"

"That's right."

"Well, maybe you'll like what we have. Let me know if you need anything." June stood there for what seemed longer than necessary. Rachel smiled at her, and June took that as a familiar sign. She turned and left Rachel alone.

Before she looked at any of the baskets, Rachel noticed some of the cute glasses that caught her eye. Rachel's taste was more on the plain side, but she saw some clear glasses with black cherries painted around the rim that she liked. She picked one up and studied it, then noticed the matching plate that went along with it. It was also clear, and the black cherries were painted along the edge. Then she saw the same style but in white instead of clear glass, which suited her taste much better. Just as she picked it up, she heard June walk up behind her.

When Rachel turned around, June appeared to be fidgety and flustered. "Excuse me dear, but can I ask you something?"

"Okay?" Rachel said.

"Weren't you and your husband in here a couple years ago, looking at picnic baskets? Your husband also bought a Porky Pig apron."

Rachel gasped and then her jaw dropped. "You remember that?"

A big smile formed on June's face. "I have a knack for it." She swatted at Rachel again. "Don't ask me how. I mean I can't even remember what I wore yesterday, and honestly, I'd probably forget my own head if it wasn't attached to my neck. But for some reason, I can remember just about everybody that comes in that door."

"That's a pretty impressive ability."

"Well, it does come in handy with customer service. How is your husband?"

Rachel's stomach suddenly floated. She released her grip on the plate and it fell to the ground, breaking into several pieces. The sound of it crashing startled her and she jumped. "Oh God, I'm sorry!"

"It's okay!" June said, quickly bending down to pick up the bigger pieces.

"I'm so sorry," Rachel said again. She bent down as well, frantically trying to sweep up the smaller bits with her hand.

June reached for Rachel's arm and stopped her. "It's just a plate, honey. Don't cut yourself. Let me go and get a broom."

They both stood up and Rachel checked her hands to make sure there were no cuts in them. There weren't, but her hands trembled. She managed to calm herself down somewhat by the time June returned with the broom.

"I really am sorry," Rachel said. "I'll be happy to pay for it."

"No, it's not necessary," June said, sweeping. "It happens from time to time. It's to be expected. Insurance will cover it."

"But I'm going to buy something anyway, and—"

"It's really okay." June stopped sweeping, and looked at Rachel with that same big smile she used when she greeted her at the front door. June swept up the last of the glass, then turned to her and smiled again. "You've got a picnic ahead of you today. Take your time and pick out a basket, if there's one you like, that is."

It only took Rachel about two minutes to decide on one. Of the three, the basket she liked best was wicker and made out of willow, and featured an integrated wooden tabletop. It also came with two hand-blown wine glasses, a small cutting board and a cheese slicer. Before she walked up to the register, she grabbed the box that contained the other three plates that matched the one she broke.

She placed the items down on the counter, and right away June saw the box of three plates. "Nope," she said. "You don't have to buy these."

"But I want to," Rachel replied.

"Absolutely not," June said. "If you really want these plates, then I'll get you a full box. I won't have my customers being cheated." She reached down to pick the box up, but Rachel placed her hand on top of hers.

"My husband…" Rachel paused and drew in a deep breath. "My husband passed away a little over two years ago."

"Oh, I'm so sorry, dear." June said.

"The thing is, I've met someone, and I don't know if it's going to work out or not, but he has a daughter. So you see, these three plates would be perfect for us."

June swallowed hard, and without saying another word, removed her hand from the plates and she scanned the basket. Then, after scanning the box of plates, she opened the top of it and placed a few pieces of wrapping tissue carefully inside to help secure them in place.

"$92.50" June said, trying to keep her voice from cracking, but not doing a very good job of it.

Rachel handed June her credit card and she swiped it. While Rachel signed the slip, June opened up the basket and placed the box of plates neatly inside.

"Thank you," Rachel said, pulling the basket off of the counter. She started for the door, a little embarrassed by the whole thing.

"Mrs. Willers?" June called out to her, probably recalling the name from her credit card.

Rachel swung around right before she reached the door. "Yes?"

"Good luck with your picnic. I really hope it works out for you, dear."

Rachel could only manage to nod in acknowledgment before she opened the door and walked out, the old bell clanking up against the glass.

Not being able to wait any longer, Rachel picked up Marc fifteen minutes early. Ten minutes later, she wheeled her Jeep into a small and secluded gravel parking lot that sat on the backside of Hunting Island. It had been several years since she'd been there and hoped it was like she remembered.

Marc grabbed the picnic basket from the back of the Jeep and stepped out. "You know," he said, looking around, "I've been to this island dozens of times, but I don't ever recall seeing this parking lot. I guess some things just blend into the background if you live here long enough."

"There's a place I want to show you, let's just hope I can find it." Rachel reached behind the back seat and pulled out a blanket.

She led Marc to a wooden platform that extended into a salt marsh about two hundred feet, then to a series of small islands. Once they reached the islands, the platform continued on for another five hundred feet or so to a deck that overlooked one of the waterways. But Rachel stopped short of that, following what looked like a small animal trail that went through the middle of the marsh. The trail was still damp from the outgoing tide.

"You sure you know where you're going?" Marc asked.

Rachel glanced back at him for a second as she walked. "No," she said, then smiled.

The path led to the near side of one of the small islands. Up and over that one, Rachel led him down yet another path, to what looked to be the furthest island in the grouping.

She glanced back at him once more, and caught him staring at her. "Are you enjoying yourself back there?" she teased.

"Well, yes. Actually, I am," he replied.

Eventually the path ended, but Rachel kept going. Hopefully the spot she was looking for would be just over the top of the hill. A few more steps revealed to Rachel that she'd remembered correctly. Actually, it was even more beautiful than she recalled.

Showing up out of nowhere, a grassy clearing about the size of a tennis court opened up to a spectacular view of the salt marsh. In the center, stood a huge, live oak that cast plenty of shade where they could have their picnic. Best of all, it was completely secluded.

"I can't believe this place," Marc said. "How on earth did you find it?"

"Just some exploring a few years ago." She decided to keep John out of it, and rightly so.

Rachel opened up her blanket, and the breeze helped her spread it out under the live oak. Marc set the picnic basket down and they took a seat on either side of it.

"Now don't get too excited," Rachel said, as she opened the lid. She took out a bottle of red wine and handed it to Marc along with a corkscrew and the two wine glasses that came with the basket. "You know I don't cook much."

"It's a picnic," Marc replied. "I'm sure it can't be that bad."

Rachel took out two of the plates she bought at the hardware store. "Still, I think a little bit of expectation control is in order here." Next she pulled out a small plastic container and opened the top. She took out what looked like a couple of yellow muffins with small ribbons of green interspersed throughout. Marc had a peculiar, if not suspicious, look on his face as she placed two of the things on each plate.

Marc finished pouring the wine, then handed Rachel hers. He cleared his throat and raised his glass, enticing Rachel to do the same. "Here's to a budding friendship," he said. "May it always be filled with laughter and good times."

As the two glasses clanged together, Rachel smirked. "You might want to wait until after you try the quiche before wishing that." They each took a sip of wine, both smiling at each other over her comment.

"Go on," Rachel said, and then sighed. "Let's get this over with."

He barely had swallowed his wine down. "Okay, okay," he said, while picking up his quiche muffin. He popped it in his mouth.

For a few seconds they both looked at each other as he chewed. Her gaze never broke away from him. She looked like a child waiting for the punishment she knew was coming. As he chewed, he smiled at her with his mouth fully closed.

A few more seconds passed, but the suspense was killing her. "Well?" she asked.

"It's pretty good," he replied, speaking through his mouth full of food.

"Seriously, how is it?"

"I like it."

Unconvinced, she situated herself a little more comfortably on the blanket. "Okay look, I'm going to tell you a story." Rachel picked up her wine glass and took another sip. "It's a very important one, so *pay attention*."

"All right," he said, finishing up the first quiche muffin. He looked intently into her eyes as he grabbed the second muffin from his plate and took a bite.

"When John and I were first married, I don't know, maybe around six months, he got on a culinary kick. It actually worked out pretty well for me, as you know, because he ended up doing all the cooking. But that doesn't mean there weren't some growing pains. The first meal he ever cooked for me was a casserole."

"I don't think I like where this is going," Marc said, the quiche still in his mouth.

"Well, you shouldn't. He found a recipe. I think it was from an old cookbook of his mother's from the 1950s or something. I guess he was trying to impress me. Actually, I'm sure that's what he was trying to do. He set the table, lit some candles, poured two glasses of really cheap wine—that's all we could afford in those days—then he called me in. You should have seen him, Marc. He was smiling from ear to ear."

Marc instantly smiled from ear to ear himself, still chewing. They both chuckled, then Rachel continued. "Being the gentleman he always was, he pulled the chair out for me. Then he sashays back into the kitchen and comes back with this gray looking casserole— canned salmon casserole—and places it on the table in front of me. He even sliced a couple of boiled eggs to put on top, you know, so it would look like the picture in the cookbook."

"It was pretty bad, huh?"

"Bad doesn't even begin to describe it. He cuts me a big, thick, wet slice and serves some green peas to go along with it. Then he did the same for himself. Honestly, I don't know how I kept it down. But I did. I couldn't bring myself to tell him how bad it was."

"Why not? I'm sure he would have understood."

"Well, that's where the lesson comes in. I just couldn't tell him, so I actually told him that it was good."

"That's a sweet thing to do," Marc said. "Just like you said, sometimes it's okay to tell a little white lie to avoid hurting someone's feelings. I think that's a good lesson."

"No, no, no. That's a mistake, and here's why. For the next year and a half, I ate salmon casserole twice a month because he thought I liked it. After that, I finally had to tell him that I didn't. I just couldn't take it anymore, you know what I mean?" She slaps Marc on the knee. "Turns out, he didn't like it either. He was only cooking it because he thought I liked it."

"Ah, I see."

"So, I want to ask you one more time, what do you think of the quiche?"

"Actually," he said, first nodding then shaking his head, "I think I'm not that crazy about it."

Rachel gasped. "What?" She pressed her tongue into her cheek and it looked like a golfball. Then she said, like a man with a mouth full of food, "You don't like my cooking?"

Marc looked at her and sort of shook his head in a feminine way, mocking her movements from last night. "I didn't say that." He picked up his glass of wine and took a dainty sip. They both laughed, and Marc almost spewed out some wine.

Rachel reached inside the basket, looking around for something. "I anticipated that you might not like it," she said, proudly. "As I said before, I'm a planner. So..." She pulled out a sleeve of graham crackers and a jar of peanut butter.

Marc smiled, and then looked out over the salt marsh, watching a congregation of white ibises flying along the horizon, probably looking for crayfish. When they passed, he turned his gaze towards Rachel as she spread the peanut butter on the crackers.

"What are you thinking about?" he asked.

"I was wondering why I find it so easy to talk to you." She passed a cracker to him. "I know we've only known each other for a few days, but I feel like it's been a lot longer than that. And not just with you, but Ellie also. I can't explain it. It just feels...right. How's the cracker?"

"It's great. I'm a big fan of peanut butter. You could put it on just about anything and it would be good."

"My quiches?" she asked.

The look on Marc's face made it seem like he wasn't sure if it was a rhetorical question or not. They both laughed.

"It's true, you know."

Rachel gasped. "What? That peanut butter would make my quiches taste better?"

"No, not that. Although I'm sure it would," he said, smiling at her. "What I mean is, it's true that Ellie is so easy to talk to. She's always been that way. She could make friends at a tax seminar."

"She must've got it from you, then."

"I think it's the other way around." Marc looked at his near empty glass of wine. "She has such a good heart. She makes me want to be a better dad, a better person…a better man." He looked at Rachel. "You have that same effect on me."

Rachel blushed, and realized she was at a loss for words. She picked up the bottle of wine and refilled both of their glasses.

For the next few hours, they sat under the shade of the live oak and talked. They exchanged stories of their childhood, talked about their parents, and about their extended families. Though the names John and Carrie came up a few times, they seemed to avoid making either of them a focal point of the discussion. Rachel was amazed how easily the conversation flowed from topic to topic.

As the sun sank over the salt marsh in front of them, they sat with their backs together, using each other for support. It was the *Magic Hour*, Marc explained, that last hour of sunlight when the quality of light was perfect for photography. Their bodies, and the live oak behind them, seemed to glow in the warm, yellow rays emanating from the sun.

"Tell me about one of your favorite pictures you've taken," Rachel said.

"Okay." He thought about it for a second, looking out over the marsh. "As you know, I've been doing a lot of local sports photography the last few years, and I was shooting a little league baseball game, just like the one we were at yesterday. Anyway, between one of the innings, I noticed this beautiful woman leaning up against the fence along the third base line. She was looking out over the outfield and the breeze had swept a few strands of hair across her face. So stunning was she, that the sight of her absolutely took my breath away. Her smile seemed so genuine. I found myself fixated on her and I wanted to take her picture, but for a few seconds I was paralyzed, unable to raise the camera to my eye for fear of interrupting the sight of her, even for an instant. But somehow, I knew I had to capture the moment. My heart raced as I zoomed in, bringing her face into sharp focus. Just before I pressed the shutter button, she looked at me. I pulled the camera down, and I could not look away from her. At that moment, I knew I wanted to spend the rest of my life getting to know her."

From their backs still being pressed together, they turned towards one another, pivoting against each other's shoulder. Their lips met and they embraced as they kissed, cautiously at first, then growing more impassioned. Rachel slid her arms around his body, and Marc grabbed her and pulled her close. But then, Marc brought his hands up and cradled her face as he slowed down, kissing her gently. He pulled away from her lips and looked into her eyes.

"This might sound a little strange coming from a man," Marc said, his breathing still heavy. "But I want to do this right. Let's not get in too deep just yet. Is that okay?"

Rachel knew he was right. She didn't want him to be, but she nodded in agreement.

Marc looked out over the marsh, the sky fading into dusk. "We should probably get going," he said.

As they headed back, Marc noticed the tide coming in, flooding the marsh and the trail they had taken. "Hurry!" he said.

Rachel grabbed him arm and pulled him back. "It looks a little deep, Marc."

"No, I think we can make it across. It's just ankle high—"

She pulled him back again. This time, she pulled him to her chest. "It looks a little deep."

Taking Marc's hand, she led him towards the grassy area under the live oak. She walked ahead, the sun throwing its orange hue on her skin: her face, her shoulders and her legs. He followed her, and as they arrived, she let go of his hand, and she laid the blanket down. She pulled the blanket taut and stood at the opposite end of it, and looked at him.

The sunlight came in sideways across her body and lit up the left side of her face. She pulled her shirt over her head then unlatched her bra, pulling it down over her breasts. Her arms fell to her waist and her chest swelled as she drew in a deep breath.

Rachel looked at Marc's body, recalling the first day she saw him on the shore, remembering how the wind pressed his shirt into his muscles. Marc took off his shirt, revealing what the wind had promised, and he held it in his hand for a second before letting it go.

He walked across the blanket and put his arms around her as she fell into his kiss. He pressed his lips hard into hers and she wrapped her arms around his waist, up and over his strong shoulders. She felt his tongue enter her mouth and she took it, feeling the silky sensation that mingled with the taste of wine. Their chests pressed together, and he reached up, prying them apart just enough to take her breast in his hand. Her head fell back, and he mouthed her exposed neck and pulled her tight into his body. Her fingers explored his strong back and her nails gently scraped across his skin.

Marc pulled her down on the blanket, and took her breast in his mouth, caressing the other in his hand. As he laid her down, Rachel's back arched and he encircled her body with his arm. She slid her hand up his back and into his thick hair, then pulled his head tighter into her chest. They made love as the *Magic Hour* passed, and as the sun sank below the horizon of the salt marsh.

The Jeep's brakes squeaked to a halt at Marc's campsite. Rachel and Marc stared straight ahead as the headlights reflected off the aluminum panels of the Airstream. The sound of their breathing almost drowned out the steady purr of the Jeep's engine.

"Hey," Rachel said, turning her head his direction. "You wanna do that again?" In concert, they swung towards each other and laid into a kiss. "My place or yours," Rachel said, still kissing him.

"Yours. We can't chance Ellie coming back."

Rachel pushed him away. "But Beverly and Charles…and Ellie? What if they see you come in?"

"They won't. I'll walk down by the beach and come in from that direction. I'm a photographer, remember? I'll be sneaky."

"Okay, but don't get caught. And *no* photography!"

Marc put his hands up, like an unfortunate teller at a bank robbery.

"Look," Rachel said, "give me a chance to walk Riley and straighten up. Maybe fifteen minutes."

Marc looked like he lost his puppy. He shook his head. "I don't know if I can wait fifteen minutes."

She reached over and kissed him again. Hard. She didn't want to stop. He didn't stop. She pushed him back.

"Okay, ten!"

"Riley!" Rachel slammed open the door of the Fleetwood and scared the poor fella right off the couch.

He barked.

"Come on boy, let's go." She leashed him up and pulled him outside. Her shoelace snagged something on the last step, hurling her out of the door. Luckily, she caught herself in time.

She dragged Riley to the woods, just outside of the Fleetwood. This was no time for a leisurely stroll, but Riley was a leisurely dog. He sniffed the bushes, sniffed the trees, and even looked as though he picked up the scent of a raccoon.

"Come on, Riley. Come on!" Rachel stomped her foot. Riley nosed up at her, not knowing exactly what to do with that command. "Okay," she whispered, "go potty. Go potty boy." Riley sniffed around again. Finally, he found a suitable tree, and Rachel felt as relieved as Riley did when he finally went.

He was still dripping when Rachel tugged on the leash and made a beeline straight for the Fleetwood. Scampering across the St. Augustine grass, she suddenly felt a lot of resistance. That's when she looked back and saw Riley assuming the number two position. "Oh, Riley!" she whimpered, stomping her foot again.

After Riley finished his business, Rachel cleaned it up, then rushed back inside and closed the blinds as she made her way to the bedroom. She threw off her clothes, and then put on a black pair of panties and a white tank top.

Rachel hurried to the bathroom and spritzed on a little perfume, then looked at herself in the mirror. She focused on her breasts. They looked perky in the thin tank top. Not too bad, she thought. She quickly brushed her teeth, then filled a cup with water to rinse. A loud knock on the door startled her, and she accidentally spilled most of the water down one side of her shirt.

"Shit!" she huffed, then poked her head out the bathroom door and yelled, "Just a second!"

Damn, that was a fast ten minutes.

She looked in the mirror again, and saw half a wet tee-shirt contest staring back at her. She considered her options. There was only one thing to do.

She wet the other side.

She scurried to the front door, and posed directly in front of it. She messed up her hair, drew in a deep breath, and flung the door open.

"Now that's what I'm talking about!" a brash female voice cried out.

"Cynthia!"

CHAPTER EIGHT

CYNTHIA'S SNORING WOKE HER. Rachel rolled over in her bed and glanced at the clock, realizing she'd slept in, at least by her standards anyway. Considering that she and Cynthia talked half the night, and the other half she spent dreaming, running around in the woods looking for a stupid lighthouse, waking up at seven didn't seem too bad.

She slipped on her running outfit, and she and Riley walked past Cynthia who lay sound asleep on the pullout couch. The blanket had all but fallen off the bed, and the sheets had bunched up over her sprawled out body. Her right arm and leg dangled off the edge of the bed. Rachel didn't worry about waking her. Since they were kids, Cynthia had always been a heavy sleeper and was definitely not a morning person.

Rachel and Riley began their run, heading north. Her legs didn't ache nearly as much as they had earlier in the week. Neither did her heart, for that matter.

Talking to Marc the last few days had certainly been emotional, but it seemed purifying at the same time, like Marc was some sort of psychological magnet, drawing the painful emotions out of her body. As proof of that, if someone had told her that in less than a week, that she'd be in the throes of passion with a man she just met, she never would have believed it.

Still, something troubled her. As glad as she was about Cynthia's surprise visit, although her timing could have been better, she could tell that something didn't feel quite right. Especially when Cynthia introduced herself to Marc last night.

Poor Marc. He had snuck along the beach just as he said he would, and showed up about a minute after Cynthia had. Cynthia nearly scared him half to death when he knocked on the door and watched it fling open, only to see Cynthia standing there, wearing a pair of skinny jeans and a Ramones tee-shirt. Rachel was in the back putting on something a little more decent, and by the time she walked to the front of the Fleetwood, Cynthia was already pulling Marc inside, introducing herself with cloyingly sweet enthusiasm.

Maybe it was Rachel's embarrassment when Cynthia showed up instead of Marc, but whatever the reason, something just felt wrong when Marc and Cynthia talked. Rachel practically shoed Marc out of the Fleetwood, mouthing to him '*I'm sorry*' as she closed the door behind him.

After her run, she and Riley went back inside. Cynthia was still snoring away, and from the rhythm of it, Rachel figured she'd be out for a while. She grabbed a shower and put on a pot of coffee, not taking any special precautions to be quiet. Cynthia hadn't moved a muscle. Looking back at her friend, Rachel smiled and shook her head. She took her coffee and her Kindle and stepped out under the awning for a little reading.

Rachel read a good bit of her book. She didn't have to reread paragraphs or go back two or three pages to recall what happened. Things were finally looking up for the hero, too, who finally realized most of his failures were created because of his own mistakes. He created a fail-safe plan to get what he really wanted, making Rachel anxious. She knew the villain surely had something up her sleeve.

"Boo!" Ellie jumped right in front of Rachel.

"Oh my!" Rachel said, not really scared, but she acted like it anyway. "Good morning." She flicked off her Kindle.

Ellie smiled from ear to ear, reminding Rachel once again how adorable she was. "Good morning," Ellie replied, the first word higher pitched than the second. She took a seat at the table and Riley walked up to her, expecting a pet, which he got. Ellie leaned her head over to one of her shoulders, still smiling.

"Wow, you sure are in a good mood this morning," Rachel said.

"Yep." Ellie studied Rachel's face for a second. "So are you."

"That's true. I am." *What a special girl*, Rachel thought to herself. She was lucky to have found someone like her. For a second, she wondered if John had anything to do with it.

Ellie's face turned inquisitive. "Is it because you're spending time with my father?"

Pow!

Rachel couldn't decide if the French-kiss-question or this one felt more uncomfortable. Well, yeah she could. This one, definitely this one. Actually, it gave last night's whole wet tee-shirt moment a run for its money.

"I think so," Rachel said, not knowing exactly what the right answer was. Ellie scrunched her lips to one side of her face, and that made Rachel nervous—as if she wasn't already. "Is that okay? That I spend time with your dad?"

Ellie appeared to ponder the question, glancing up at the awning. To Rachel it seemed like a full minute, but actually, only a second or two passed before Ellie's infectious smile came back, and she nodded. Rachel let out an audible sigh, and Ellie giggled.

"You wanna know why I'm in such a good mood?" Ellie asked.

Rachel wasn't sure. Ellie had come up with some tough ones lately, but she nodded anyway.

"Well, last night after I beat the pants off of Aunt Beverly at Monopoly, me and Jonathan sat on the beach for a while."

"Oh really?" Rachel's reply was drawn out a bit, but in the back of her mind she was hoping Ellie didn't see her dad sneaking over to the Fleetwood.

"We didn't kiss or anything like that. You know…in case you were wondering."

"Who? Me?" Rachel placed her hand over her heart. "I wasn't wondering."

Ellie's eyes widened and she spoke faster. "Don't get me wrong though, it's all part of my plan. But like you said, this is serious business, and I thought it was best to get to know him a little better before just kissing him. I mean, I don't want to be like your cousin Kelly or anything like that. It doesn't make me a tramp just because I *want* to kiss him, does it?"

Rachel was about to shake her head, but Ellie continued on. "No. It doesn't. But just because I want to, doesn't mean he gets one. He has to spend quality time with me first, you know? Get to know me. I need to know him. Do you know what I'm saying?"

Rachel nodded quickly during Ellie's breath, knowing more was coming.

"Did you know, for instance, that Jonathan collects animal teeth? Gross, right? But he does. He also plays trumpet in the band. And guitar. But not in a band or anything like that. And get this…" She looked around, checking to see if anyone else was near. "He's got a grandmother that only has two toes on one foot. Ewww!" Ellie shook her head, and made a face like she just sucked on a lemon wedge. "Something to do with a hoe when she was a kid. I don't know. I blocked him out during that part." Ellie swiveled her head up towards the camper. "Hi!"

Cynthia walked out with her hair all frizzed, wiping the sleep out of her eye with one hand, and carrying a cup of coffee in the other. Her tee-shirt had one of those big, yellow smiley faces on it, but with a bullet hole in the forehead.

"Good morning sleepy head," Rachel said. "Ellie, this is my friend Cynthia."

Ellie waved and smiled.

"Oh, man. Not another morning person." Cynthia winked at Ellie. Or maybe she didn't. It was hard to tell. In fact, her eyes might've still been closed.

"Cynthia, it's almost nine-thirty," Rachel said.

"I know, right? Pretty good for me." Cynthia shuffled her feet to the picnic table and sat down. She took a sip of her coffee. "Ah, that's good." That seemed to do the trick because she glanced over at Ellie. "So, you're Ellie huh? Rachel sure has told me an awful lot about you."

"Did she tell you that I play guitar?"

"Yes, she did. In fact, she told me that you were a quick learner, and that you try very hard. She said she's never seen such passion from someone."

"That's true." Ellie nodded. "The way I see it, if you're going to do something, you might as well go ahead and put everything you've got into it. I mean, otherwise why do it at all? You never know just how long you've got, right? Sort of like painting. You can't just sit around thinking about it too much. The paint will just dry up on you. Nope, you have to take the brush, dip that sucker in the paint, and just go at it!"

Cynthia turned towards Rachel, sort of hidden behind her coffee cup, and widened her eyes. She mouthed silently "Oh, my God!"

"So," Rachel said, giving Cynthia the I-told-you-so look, "what do you ladies want to do today? I was thinking we could hit the beach."

Ellie and Cynthia both looked at each other and nodded. Then they turned towards Rachel and nodded some more.

"Ellie, you want to ask your dad to come? You know, if he's not too busy."

Ellie smiled and shook her head. "He won't be too busy."

By noon, it was ninety degrees. Cynthia was no stranger to the sun, or tanning salons for that matter, and eager to get to the beach. It was flourishing with activity when she and Rachel set their chairs in the sand. Rachel knifed the umbrella between them, and then sprayed on some SPF 30 sunscreen. Cynthia put on some Banana Boat Dark Tanning Oil. Rachel opened the cooler and took out a bottle of water. Cynthia pulled out a Perrier. Rachel turned on her Kindle. Cynthia opened up *Under the Frozen Tundra*.

"Cynthia!" Rachel sat up in her chair.

"What?" Cynthia mimicked her tone.

"*Under the Frozen Tundra*? Really?"

"What? Like you don't read romance novels or something?" Rachel didn't say anything. Cynthia pulled her sunglasses down over her nose, waiting for her reply.

"I don't. Not like those, anyway." Rachel slid back down into her chair, raising her Kindle up and pretending to read, but then Cynthia snatched it out of her hands.

"Hey!" Rachel leaned over trying to get it back.

"Nope!" Cynthia swung the Kindle over her chair and out of Rachel's reach, working the menu with the keyboard. "We're going to find out, right now. You see, that's the problem with a Kindle. I can find out everything you've been reading." It only took Cynthia about five seconds to find what she was looking for. "And there it is. Fifty Shades of Grey. Yep! The whole trilogy!"

Rachel folded her arms, and huffed. "Well, I haven't read them."

Cynthia kept working the menu. "Oh, what have we here?" Cynthia gasped and handed the Kindle back to Rachel. Then she said, "Furthest page read says *the last page*…on all three!"

For a few moments, Rachel didn't say a word as she pretended to read again, and Cynthia let her stew. Finally she turned to Cynthia. "It's an excellent story, you know."

"Uh-huh."

"Well, it is."

"I know." Cynthia said. "I've read it too."

Rachel looked over at her and smiled. She dwelled on her thoughts for a moment before speaking. "I never used to read anything like that, you know. But the last few months…" Rachel looked down, almost embarrassed. "I don't know. You know how much I miss John. That never changes. It never will. But the last few months I've been really lonely." Rachel looked up and noticed a cargo ship crawling along the horizon. "You know I've always been a reader."

"Yeah, you have. I don't think I've ever seen you without a book within arm's reach. Except, after…" Cynthia tried to finish the sentence, but didn't.

"Yeah, I know. After John died, I just couldn't enjoy anything. Food, sleep, books…life. Honestly, I wanted to die." Rachel looked over at her friend. "Well, you know."

Cynthia nodded.

Rachel thought about the weight loss, the depression, the constant feeling of falling, and the guilt of not being able to give John a child. Without question, it was the lowest point in her life, and honestly, at the time, she didn't think she'd survive it. She still wasn't sure she could.

"After you saved me…" Rachel's voice strained, and the corners of her mouth turned down. She looked away for a second, trying to keep it together. That's when Cynthia placed her hand on top of hers, and Rachel started to cry. Rachel wedged a hand under her sunglasses and wiped away the tears. Looking over the water, she tried to focus on the cargo ship. "I just got so lonely. I can't even tell you the first book I read, but I suddenly found myself reading all the time. It was an escape—a fantasy. I started reading romance, and the words seemed to give me back a piece of myself." She looked down once more. "A piece I didn't think I'd ever have again."

"Rachel, you don't have to feel bad about that. Everyone needs an escape. Especially you, considering everything you've been through. And now look at you. You're *living* a romance novel."

Rachel sat up quickly and turned towards Cynthia, leaning in her direction. "Well, what if I'm just living out another fantasy? Just another escape? Is that fair to Marc? Is it fair to Ellie? Is it even fair to me? Eventually, you have to finish the novel. Whether it's one hundred pages or one thousand pages. It has to end Cynthia. The real world comes back. Pain comes back. Fear comes back. Loneliness comes back. It's all real."

Rachel fell back into her chair, looking at the cargo ship that continued to crawl along the water. She shook her head. "Real life always comes back. How do you prevent that from happening? Tell me. How?"

"Okay, I will." Cynthia pulled off her glasses and turned to look at Rachel. Rachel's sunglasses were dark, but Rachel knew Cynthia found her eyes nonetheless. It was then that Cynthia said something very profound, something that troubled Rachel, yet later she'd hear again, and remember for the rest of her life. "Don't stop reading. Ever."

Cynthia put her glasses back on, and leaned back in her chair, pulling her book up to read. Not ten seconds later another copy of *Under the Frozen Tundra* showed up.

"Excellent book!" Beverly said, showing Cynthia her copy.

Cynthia mocked a gasp, then turned to Rachel. "See what I mean?"

"Hi Beverly." Rachel said. "Meet Cynthia, my very best friend in the whole world."

"Hello. Nice to meet you, dear." Beverly set her chair down next to Cynthia and plunged her own umbrella into the sand before taking a seat.

"Beverly is Marc's aunt," Rachel said.

"Yep," Beverly replied. "And now you know where he gets his good looks from!"

"Is Charles joining us?"

"No, I'm afraid he has to work today." The way Beverly said it, Rachel wondered if poor Charles *ever* got a day off.

"So," Cynthia turned to Beverly, "what chapter are you on?"

"Chapter twenty-seven. You?"

"Just finished seventeen."

Beverly gasped. "Oh, that was a hot chapter wasn't it? That's right when Felecia realized that Jeremy's—"

"Boom!" Ellie slammed down in the sand next to Rachel, startling her—and not a moment too soon. Rachel looked back over her shoulder and saw Marc walking towards them. As quickly as she came, Ellie jumped up and started towards the ocean. "Come on! Let's swim!"

"Okay, just a second." Rachel watched Ellie as she ran towards the water, thinking she looked a little thin. Rachel stood up about the same time that Marc arrived.

"Hi," she said, smiling up at him

"Hey," he replied, unable to take his eyes off of her. Finally, he glanced over at Beverly and Cynthia. "Ladies." They waved at him and dove right back into whatever Felecia had realized about Jeremy. Marc didn't have any chairs with him, but he unfolded a beach blanket and Rachel helped him lay it out next to her chair.

"How'd you sleep last night?" Rachel asked.

"Hard."

Rachel blushed, and after reading the expression on his face, she decided it was best not to question him about it any further.

"Come on daddy!" Ellie yelled from the water as the waves crashed over her thighs.

Marc looked at Rachel and motioned towards the ocean. "Wanna go for a dip?"

"Sure." Rachel watched him while he pulled his shirt over his head, and she admired his body, thinking about last night. But then she heard Cynthia's voice in conversation with Beverly, and for some reason she looked away. Her stomach felt like it did last night when she saw Cynthia and Marc together.

As they made their way to the water, she looked back at Cynthia and Beverly. The two of them were oblivious they she and Marc had even left. Rachel knew that Cynthia and Beverly would hit it off instantly. But this feeling she was having? It felt somewhere between guilt and apprehension.

Marc's hand inadvertently brushed up against hers, or maybe it wasn't inadvertent. Either way, Rachel didn't take it.

"Are you okay?" Marc said.

"I'm fine. Why do you ask?"

Marc studied her face for a moment as they walked. "I don't know. Something doesn't seem right."

Ellie splashed them when they got to the water, and Marc ran towards her yelling, "Oh, no you don't!" He leapt into the water like a shark, then came up and grabbed her waist from behind. He roared like a monster and she screamed. He swung her around, her legs thrashing about in the water. Then he threw her a little ways and she crashed into a wave. When Ellie popped up, Marc held his nose and said, "Marco!" before plunging under again.

For a while, the three of them played in the water. They bodysurfed, seeing who could stay up the longest. They floated on their backs. They went out beyond the surf, and walked on the sandbar, watching the fish. Ellie would stand up on her dad's shoulders, and then launch herself into the water. All in all, they had a good time.

Every now and then though, Rachel would look back to the shore towards Cynthia and Beverly. Sometimes they'd see her and wave, sometimes not, but without fail, Rachel felt that feeling come over her. It was really starting to bug her. A few moments later, Rachel found out why.

They were floating along in the water, taking a break from the splashing and playing around. Rachel looked back to the shore and Cynthia waved. Just as Rachel waved back, a large swell of water pushed her right into Marc's arms. Right then, that feeling seemed amplified by a thousand. Marc must have sensed how she felt, because he released her almost instantly.

But why did she feel that way? Was it because Cynthia had known John? Was there some sort of subconscious thing going on, that somehow Cynthia seeing her with Marc made her feel guilty?

Rachel saw Marc looking at her as if she was a ghost. He looked confused, almost as confused as Rachel felt. "Marc, I'm sorry. I don't know what's going on."

"Daddy?" Ellie said in a weakened voice. Rachel thought she looked pale.

"What is it sweetheart?"

"I don't feel good."

Marc rushed to his daughter. "What doesn't feel good, honey?"

"I don't know. I just feel yucky. I feel like I'm going to throw up."

Marc put his hands on Ellie's shoulders and guided her through the water. Rachel followed.

As they reached the shore, Ellie held her stomach. She walked slowly and a bit wobbly. Marc steadied her with his hands. "Aunt Beverly!" Marc yelled.

Beverly looked up and sprang up out of her chair. "Let's get her in the shade." Cynthia jumped up as well, and as Beverly reclined her beach chair, Cynthia made sure the umbrella was casting shade over it.

Ellie laid down and put her forearm over her eyes. Marc reached into his cooler and pulled out a bottle of water. "Here, drink some of this, sweetheart." Ellie lifted her head up enough to take a few sips, and then put her forearm back over her eyes again.

"I feel better, just give me a minute," Ellie said.

Marc gave her two seconds. "Tell me how you feel, angel."

"My stomach just feels achy."

"Yeah, I know, but how?"

"Dad, I told you already!" Ellie snapped. She must have realized it too, because her next words came out much nicer. "I'm just a little nauseous, okay? That's all."

Rachel realized what was going on and tapped Marc on the shoulder. When he looked back, she pointed towards her waist and mouthed silently, "Period."

Beverly saw what Rachel had gestured. "Oh," she said, and placed her fingers over her mouth.

Marc looked at Beverly, then back to Rachel, then back to Beverly. His head fell to his chest and he sighed. He closed his eyes and pinched the bridge of his nose. After a couple of seconds, he nodded his head, as if to convince himself that everything was all right. He looked up, appearing relieved, if not still a little frazzled.

Ellie started feeling much better after a few minutes, and Beverly and Cynthia began taking to each other again about the *Tundra* book, but in innuendoes so Ellie wouldn't understand. Rachel glanced over at Marc who still looked a bit shaken up. "You want to go for a walk?" she asked.

They walked slow, watching the children play in the pools of seawater left behind by the outgoing tide. A few clouds passed under the sun, casting a much-needed shade over the hot beach. Marc gazed up at the clouds, and then to the western sky as if evaluating the coming sunset.

For the first time since Marc and Rachel met at Beverly's Winnebago, Rachel found herself speechless in his presence. She wanted to say it was only because Cynthia was here that she acted as she had. But as truthful as it seemed, to tell him felt wrong. She wanted to reassure him that they could battle through anything, and that she was going to be there for the long haul, but she knew it would be insincere. Instead she simply took his hand and they walked in silence, hoping that her feelings would say everything she wanted. When they returned and Cynthia came into view, Marc let go of her hand at almost the very instant Rachel became anxious.

After Rachel and Marc's walk, Cynthia and Beverly continued to talk, of course, and Rachel tried to read, but she kept watching Marc and Ellie build a huge, elaborate sand castle. She was certain it should win some kind of award or something. The two of them seemed so perfect together, and Marc made sure not to take over. He let Ellie be the architect and make most of the decisions about where to place the towers, or decide how thick the walls should be. When it was time to fetch water for the moat, it wasn't Ellie that had to run back and forth like that little girl Bella had to do, but Marc. And like Bella had done to her brother, Marc dumped water on Ellie's head, and then ran away. Ellie screamed, then chased him, and when she got close enough to catch him, Marc turned into a monster and chased his daughter into the ocean.

It was the kind of afternoon Rachel always dreamed of having with John. She glanced over at Cynthia, her best friend her entire life, and to Beverly, who reminded Rachel so much of her own grandmother. She watched Marc—the monster—grab his daughter's leg and pretend to gnaw at her calf, splashing water around her like it was fake blood, while Ellie flailed in an attempt to escape. Ellie laughed and screamed at the same time, knowing that when the monster releases, she'd let him attack her again.

The hot sun, the warm sand, the sound of the waves breaking, the salty breeze blowing, the children playing and laughing, and escaping from monsters.

All without John.

No one could see the tears that had welled up inside Rachel's eyes, hidden behind her sunglasses.

"I'll be back in a few minutes," Rachel said, trying not to sound upset.

"All right." Cynthia replied, watching Rachel push herself up and out of her chair. "Everything okay?"

"I just need to walk Riley."

"Okay sweetie."

Rachel sensed the two of them looking at her as she walked away. She told herself to calm down, to relax. She took off her sunglasses and dried her eyes, then put them back on again. She took deep breaths and concentrated on the warm sand beneath her feet. Soon, the sand gave way to the gravel walkway that led to her camper, and she didn't even notice that she'd left her sandals behind.

She opened the door to the Fleetwood, and the cool air from the air conditioner engulfed her body, and she realized how hot she felt. Riley greeted her as she opened the refrigerator and pulled out a bottle of water. She plopped down into the seat at the dinette, unscrewed the cap, and took a few big gulps. Reaching up with her hand, she took off her sunglasses and slid them across the table where they suddenly stopped after coming into contact with an object.

Tripp Blunschi

As she looked at it, she could feel the pain from the bottom of her gut begin to surface. Her vision started to blur, and the breathing she'd tried so hard to control while walking from the beach, increased. She reached for the object and pulled it into her chest. It was then that she just couldn't stop the tears from streaming down her face and running down the side of John's wine glass.

CHAPTER NINE

IT'S OFTEN TIMES SAID that when you graduate from high school, you're lucky to have one true friendship that will last a lifetime. For Rachel Willers and Cynthia Georgopoulos, that friendship began at the beginning of second grade. Perhaps it was the fact that they were complete opposites, Rachel always the quiet and shy goodie-goodie, and Cynthia the loud and boisterous troublemaker, that drew them together like opposite ends of a magnet. They've always been there for one another and knew each other inside and out. This fact was no doubt the reason Rachel heard the door to the Fleetwood open so soon after she started crying.

"Oh sweetie," Cynthia said, sliding into the dinette. She wrapped her arms around Rachel and drew her into her body, almost like a child. Rachel still clutched the wine glass close to her chest, and she continued to cry. Cynthia said nothing, occasionally stroking Rachel's hair, comforting her like she always had.

"Oh God," Rachel said, as she pushed herself off of her friend's shoulder. She put the glass down on the table and rubbed her bloodshot eyes. "I'm so sorry Cynthia. The last thing I wanted was for you to come down here to the beach, and me act like this."

"Don't be sorry. I'm not here for the beach. You know that. I'll always be here for you."

"I know." Rachel stared down at the wine glass. She knew Cynthia didn't know its significance, yet she obviously knew it had something to do with why she was crying.

"You want to talk about it?" Cynthia asked.

Rachel shook her head. "No, definitely not." They sat in silence for a moment as if Cynthia was daring her to speak first.

Rachel studied John's glass. Oh, how she wanted for it to be full of wine, right up to the rim, and John sitting on the other side of the table, leaning forward to sip it, touching it only with his lips to avoid spilling it. He might even do something funny, like lap it up like a cat, or pretend to be a pretentious wine snob, sniffing it, testing for aroma, before swishing it around in his mouth.

But how ridiculous was that? Dead people can't do anything. She realized for the thousandth time she was never going to see him or be able to talk to him, that he'd never make her laugh again. The tears started to well up in her eyes once more. She folded her arms on the table and placed her forehead on them, trying not to cry loudly. But then Cynthia rubbed her back and she couldn't help it.

Embarrassed, Rachel quickly sat back up and placed her hands over her face, willing herself to stop—to stop acting like a baby. Cynthia was right. She had to talk about it.

"I miss him so much."

"I know," Cynthia said softly, trying to hold back tears of her own, as one began to trickle down her face.

"He's supposed to be here with me, don't you see?" Rachel glanced over to the glass. "This glass, this stupid glass, is John's. How can I share that? How am I supposed to pretend it's someone else's?"

Cynthia nodded, and she took Rachel's hand and held it.

"It's not someone else's, Cynthia. It's just not." Rachel started to cry again and her voice broke up as she spoke. "And when I see Marc on the beach with Ellie, all I can think about is how it should be John and our daughter out there. We're the ones that are supposed to be living this life."

Rachel felt foolish, crying like a baby in her friend's arms for the third time in only a few moments. It wasn't like she hadn't many times before. Lord only knows how many tears she'd cried with Cynthia by her side since John's death. She'd been supportive for so long, and never, not even once, complained about it. The strange thing was, she understood that Cynthia never minded, because Rachel knew she'd be there giving the exact same support to

Cynthia if she ever needed it. But this time seemed different. For some reason, Rachel felt ashamed, like she was taking advantage of her best friend.

A loud knock on the Fleetwood's door startled them both, causing Cynthia to jump a little in her seat. She got up from the dinette, walked over and opened it.

"Everything okay?" Marc asked.

"Yeah, everything's fine." Cynthia was a lot of things, but a convincing liar she wasn't. Especially considering that her eyes were red and she sniffled after she spoke. Marc peered inside the Fleetwood with a concerned look on his face. Cynthia shifted to block his view.

"Okay," he said, trying to look around her. "Rachel left these." He lifted her sandals up in the air. "I thought she might want them for when she came back down."

Cynthia quickly took the sandals. "We're not coming back down, Marc. I think we're going to go into town this afternoon. You know, just some girl time."

Marc scratched his head and looked out towards the beach. "Do you want me to bring your things back up?"

"That'd be great. Tell Beverly we'll finish up our *Tundra* talk a little later, okay?"

"Sure thing," Marc said, barely getting the words out before Cynthia closed the door.

"Come on girl," Cynthia said as she walked past Rachel. "Let's go shopping. Don't want me to lie to him, do you?"

"Shopping? Oh Cynthia, I don't think I can."

"It's not a suggestion."

Shopping at the mall with Cynthia was work. Not that Rachel didn't like to shop or anything, they used to shop all the time before John died, but to be a bit more truthful, Cynthia did most of the shopping. Rachel tagged along for support if Cynthia started to spend too much money. Cynthia liked to look at every stitch of clothing in every store, and it didn't matter if she'd been there the week before or not. There was no telling what had gone on sale, or what new inventory had arrived, and she didn't want to miss a thing.

Today though, Rachel was actually thankful for the extended shopping. It calmed her down quite a bit, and took her mind off of the events of the last few days. She didn't think of John again, and the only time she thought of Marc was when she bought a cute short outfit and wondered if it was something he might like.

After the last store had been shopped, and Cynthia's credit card was finally safe and sound in her purse, at least for the moment anyway, the two stopped for dinner at one of the chain steakhouses near the mall.

Rachel wasn't all that hungry, but she ordered a baked chicken breast with a side of asparagus so that Cynthia wouldn't complain about her appetite.

There wasn't anything wrong with Cynthia's appetite, because she ordered the deep fried whole onion as an appetizer, along with a ribeye and loaded baked potato for her main course.

"You know," Cynthia said, chomping on the first piece of rare steak she'd just cut, "Marc seems like a really nice guy."

Rachel felt a knot swell up in her throat, and it wasn't because of the chicken she just swallowed. In the back of her mind, she knew they'd talk about it, but she hoped it might've come after dinner.

"And Ellie is so adorable," Cynthia continued. "Seems like you two have really hit it off."

Rachel nodded.

Cynthia was the type of person that had to completely eat each individual item before moving on to the next. She didn't say anything, apparently daring Rachel to speak first. She was just finishing up the last bite of her steak when Rachel finally broke the silence.

"But don't you think it's too soon though?" Before Cynthia could finish swallowing, Rachel answered her own question. "I know it's not *really* too soon, there's nothing wrong with a widow having a relationship after a year or so, or even earlier if that's what she wants. What I mean is, don't you think it's too soon for me?"

"No one can answer that but you, sweetie. You know that." Cynthia stirred the sour cream, butter, and pieces of bacon floating on top of her baked potato. "But if you ask me, I really don't think you could find a better setup if you tried." Cynthia put her fork down and leaned in towards the table a bit. "Did you ever think about why that might be? You came down here, and within days, you find, not one, but two people that seem to really enjoy spending time with you. Not only that, but you enjoy spending time with them."

Cynthia plunged her fork into the potato and scooped out a large bite. "And from what you've told me, and from what I saw when I first got here—with your wet boobs and all—you think all of that is just a coincidence?" Cynthia leaned back in her chair and pushed the fork full of potato into her mouth. "I think not," she muttered.

The drive back to Hunting Island was anything but quiet. Cynthia was wound like a Timex watch, and they talked all the way back, not about John or Marc or Ellie, but about anything else.

After they reached the Fleetwood, and Rachel walked Riley, she told Cynthia goodnight. It had been a busy day. Spending time at the beach, practically having a nervous breakdown, then shopping for several hours was enough to make any girl weary.

Rachel showered, put on her pajamas, and slipped into bed. She heard Cynthia flipping through the channels on the television, pausing for a few seconds when she reached one of the shopping networks.

As Rachel lay in bed, staring up at the ceiling, she thought about what Cynthia had said at the steakhouse; about it not being a coincidence that she'd met Marc and Ellie. At first it didn't seem to make sense.

When she was young, she frequently went to church, but mostly because her parents had been taking her for as long as she could remember. She never actually decided on her own how she felt about God, just taking it for granted that it was truth. But after her inability to have children, and certainly after John died, she'd made up her mind. There was no such thing as truth, and she was okay with that.

Still, she couldn't help but to consider it. Was it possible? Could John really have something to do with Marc and Ellie showing up in her life? What about her dreams? Were they some sort of sign from John, that he was guiding her, that he was telling her it was okay to move on, and she just wasn't listening?

Rachel's eyes finally closed, and the sound of the television slowly faded from her consciousness. The first visions of a dream that she'd have entered her mind—dreams of her and Marc making love under the beautiful live oak.

Then the branches smacked her in the face and the underbrush cut into her skin as she searched for the lighthouse in the dark.

The next morning started exactly the same as the morning before. Rachel and Riley finished their run, and she found herself sitting under the awning, sipping coffee and reading her Kindle while Cynthia slept. Rachel could hear her snoring away, vibrating the windows off the Fleetwood.

But the similarity to yesterday morning came to an abrupt halt when Ellie ran around the corner, crying. Rachel managed to put her Kindle on the picnic table before Ellie fell into her lap, and sobbed on her shoulder.

Rachel put her arms around her thin body. "What's the matter?" Rachel asked, but Ellie continued to cry as if she didn't hear what she said. "Ellie, what's the matter?" Rachel nudged her a bit to get her to look up, but all Ellie did was drop her chin to her chest and sob. "Calm down, sweetheart." Rachel pulled her into her body and rubbed her back.

After a few moments Ellie sat up, her eyes and face red. She sniffled, and tried to compose herself. She took a couple of deep breaths before she spoke. "Jonathan...went...home!" Her eyes filled back up with tears, and then streamed down her face again. She fell back into Rachel's body.

"Oh, honey. I'm so sorry." Rachel rocked her as best she could in the camp chair. She heard the door to the Fleetwood open, and Cynthia stepped out. Rachel shook her head. Cynthia got the message and stepped back in and quietly closed the door.

"I didn't even get to kiss him," Ellie's muffled and crying voice said into Rachel's shirt.

"It's okay, there will be other boys."

Ellie popped up and shook her head. "No! No! No! There won't be!" She fell back into Rachel's chest again. For a few more moments, Rachel tried to soothe her and eventually, Ellie's crying slowed.

Ellie pulled herself up and sniffled. "He told me last night to meet him on the beach this morning because his family was leaving early today. So I met him and we walked. I could tell he was thinking about kissing me because he was so quiet. We hardly said anything to each other. When we got back, he looked at me and said he wished he didn't have to go, and thanks for being his friend." Ellie's eyes started to tear up once more and her lower lip began to tremble. "So I closed my eyes and waited for him to kiss me. But then he just ran away." She cried again in Rachel's chest.

Rachel continued to rub her back, and it took a few more moments for Ellie to stop crying. Rachel held her, and let Ellie decide when she was ready to talk.

Ellie finally lifted her head. "Can I ask you something?" She shook her head, and swallowed. "And please don't lie, okay?"

Rachel looked into Ellie's innocent blue eyes. "I would never lie to you."

"Am I ugly?"

"No, of course not!" Rachel put her hands up to Ellie's cheeks, wiping away her tears. "I think you're one of the most beautiful girls in the whole world. One of the most special people I have ever met in my entire life. I promise. Ellie...you are *so* beautiful."

"Really?" she whimpered.

"Yes, you are sweetheart. And don't ever forget that. I'm sure Jonathan wanted to kiss you too, but he was just scared. Just like my friend Kelly was. That's all that happened."

Ellie looked down and nodded.

"Come on," Rachel said, standing up, "let's take a walk."

She took hold of Ellie's hand and they walked towards the beach. The sky was covered with thick, puffy clouds, but as Rachel glanced out over the ocean, she noticed how dull and gray the horizon looked. They reached the water and turned north, walking along the shore. For a few minutes, Ellie seemed quiet, but Rachel could tell she was in deep thought about something. That worried Rachel— and for good reason.

"Do you think there's a heaven?" Ellie asked.

If ever there was uncertainly in Rachel's mind about which of Ellie's questions was the most difficult to answer, this one certainly removed all doubt. At first Rachel didn't know how to respond. Their relationship had grown, true, but this hit a new level. Was it her place to say anything at all? Ellie trusted her. Was it fair for her to influence Ellie's beliefs because of her own? Carefully, she considered her options. Then she decided.

"I don't know," Rachel said, feeling guilty because it bordered on a white lie.

"I think there is." Ellie said. "When I die, I hope I get to be an angel. I know I'd be good at it. I just know it. Do you think I'd make a good angel?"

"I do," Rachel replied.

"I'll tell you one thing," Ellie continued at break-neck speed, "Jonathan will be sorry he didn't kiss me. I mean, I'd help him if he was in trouble, but how often does a boy get a chance to kiss an angel? I've never heard of it. Besides, if I'm an angel, kissing a boy will be the last thing on my mind. Just think about all the cool stuff I'll be able to do." Ellie tugged on Rachel's hand. "I think I can change the world!"

After about an hour on the beach, Ellie talking to Rachel about anything and everything under the sun, Rachel walked Ellie back to the Airstream.

"Thanks for the talk," Ellie said, her smile as wide and as large as the dreams she spoke about. Rachel was beginning to think she was learning far more from Ellie than Ellie was from her.

"Will you ask your dad to come out?" Rachel asked. Ellie nodded, and then ran inside. A few seconds later Marc stepped out.

"Hey," Rachel said. "I'm really sorry about yesterday."

"It's alright."

Rachel didn't elaborate; somehow she knew that Marc understood. "Maybe we just need more time together. Let's pick up where we left off Friday night. Cynthia is going back home this afternoon. You want to come over for dinner tonight?"

Marc grinned. "What are you cooking?"

Rachel put her hands on her hips. "Does it matter?"

"It might."

"What, you didn't like my graham crackers and peanut butter?"

"Loved them."

"Well, I promise, this will be just as good."

When Rachel returned to the Fleetwood, the television was tuned to the shopping network. Cynthia quickly put her billfold back in her purse, then snatched the remote control and turned it off. "Beach?" Cynthia said, smiling and trying not to look suspicious. "I've still got a few hours before I have to leave."

They gathered their beach equipment that Marc brought up to the picnic table yesterday, and headed back to the sand. For the duration of the afternoon it was just the two of them, the sun, a little reading, and a lot of good conversation, none of which focused on anyone Rachel had just met. Well, none except for Beverly, who the two mutually agreed they adored.

After their day at the beach, they said their goodbyes, both a little teary eyed, and vowed next time to spend a little more time together. Rachel waved as Cynthia pulled out of the campground. She looked up and noticed the gray sky that she saw earlier had darkened, and hoped Cynthia would have a safe trip back to Atlanta.

Marc knocked on the door promptly at seven o'clock.

"Come in!" Rachel said. She stood at the sink, cutting some vegetables.

Marc opened the door, one hand behind his back. "It smells delicious in here."

"I thought we'd eat inside tonight. It looks like it might rain." Then she spun towards him and smiled, throwing her hands in the air. *Tada!* "It's DiGiorno!" She said it just like the commercial.

"Ah, pizza. Excellent choice."

"I like to think of it as Italian. I'm even putting together a salad. Salad...I can do."

"And I like to think that these..." he pulled out a large fistful of flowers, "are for you."

"Oh Marc, that's so sweet. Let me get a vase." But when she thought about it, she realized the only vase she had contained the fresh cut flowers. She walked over to the dinette and picked them up. They were mostly wilted and dried now, perhaps a few stems still hung on to a bit of life.

She pulled the dead flowers out of the vase and dumped them in the trash. For a second, she looked at them. She thought about her first night in the camper, how she placed those flowers on the dinette table like she'd done several times before when she and John had camped. It was their tradition. But now, as she put Marc's flowers into the vase, it felt wrong. The flowers were certainly pretty—a small array of assorted tulips—but replacing the fresh cut flowers with them seemed so...final, like a metamorphosis was taking place in her life she wasn't ready to accept.

She walked to the sink and filled the vase half way with water, then placed the flowers on the counter next to her. She went back to cutting the cherry tomatoes and cucumbers for the salad. Marc walked up behind her and placed his hands on her waist.

She stopped cutting. "I'm sorry, Marc. It'll be ready soon. Why don't you have a seat and we'll eat in a few minutes."

"Okay," Marc said. He took a couple of steps back. "Is everything okay?"

"Sure," she said. "It's just that I've got a sharp knife and I don't want to cut myself." She looked over her shoulder and smiled. "I need to concentrate on what I'm doing. That's all."

Marc walked over to the couch, but he didn't sit. He gave Riley a pet on the head then looked out the window. "I hope this weather holds off, but it sure doesn't look like it's going to."

"As long as it holds off until Cynthia can get home, I'll be happy."

"Did you two have a good time yesterday?" He looked around the room, checking out the Fleetwood.

"We did." Rachel sliced her knife through a head of romaine. "We went shopping, and let me tell you, that girl can shop. We went into this one place...you should have seen the baby clothes they had in there. Maria's." She put the romaine in a bowl then started slicing some mushrooms. "Have you heard of it?"

"I don't think so. Is it new?" Marc walked over to the dinette, eyeballing a bottle of wine. "Chianti Classico," he said, reading from the label.

"It didn't look new, but what do I know." She popped a piece of mushroom into her mouth. "They had the cutest little knitted onesies, blue or pink, with an adorable hoodie on top. They even had them in green in case you were shopping for someone and didn't know if it was a boy or girl yet."

"Sounds fun." Marc picked up the corkscrew sitting next to the bottle, and he started twisting it into the cork.

"Of course, Cynthia tried to buy everything in the store. Honestly, I don't know how she ever has any money. She's a shopaholic in the worst sense of the word. Have you ever had to deal with someone like that?"

Pop. Out came the cork.

"Nope," Marc said. "I take that back. I dated a girl like that in high school, but it didn't last. I couldn't afford it." Marc grabbed a wine glass sitting on the dinette table and poured a healthy glass full.

"I can see why," Rachel said. She took the tomatoes, cucumbers, and mushrooms and placed them in the bowl with the romaine. Then she went to work on the carrots with a peeler. "I don't know if there's a shopaholics anonymous or not—actually, I'm sure there is—but if she was anything like Cynthia, I hope she had a good support system in place."

Marc twirled the wine around in the glass, and then buried his nose in the top of it, sniffing the bouquet.

"You know," Rachel continued, "It's an addiction like anything else. Like being addicted to gambling, or drinking, or whatever."

"I'm sure," Marc said. He took a drink from the glass, and then swished it around in his mouth, studying its character and body.

"Clearly, people like that need help." Rachel swept the carrots into her hand and put them in the salad. Next she opened up a jar of olives, filtering the liquid into the sink. "I've tried to tell Cynthia that she has a problem, and she probably knows it, but I think sometimes people with addictions have to tell someone else. You have to admit it to others before you can admit it to yourself? Don't you agree?"

Marc gulped the wine, "I do. Hey, this tastes pretty good. Got another glass? I'll pour you some."

"Cabinet above the recliner. The thing is, some people won't listen to just one friend." Rachel dumped the olives from the jar right into the salad. "I think the only way to help people like that, is to surround them with the ones you love. An intervention."

Rachel picked up the salad bowl and turned around. She saw Marc reaching up towards the cabinet above the recliner with one hand, and holding a glass of wine in the other.

The external events of their conversation rushed through her mind: Chianti Classico, the cork popping from the bottle, the sound of Marc swishing the wine around in his mouth.

This tastes pretty, good. Got another glass?

Rachel's eyes darted to the dinette table. Her eyes widened. She looked back at Marc, and he was about to drink from the glass.

"No, don't!"

But it was too late. Marc took his lips off the wine glass—John's wine glass—and he swallowed. He looked confused, and even frightened. Rachel dropped the salad bowl and rushed towards him. She reached for John's glass and it fell, bouncing off the recliner. It hit the Fleetwood's marble flooring, shattering into pieces, scattering shards of glass and wine all over the tile.

"John!" Rachel cried, as she reached out towards the floor. She dropped to her knees and she put her hands over her mouth, trying not to cry, but there was no stopping it.

Marc took a couple of steps back from her. "I'm sorry Rachel." But she didn't hear him, and for a second or two, he watched her as she sobbed into her hands. "I'm sorry. I don't know what to say." Marc knelt beside her. "It's okay." He put a hand on her shoulder. "We'll get some more glasses."

"No, we can't!" Rachel cried. Marc stepped back.

"Rachel," Marc paused for a moment. "I don't understand."

And how could he? As Rachel looked at the pieces of glass and wine spreading out over the tile floor, she became aware of the absurdity of the situation, grieving about something as trivial as a broken wine glass. But worse than that, as ludicrous as it looked, the pain she felt tearing a hole in her heart was real. She realized how little she had recovered.

And Marc, it wasn't his fault, and she knew it. Though she couldn't deny she had feelings for him, it certainly wasn't fair to drag him along in the wake of her own suffering. Thinking back on it now, she realized how foolish she'd been for letting things get this far.

Rachel lifted her head, and turned slightly, but she didn't look at him. She couldn't. "I think you should go."

"Rachel. Don't." He started to reach for her, but her slight movement made him stop.

"I'm sorry Marc. I thought I could do this, but I can't."

"If you could just help me understand, I know we can work it out."

"There's nothing to understand. I told you in the beginning that I couldn't make any promises. Now please go." She waited, listening for his footsteps, praying for him to leave her, to find someone else that deserved him. But the footsteps didn't come. "Please, Marc."

Marc walked to the door and opened it. For a moment, all she could hear were the first drops of rain starting to come down.

"Rachel?"

"Please," she pleaded.

She didn't want to hear the door shut, and for a moment it didn't, but when it finally closed, so did her eyes and the tears fell once more. Through her blurry vision, she looked at the shards of glass mixed with red wine, and just like the pieces of her broken heart, there was nothing she could do to mend it.

CHAPTER TEN

SHE STOMPED THE ACCELERATOR. With Riley strapped in the passenger seat, the Jeep launched forward, slinging gravel everywhere as it exited the campground on Hunting Island. By the time Rachel reached the drawbridge, the storm out of the east was in full force. She had a hard time telling if it was the rain or her tears making it so hard to see, but she didn't care. She didn't care where she was going, only that it wasn't anywhere near the beach, the lighthouse, the Fleetwood, or anything related to Hunting Island, South Carolina.

As she drove through Beaufort, she thought about the plates she bought at the hardware store. Three stupid plates. They weren't *meant* for her, Marc, or Ellie. They weren't *perfect* for them at all. It was only an incomplete set, nothing more and nothing less. The fact that she dropped one of the plates when that woman asked about her husband only proved how completely pathetic Rachel was. Maybe she should've dropped another one. Then she could have finagled a set of two out of that nosey old woman—one for her and one for John.

God, she missed him so much. As her tears fell, she halfway thought about slamming into the sidewall of the bridge that spanned Port Royal Sound, hurling the Jeep along with her suffering towards the salty water below. If God was real, surely he could help her find comfort in John's arms again, to feel his heart beat next to hers, to be able to hold his hand, to hear his voice whisper in her ear—*I love you Rachel. I love you.*

And if there was no God? Then fuck it! She'd no longer have to live with the great curse of love. She'd sink to the bottom of the ocean, letting her deplorable body bloat and swell. The fish could have their way with her flesh, and her soul could rot in hell.

But as she drove through Savannah, the inside of her Jeep remained dry and above ground because of a promise—a promise to John that she'd find happiness and love once again, that she'd somehow grow old in the arms of another, with passion that equaled or exceeded what she and John had, and to live out the dreams they had always wanted to live out together. In his last days, John made her promise these things. A promise that she knew was impossible to keep. A promise she *couldn't* keep.

But she tried, hadn't she? She really tried to keep the promise. When she first bought the Fleetwood, she naively thought it would drive her in the right direction towards happiness, to help her face her fears head on, to help her find her creative streak as an author. But now she found herself driving through Macon, Georgia, driving away from her expensive experiment, crushing her and John's dreams at the same time, and abandoning the promise. She felt like a failure. She had failed herself, and worse, she had failed John.

And what about Marc? Had she failed him as well? She told Marc up front she couldn't promise anything. She was clear to him about that, and she warned him. He shouldn't have expected anything from her. But deep down, when she really thought about it, she knew that was just a facade. Maybe at first that's what she meant, but it grew into something much more than that, and she knew they both felt it. She *did* feel something for him—something more than just sex, more than just a stupid romance novel that abruptly ended. But that feeling could *never* match what she and John had. The fact that she led herself to believe there was a possibility of love like that was like telling John he would never die of cancer. Absurd! It's all just a big lie. All of it!

Rachel cursed Beverly. Who did she think she was, conniving, and tricking her into falling for Marc? What business was it…no, what *right* did she think she had to impose her will onto Rachel's life? How dare she play with Rachel's emotions by using Ellie as bait to draw her in.

But what about Ellie? Her sweet Ellie. Was she not the big contradiction then? Ellie's heart seemed as pure as Rachel and John's love for one another.

Rachel drove through Atlanta, and the storm followed her, intensifying and pounding the thin sheet metal of her Jeep, but she couldn't hear it at all. All she could hear were the sweet, soulful vibrations emanating from John's guitar, as Ellie strummed the chords to *Unchained Melody*. Even imperfect as the notes Ellie created were, it sounded beautiful because it came from her soul, and hearing it now pained Rachel's heart.

Soon, Rachel found her heart was just as lost as she was, and she drove aimlessly along back roads, slinging muddy clay across the windshield. The wind howled, and the rain came down so strong it sounded like a machine gun spraying bullets on the top of the Jeep. She slid into a driveway, a long winding one, with pastures on each side. The lightning flashed around her, revealing the outline of a farmhouse, and the thunder clacked with ferocious intensity.

Rachel reached the end of the driveway, and flung open the door of the Jeep. Shielding her eyes from the sideways rain trying to blow her down, she ran up to the house, splashing through the mud. She pounded on the screen door, but no one came. She screamed louder, trying to be heard over the wind. The rain sheeted down from the roof above, splashing mud over her legs and hips. She pounded on it again, crying and kicking.

Finally, a light came on and she held her breath. The door opened and the outline of a face appeared, buried behind the screened door, diffused by the light.

"Rachel?"

The screen door opened, revealing the face of a man, and Rachel cried inconsolably as she fell into John Willers' arms.

The smell of cornbread cooking in a cast iron skillet has a way of penetrating every crevice in a house, and in particular, finding its way upstairs and teasing anyone up there with its aroma. Rachel didn't know if it was the bread, or the sunlight that beamed through the cream, lace curtains that woke her. Sweat beads formed on her forehead and lip, and for a moment, she focused on the ceiling above to let her eyes adjust.

She swung her legs over the edge of the mattress, and her feet barely touched the dark, almost black, hardwood flooring. On the nightstand sat an old brass alarm clock, the kind with bells attached to the top. It read eleven-thirty. The floral patterned wallpaper was yellowed, and peeled in places around the top, but still nice looking.

Riley got up from the floor and stretched his back, then placed his head on the bed. Rachel rubbed him on the snout. She didn't remember bringing him up, but then again, she wasn't quite sure how she got here in the first place.

Rachel stood and shuffled over to the antique dresser, wiping the sleep from her eyes. She looked at her blurred reflection in the stained, plate glass mirror, unhappy with what she saw. Her eyes, normally sunken and blue, looked puffy and red.

On the dresser, she picked up a small, framed picture of John as a child. It was a faded color photo of him swinging in a tire in front of his house—a house Rachel hadn't seen since before John died.

Until last night.

After John's funeral, Rachel had called John and Eileen Willers a few times to see how they were doing and to catch up on things. She loved them so much, but she couldn't bring herself to face them. For one, John Sr. looked so much like his son. Just looking at him would surely bring tears to her eyes, and she didn't want them to see her like that again. John's service had been hard on everyone.

But the other reason ran much deeper.

John and Eileen had accepted Rachel right away into their family when she and John were first married. Or course, they had known Rachel since she was sixteen and had always treated her as one of their own. Sure, they offered their opinion from time to time on issues concerning John and Rachel's big decisions, but not unless solicited, and even then it was offered gently and without pressure. They had been the best in-laws a girl could ask for.

That thought lingered in her mind after she dressed and began to walk down the staircase. She looked over the dozens of framed photos that hung on the wall: old black and white photos of the Willers' from the turn of the twentieth century, John's great grandparents, Eileen's parents and her two sisters, John's uncle, and pictures of John when he was young. Next to those, hung John's high school pictures, Rachel's wedding photos, and photos of John's cousins and their kids. It was a storybook of the Willers' lives.

But then the mosaic of photos came to an abrupt end, though plenty of room remained. Rachel placed her hand on the wall where pictures should've been. Missing were pictures and memories that could never happen, and it was all her fault. She deprived John and Eileen of the same gift Rachel couldn't give to her husband.

John was an only child, so when he died, any chance of the Willers having grandchildren died with him. Having to face them, knowing that she was the reason their blood—the extension of their lives—would cease to exist, was too much to handle. They say guilt is a rope that wears thin, and in Rachel's case, too thin to support frames upon the wall of the Willers' staircase.

But Rachel *was* here now. As she reached the last step, she wondered why? She didn't recall making a conscious decision to come, yet here she stood in their home, the smell of cornbread luring her into the kitchen.

She froze when she saw Eileen on the other side of the counter, rolling out some dough. Rachel noticed that Eileen looked thinner than she used to be, and the color of her hair, once long and brown, had turned mostly gray. Seeing how much older she looked, Rachel regretted not visiting the last two years. Rachel took a couple of nervous steps forward, when one of the floorboards squeaked, and she stopped, wondering how Eileen would react when she saw her. Eileen glanced up, and at first she looked vacant, like she'd seen a ghost.

"Hi Eileen," Rachel said.

For another second, Eileen's expression went unchanged, and Rachel began to think she shouldn't be here. But then, Eileen's face lit up. She sat her rolling pin down, scurried over to Rachel, and hugged her. Rachel detected the sweet scent of pastry dough on her apron.

Eileen pushed Rachel back, but held on to her arms. "Let me look at you." She studied Rachel's face and body. "Yep. I was right. You've lost too much weight." She pulled Rachel in for another hug.

160

"Eileen," Rachel said, a touch of sadness in her voice. "I'm sorry I haven't visited sooner."

"Oh, never mind that. You're here now, aren't you? Let me get you some sweet tea. How did you sleep? If I would've known you were coming, I would have washed the sheets. No one's slept in that bed in ages."

"I slept fine," Rachel said, taking a seat at the kitchen table. "I'm sorry for not calling. I wasn't even sure where I was going last night."

"Well, you gave us quite a scare." Eileen set the tea down in front of Rachel. "John thought someone was breaking in the house. He almost grabbed his shotgun."

Rachel huffed. "At least then he could've put me out of my misery."

Eileen swatted her hand. "I doubt it's loaded. And even if it was, John couldn't hit the broadside of a barn these days." She pulled out a chair from the table and took a seat across from Rachel.

Rachel fiddled with her fingernails in the silence. Eileen was always a good listener. Maybe too much. "What smells so good?" Rachel finally said.

"It's a ham, for supper. You looked a little hollow-cheeked and I thought you could use some good home cookin'. I've got collards, Crowder peas, dressing, and some fresh tomatoes. Just picked them off the vine myself. I'm also fixin' that apple pie that you used to like so much."

"Thanks Eileen. That sounds great."

After some much needed gossip with Eileen, Rachel stepped outside to get some air and to say hello to John. Eileen said he'd probably be in the barn. As Rachel pulled back the hefty doors, the smell of old leather and tack, combined with the sun's rays spilling in, lit up the inside of both the barn and her heart.

That cheap radio still hung from the same nail, and she walked over and flipped the switch. It surprised her when it came on, playing country music. Rachel closed her eyes, listening to the music, remembering that night she danced with John.

"How you doin' kiddo?"

Startled, Rachel spun around, and John Sr. stood in the doorway. "John, you scared me." He looked just like his son. Older, thinner, and perhaps a little more hardened from years working a farm, but his brown eyes and high cheek bones had unmistakably been passed down to his son.

"Well, consider us even, then." He smiled and walked to her with his arms out. Rachel ran to him and gave him a hug. She knew it was as close to John as she'd ever get.

"It's good to see you Rachel. We've missed you."

"I'm so sorry about that. I know I should've stopped by sooner, it's just that—"

"Ah, no need to explain. You know we're always here for you, and if that means staying away for a while, then that's what it means. You're always welcome. You know that."

He pointed to the radio as he walked past it. "I keep batteries in that thing for when I'm in here. I keep waiting for it to die, but it won't. It's been on that one station for so long, it won't play anything else. Stubborn I suppose." A pail hung on the wall next to the middle stall, and John pulled out a fist full of sweet feed. "Sort of like you." He winked at Rachel, then put his hand in the stall and fed an American Paint horse. "This here's Chester. Our newest addition."

John's eyes started to moisten, and Rachel put her arm around him. Chester had been John's middle name.

"We bought him a couple of years ago. What good is a farm without a few good horses?"

"He's beautiful," Rachel said. John reached up and patted the horse's jaw, then rubbed its forehead with his fingers.

Apparently, John had managed to tractor in a load of hay before the storm yesterday. He walked to the other end of the barn, slipping on a pair of leather work gloves, and grabbed a bail off the trailer and started stacking. "Eileen tells me you bought one of those fancy motorhomes. How's everything working out with that?"

Rachel sighed. "I don't know, John. For some reason, I had this idea that going back to the beginning would somehow allow me to move on. Plus, I thought focusing on something like trying to write a novel might take my mind off John. You know I've always wanted to be an author. But every time I try, it's just junk. I cry. I get angry. More than anything, I think I'm just confused. I'm worried if I made the right decision. In fact, I think I've made a huge mistake." Rachel looked at the ground. "I miss him so much, John."

John stopped stacking. "I know you do. Come here." He sat down on the trailer and offered a seat next to him, and Rachel took it.

He looked up at the loft, stacked high with hay, and pointed. "You know, John used to spend a lot of time up there writing you all those letters." He kind of laughed to himself, as if caught up in a vision of his son. "I swear, he'd sit up there for hours, saying it was *easier* for him do his homework up there. He wasn't fooling anybody. He sure wasn't doing his homework. We could tell that much from his grades. It's a wonder that boy got into Georgia at all. He was crazy about you from the very beginning." John put his arm around Rachel, lightly squeezing her. "I sure am glad he was."

Rachel smiled at him and she placed her head on his shoulder.

"You know," John said, "I think if you'll stop trying so hard, you might find that he still writes those letters to you. You just gotta learn how to read 'em."

Rachel looked up to the loft, wishing she could open just one more letter from him. Maybe it would tell her everything she needed to know, how to go on living without him, how to move on, how not to forget him—how to be happy.

"Come on," John said, "I know Eileen's probably got supper on the table. You know how she gets if we're late."

After supper, Eileen and Rachel cleaned off the table and sat down to a game of progressive rummy, a card game all four of them enjoyed playing when Rachel and John used to visit.

"How are things going on Hunting Island?" Eileen said, discarding.

Rachel looked in her hand, and then picked up a card from the deck. "All things considered, not bad I suppose. I met this pretty amazing eleven-year-old girl. I've been giving her a few guitar lessons. Just showing her some chords, is all." She glanced up at Eileen and smiled, then discarded.

Eileen drew a card off the deck and placed it in her hand. She peered at Rachel over her reading glasses. "Is that girl the reason you came here in the middle of the night, in a rain storm?"

Rachel didn't say anything at first, studying her hand. "No, I guess not," she said, sort of dispassionate. She rearranged some of the cards, trying to match up the suits.

Eileen pursed her lips together, and then looked at her own cards. "You know Rachel, you've always been like a daughter to me. John feels the same way. I want you to know that." She discarded the king of spades.

After peeking at Eileen's discard, Rachel's eyes bounced from card to card in her hand. She already had the king of clubs, and glanced up at Eileen as she picked up the discard. "I know. You've always made me feel like a member of the family." She discarded.

Eileen took the top card from the deck, and then looked at her hand for a moment. But then, she shook her head. "You've met someone haven't you?"

Rachel continued to study her cards. She already had three jacks. She just needed another king to go with the other two, and then she could lay down.

"Rachel?" Eileen said again.

Rachel's eyes watered, and she wiped them dry so she could concentrate on her cards. She didn't need the two of clubs, the six of diamonds, or the ace of spades she held. If only she had a king.

"Put your cards down honey," Eileen said. "Rachel, look at me."

But Rachel kept looking for the king. She looked at the discard pile, and nothing was there. She wiped her eyes again, and glanced up to Eileen. "It's your go."

Eileen put her cards face down on the table, and slipped off her glasses. She dabbed her eyes before she spoke. "You have to let him go, Rachel."

A tear streaked down Rachel's face. "Eileen, I don't know if I can."

"You know that's what John would want."

"I know. We talked about it, but it's so hard."

"I understand, but darling, you have to. I don't mean forget. Don't ever forget. I think tomorrow, you and Riley need to head on back down to that island, before it's too late."

"Eileen, I don't think I should. If I can stay here a few days I can figure it out. Take some time, you know?"

"No, you don't need to do that. You know what this old place looks like. What you need to do is get back down there. If you're looking for my permission, then you have it, but please don't spend the rest of your life miserable, when you can be happy. That's what John would want. That's what we all want."

Eileen picked up her cards, a signal to Rachel that she was done talking about it. It only took Eileen a second to find the card she was looking for, and then she discarded the king of hearts.

Before the sun had a chance to spread its morning rays on the Willers' farm once more, Rachel had kissed John and Eileen goodbye, and started back for Hunting Island. She had two goals in mind. The first was to beat Atlanta traffic—a pretty impressive feat even at six-thirty in the morning. The second was to make up her mind about Marc.

It wasn't fair to herself or to Marc, or even Ellie for that matter, to sit on the fence toying with everyone's feelings. Besides, a plan seemed logical. She needed to make a decision one way or the other, and pursue it. That way, she'd avoid being blindsided by her own feelings, like what happened with John's glass. Either find Marc right away and tell him she was all in, or pack up the Fleetwood and move on.

She met her first goal with relative ease, taking some backroads that lead to the airport, south of Atlanta. As she considered the second goal, she wondered if there was a special reason she'd met Marc in the first place. She thought about what John Sr. had said to her in the barn, that he believed John was still writing her, and how it was up to her to figure out what he'd written. Then there was Cynthia's theory that it wasn't just coincidence Rachel had met two people who enjoyed spending time with her, and she with them.

Did John, in fact, somehow have some sort of divine influence on the situation? She seriously doubted it, but she had to admit that

Marc and Ellie would've been perfect choices. Marc was handsome, funny, and unafraid to show his emotions. Not only that, as Marc had even mentioned, they both had endured a similar loss, and were sensitive to each other's feelings. More importantly, he truly seemed to enjoy spending time with her. Plus, he was a dynamite cook!

And how about Ellie? Rachel simply adored her. She was everything Rachel could've asked for, had she had a daughter of her own. She was spirited, passionate, grateful, and even inspirational. Rachel seemed to need her just as much as she needed Rachel.

By the time she drove through Savannah, she realized what a fool she'd been. Marc and Ellie had been practically dropped in her lap. Whether John had anything to do with it or not, through some sort of divine intervention or not, she thought about what it would be like to *not* have them in her life. As she answered that question, pressing the Jeep's gas pedal closer to the floor, she knew she'd met the second goal.

All in.

When she got to Hunting Island, she pulled up to the Fleetwood and went inside. It felt like a sauna. It was already two o'clock and the air conditioning hadn't been on in a couple of days. She flipped on the air and went outside to walk Riley.

She wanted to see Marc right away, but first she stopped by Beverly's to let her know she was back. She didn't want her to worry. She knocked, but no one answered. Then she walked over to Marc's airstream, and he wasn't home either and his truck was gone.

As Rachel walked back to the Fleetwood, wondering where everyone was, she saw Charles talking to one of the campers. As she approached, Charles caught a glimpse of her and quickly finished up the conversation. He started walking towards Rachel, and right away, she noticed something unusual, something about the way he walked or the expression in his face. Perhaps the heat?

Feeling anxious, Rachel spoke before he reached her. "Hey Charles, I'm trying to find Marc. I stopped by, but didn't see his truck. Do you know when he's going to be back? I would've asked Beverly, but I couldn't find her either."

Charles didn't reply. As he walked up to her, Rachel definitely knew something wasn't right, and it wasn't the heat. She almost didn't want to ask. "Charles, is everything okay?"

Charles took a rag from his back pocket and dabbed the sweat over his lip. He looked like he was stalling. He placed the rag back in his pocket. "I'm afraid not," he finally said. "Marc and Beverly are both up at the hospital."

Rachel felt sick. Her heart sent an initial shock to her chest, and then it tripled in speed. "Oh, my God! What happened? Is Beverly okay? Is it Marc?"

She started to back away when he didn't say anything. She looked into Charles' eyes and placed her hand over her mouth, unaware that it shook. Charles seemed unable to speak, and Rachel didn't want him to. But as a foreboding thought entered her mind for a microsecond, she became terrified, somehow knowing what he was going to say—as if she'd always known it.

"It's Ellie."

CHAPTER ELEVEN

LIKE HER HEART RIPPING, the doors of the elevator opened, and a flood of wretchedness surrounded her and made her gasp. She backed away from the doors until she felt the metal railing that surrounded the walls of the elevator. She grabbed it, trying to somehow convert its cooling effect into comfort. She turned her head and covered her mouth, not because of the sickly scent that she drew into her lungs, but simply to forbid a scream. The doors of the elevator began to close, and in her mind she didn't move, hoping instead that she'd be crushed by them. The alternative seemed much worse. But the doors closed behind her, and she found herself standing on the white tiled floor of the Beaufort Memorial Hospital Cancer Center.

As she walked past the rooms, her gut tightened. She read the names on the doors: Anne Fletcher, Louise Anderson, Jackson Smith...*John Willers*. Some patients had visitors talking to them about such things as the weather, how their work was going, or what so-and-so was doing—anything to avoid talking about the dying elephant in the room. Other patients received no visitors. In those rooms, Rachel only saw lumps of covers and feet, some old, some young, some even with polished toenails, as if there was such a thing as hope.

Rachel saw Marc, and the pounding of her heart pulsed in her head. He was talking to a couple of doctors at the other end of the corridor, behind a glass door, and one of the doctors was spewing out information. Rachel couldn't hear what he said, but she could tell by the way he fidgeted it wasn't good news. Rachel had become quite good at reading their body language. The doctor stopped talking and he put his head down, as if trying to find his next words. He finally looked up at Marc, and spoke a single, short sentence. Rachel tried to read his lips, but couldn't make it out. The second doctor remained quiet, her eyes glued on Marc.

Marc didn't move a muscle. He stood there, looking at the first doctor like he hadn't heard a thing. The doctor took his glasses off. This time Rachel could read his lips when he spoke.

I'm sorry Marc.

Marc reached behind him, searching for the wall, and he found it, then slid down to the floor. The second doctor sank down with him, and she put her arm around him.

"Four hundred dollars, please." A girl's voice sounded from inside the room next to Rachel. She glanced at the name on the door. *Eleanor Sanders.*

"Four hundred dollars?" It was Beverly.

"Yep! What did I say? The person that owns Boardwalk always wins the game."

Rachel didn't want to, but she moved towards the room. She looked back at Marc. He hadn't moved; the second doctor still had her arm around him.

Before she knew it, Rachel had walked inside Ellie's room. She was frightened by what she saw in the corridor—and it was serious, that much she knew—yet everything seemed so gleeful inside. Ellie and Beverly looked like this was just another part of their lives, like it had always been a part of their lives.

Rachel fixed her gaze on sweet Ellie. Her short hair, pale skin, her beautiful blue eyes—there was something about those eyes. She'd seen something in them before, when they first met. She had decided Ellie reminded her of herself. But looking at them now, she realized that wasn't the case at all. They reminded her of John!

Beverly looked up at her, and apparently saw the grave look on Rachel's face, and gasped. At her aunt's sudden movement, Ellie looked up and saw Rachel too. Instinctively, Rachel smiled.

"Rachel!" Ellie said, smiling from ear to ear.

Rachel raced up to her, trying desperately to keep the smile on her face, to act normal like Ellie and Beverly had. Rachel gave her a hug, tight and long, but not too long. She pulled back and looked into Ellie's eyes. Those eyes. Those same eyes! It was everything she could do to avoid sobbing. She wanted so bad to scoop Ellie back up in her arms and hold her, to tell her everything was going to be okay.

"We tried to find you yesterday," Ellie said, "but daddy said you left."

"I had some things to take care of," Rachel said. "I should have told you. I'm sorry."

"It's okay," Ellie said, rolling the dice again.

But it wasn't okay. At the moment, Rachel didn't know what to ask, what to say, what to expect. How much had Beverly known? How about Ellie? Did neither of them know what was going on?

Rachel watched Beverly and Ellie play Monopoly. It looked like Ellie was winning, but after a few turns, Rachel could tell that Beverly wasn't playing very hard. She was letting Ellie win.

"Rachel?"

Marc's voice startled her. She whirled around and saw him, his eyes looked red and defeated. A million thoughts went through her mind. She had wanted to find him at Hunting Island, throw her arms around him and say how sorry she was about the other night, to tell him how special their time had been together, and how foolish she'd been. They could make it work. She was sure of it. But now, none of that mattered. Rachel suddenly felt out of place, like watching an intimacy that wasn't meant for her. She realized how little she'd been a part of their lives.

"I should go," Rachel said. She stood up, but before she could take a step, Marc spoke.

"Actually," he made a quick move towards her, but stopped short. "Do you mind staying for a little while?"

Rachel saw the desperation and fear in Marc's eyes. She felt so selfish and small. What right did she have to be here? She hadn't *earned* the right to be here. But he was begging her and she couldn't refuse him.

"Hey Bev," Marc said. "Can I see you for a second?"

Beverly's voice crumbled when she tried to respond. She nodded instead. A little unsteady on her feet, she stood up and cleared her throat. "Rachel, honey, will you go ahead and play for me?"

After the two of them walked out, Rachel looked at Ellie, watching her study the board.

"What happened, Ellie?" Rachel asked.

Ellie glanced up at her for just a second, like she'd been caught doing something bad, like stealing, or worse…lying. She took the dice and shook them in her cupped hands. "It's cancer," she said. The words rolled off her tongue just as easily as she rolled the dice. Snake eyes. "I've probably relapsed again. I can tell because everyone's being so nice to me." Rachel's throat tightened as Ellie tapped the little silver dog twice on the board, landing on Community Chest.

Go directly to jail. Do not pass go. Do not collect $200.

Drying her eyes, Rachel grabbed the dice and rolled a seven. She picked up Beverly's silver top hat and moved it without tapping the board, landing on Chance. She drew a get out of jail free card from the top of the pile.

"I'm sorry Ellie," Rachel finally managed to say through the lump in her throat.

"It's okay. I'm not scared." Ellie paid her $50 to get out of jail and rolled the dice again. Eleven. She tapped the little silver dog again on the board. She just missed Free Parking. "I'm sorry I didn't tell you sooner, but daddy didn't want you to be upset." She stopped, and looked up at Rachel. "You know…because of what happened to your husband."

Beverly and Marc came back in, and Beverly's eyes looked bloodshot. She tried her best to appear normal, but was doing a terrible job of it. Marc looked at the game board for a moment, acting like he was interested, then turned to Rachel. "Hey, you want to get something to eat?"

Marc and Rachel walked out of the room and down the corridor, and Marc didn't say a word. He looked at the floor in front of him, as if reminding himself to put one foot in front of the other.

Rachel put her hand on his forearm. "Marc?"

"Let's go outside first, okay?"

They reached a small gazebo out behind the smoking area of the hospital. They sat down on a bench, and for the longest time, Marc stared out across a pond, where a couple of ducklings were swimming, following their mother. The warm breeze came in through the gazebo and pressed his shirt against his chest, just as it had the first time Rachel saw him. She remembered that day on the beach. He looked so confident and peaceful. Now he looked cut down and crushed.

Marc tried to speak a couple of times, but stopped short of making a sound. He leaned forward and placed his elbows on his knees, looking down at the aging wood beneath his feet.

"Ellie told me she had cancer," Rachel said, no longer able to handle the silence.

Marc nodded, then closed his eyes and dropped his head into his hands. He began to cry. Rachel put her arms around him, and he slumped down into her body, and for a moment, they both sobbed, holding each other.

Marc sat up and looked out over the pond again. The ducklings had reached the edge, and their mother squeezed in between her babies and the grass, protecting them.

"Ellie was five when she was first diagnosed. She had beaten it three times since then. She's been cancer free for the last year. I thought we got it all." He looked down to the floor—a floor that had a hole Rachel knew was opening up for her. "When you told me she had started her period, I really thought we had won, you know? She was going to grow up and be a normal, healthy, beautiful woman."

Rachel placed her hand over her chest, desperately searching for her heart. She wanted Marc to stop, but knew he wouldn't, and she had to listen.

"But the other night after you left, when I got back to the camper, Ellie was lying on the couch, holding her stomach. She played it off as nothing, but then she let out a couple of short cries, and pulled her knees up to her chest. She tried telling me it was only cramps. She argued with me the whole way to the hospital."

Marc stood, and walked to the other side of the gazebo. He looked out over the parking lot reserved for doctors. "She's relapsed for the fourth time," he said. His voice changed, sounding impersonal and clinical. "Cancer is usually more aggressive when it comes back. But for children, even more so. It's in her stomach and spine. But mostly..." He stopped and covered his mouth, doubling over slightly. He grabbed the rail of the gazebo, and steadied himself. "But mostly it's attacked her cervix." Marc turned, looking at Rachel. "She never started her period."

Rachel's body trembled. She tried wiping her tears, but they kept coming, dripping into the widening hole beneath her. She couldn't listen to his next words, and she needed to tell him that, but her throat clamped down, and all she could do was weep.

Marc staggered over to her and dropped down on his knees, taking Rachel's hands into his. "They don't think she's going to make it this time," he said, crying.

Rachel shook her head, slowly at first, but then more quickly. "She'll make it. She has to." Rachel withdrew her hands from his grasp, and stood up. She walked to the other end of the gazebo, and paced back and forth. "What about chemo?" she said. "Radiation? Alternative treatments? There has to be something!"

Marc shook his head, and Rachel huffed. She gripped the rail of the gazebo and looked out over the parking lot of Jaguars, Mercedes, and Audis. What the hell were they getting paid for?

"There has to be something they can do. Tell me, Marc!" Rachel looked at him, waiting for him to speak, to move—anything. But he remained motionless, his head still in his hands.

"Right now, Marc. Tell me!" She ran over to him and grabbed his arms and shook him. "Now goddammit! Tell me now! Please tell me!"

When he didn't respond, she backed away, staring at him in disbelief.

How could he not know the answer? Ellie was his daughter. That was his job, to protect her, and to keep her safe. He'd even said so himself. He held her as a baby when she couldn't go to sleep. That's what he said. Ellie was as safe as she could ever be, right there in his arms, dancing.

Rachel had danced too—with John. She knew what it felt like to love with every fiber of her heart, to feel happiness only when he was happy, to feel whole only when he was beside her. Rachel knew what it felt like to see her loved one in pain, to want more than anything to take it from him—to transfer it into her own body and let his pain become hers.

She knew!

The full truthfulness of what Marc said began to sink in. Ellie was just eleven. Rachel had only known her for a week, but already, she had made Rachel feel hopeful again, to feel needed. She was the star that brightened up Rachel's life. Now, she was vested.

"Why didn't you tell me?" Rachel said, quietly at first. Then she got angry. "Why didn't you tell me?!"

Marc—he just stood there, unmoving, appearing cowardly. She wanted to hit him, force him to man up and tell her why. Why didn't he tell her? He knew! He knew what Rachel had gone through, and now, he was forcing her hand, forcing her to relive it again. It was his fault. All of it!

"Marc!" she yelled at him.

Marc looked up. He studied her face and sulked. "I was going to," he said. "After I found out what happened to John, I don't know...I just couldn't. And at the time, I thought it was behind us."

Rachel shook her head, stepping away from him again. "All that talk about telling the truth. It was just bullshit, wasn't it?"

"Of course not. I didn't want to hurt you. That's all. Rachel, please understand. Don't do this now."

"I can't do this again, Marc. I just can't."

Rachel stepped around him, crying as she walked away.

Rachel slammed the door to the Jeep, and cranked it. The six-cylinder engine whirred to life, then puttered out when she shut it back off. She pounded on the steering wheel twice, and shock waves bolted through her shoulders and jarred her neck.

She cranked it again. Shut it off again. She sucked the sun-baked air into her lungs and screamed as loud as she could. She placed her head on the steering wheel, sobbing, trying to make sense of what just happened.

Why did it happen again?

Again!

Was this the sign she was supposed to be looking for, or was this some sort of punishment from God? What did she have to do? Was it not enough to watch the love of her life—her only love—dwindle away from a healthy, loving and passionate man, to nothing but ash? And now, this God was forcing her to watch it happen all over again. She didn't deserve that. Ellie sure as hell didn't deserve it. All things happen for a reason, huh?

Tell me goddammit! Tell me what the fuck those reasons are!

How could the world be a better place without Ellie in it? Who's going to swoop down from the sky and help that little old lady cross the street? Who's going to save those turtle eggs and fly around giving food and medicine to those who need it?

Tell me, who?

And Marc. He'd already lost his wife, and now his only child too? How was that fair? What had he done? He'd never been anything but nice to Rachel.

That turned her stomach. It wasn't fair what she'd said to him— those vile, malevolent things. How could she have reacted that way? She knew she didn't mean them now, but she *had* said them. Perhaps God was testing her. Maybe John was. Either way, she knew she had failed.

The heat from inside the car stung her lungs and a wave of nausea sickened her. She flung open the door and the tepid, salt air washed through her hair, mildly cooling her face and neck. She slumped against the side of the Jeep, staring up at the hospital in front of her.

In there, they were hurting, Marc, more than he needed to, and it was because of her. She couldn't leave things like this. That much she knew. It wasn't fair to have treated Marc that way. He deserved better, he deserved better than her, and he certainly deserved an apology.

The elevator doors opened, and the clinical scent of the hospital corridor surrounded her again, almost making her gag. She looked at the floor, concentrating on putting one foot down in front of the other as Marc had done.

She passed by the rooms she'd walked so slowly past before, but this time she didn't look inside. She couldn't bear to see them. A nurse asked if she could help her. She ignored her. A feeble old man walked towards her, taking half-inch steps, holding on to his portable IV stand for dear life. He looked at her with dead, hopeless eyes.

Down the corridor, she saw Ellie's door, and it was closed. Rachel started to cry as she neared it, softly at first, but then with each step towards Ellie's room, a little louder. She placed her hand on the doorknob, but stopped, then reached up to dry her tears away. She realized there weren't any. She wasn't crying at all. Ellie was.

Rachel backed away from the door, searching for the wall, the floor, a bench—anything to keep her from falling. Her body trembled at the sound of Ellie's crying, and Rachel fell through the black hole beneath her, rushing after her heart she was sure she'd never find again.

CHAPTER TWELVE

RACHEL'S MIND WAS VOID. She slept until nine-thirty, and really, she only woke up because Riley nosed her foot. Haphazardly, she threw on a pair of shorts and a shirt. She knew there'd be no running this morning, and honestly, if it were completely up to her, she'd just stay in the camper. But of course, Riley needed to be walked.

While Riley did his business, Rachel held on to the leash, sitting on the picnic table bench outside of the Fleetwood, staring at the ground. She disallowed any thoughts whatsoever to enter her mind. She didn't want to think, she didn't want to hear, or see, and for the love of God, she didn't want to feel anything. The longer her mind remained devoid of thought, the longer she could delay the pain of answering what had happened.

It didn't even register to her that Charles had called out to her a couple of times until he touched her on the shoulder.

"Are you okay?" Charles said.

She glanced up at him, then looked back to the ground, back to the nullity of her mind, back to her safe zone where the world couldn't reach her.

Charles dropped his head and sighed. He took a seat next to her, and Riley plopped down next to his feet. He reached down and gave him a good pet, and for a moment, he sat there, stroking Riley's back.

"I had a lab once when I was kid," he said, "but I don't think he was as well-mannered as Riley though." A little smirk formed on his face, apparently recalling an old childhood memory. "Actually I'm quite certain he wasn't. He wasn't yellow either. He was brown. You've heard of the Buster Brown comic strip, right?"

A few seconds went by before the string of words actually entered Rachel's mind. She knew Charles was just trying to make her feel better. "I think so," she said, glancing at him for a second, trying to appear interested.

"Buster Brown was a mischievous little kid," Charles continued. "Always up to something, playing some practical joke or causing trouble. Usually there was a moral at the end of the story or whatever. But that's not why you read the comic.

"Anyway, when I was eight, my dad came home with this brown puppy that we eventually named Buster, because he was just like Buster Brown. Always into trouble, tearing up everything in sight, crapping all over the house, running over freshly mopped floors…the whole bit. And I mean there wasn't nothing he couldn't eat. Shoes, pillows, laundry…his own dog house. He drove mom crazy.

"By the time I was eight, I was already a handful, but the two of us together? I'm surprised mom survived as long as she did considering what we put her through. If there ever was a matched pair between man and beast, it was the two of us. Our personalities were just alike, and we were practically inseparable. School was about the only time we weren't together."

Charles looked over at Rachel, her eyes still fixated on the ground. He became excited as he continued, shifting slightly to give Riley another pet.

"You know, I can see him in my mind as clear as I can see Riley right now. So many good memories. Fishing, hunting, exploring. He was always there. My dad worked a cattle ranch right next to where we lived, and there wasn't a single square inch of that place me and Buster didn't cover. I know I don't show it now, but when I was a youngster, I was hell on wheels. Even so, that dog of mine wore me slap out. He was non-stop, all the time." Charles shook his head, sporting a smile so big, it would put a child's to shame. "He was the best friend I ever had."

Charles sat back against the picnic table, looking out over the pines, the same direction as Rachel. The smile slowly faded from his face, and sadness filled his eyes.

Rachel knew how the story ended, and Charles didn't finish telling it. He sat there and continued to pet Riley, who was almost comatose from it.

"It's never easy," he finally said. "God knows I don't know what I'd do if something ever happened to Bev, and it sure isn't fair what's happening to poor Ellie and Marc. But I do know this— Buster taught me everything I ever needed to know about love. It would've been a shame if I never put it to good use again."

Charles reached down and patted Riley three times on the belly, signaling an end to his petting. "Well," Charles said, slapping his hands down on his knees before he stood up. "If there's anything I can do, just let me know." He paused for a moment, waiting on some acknowledgement from Rachel, and then turned to leave.

"Charles?" Rachel said.

He stopped and turned around. "Yeah?"

"Thanks."

Charles nodded, and walked away.

Later that afternoon, Rachel drove to the hospital to visit Ellie. As she entered Ellie's room, she saw Marc sound asleep in a chair in the corner, his head propped up against his fist, and his jaw hanging down.

Ellie sat with her legs crossed, watching *The Price is Right*, the one hosted by Drew Carey.

"I just don't think it's the same without Bob Barker," Rachel said, trying not to wake Marc.

"Rachel!"

Ellie got up on her knees as close to the edge of the bed as she could without falling over, and they hugged. The IV in Ellie's arm tugged at the two drip bags on the far side of the bed, one clear the other red, but Ellie didn't seem to care. Then suddenly, Ellie pulled away from Rachel.

"What is it Ellie?" Rachel said.

"Who's Bob Barker?"

Rachel sighed, and pulled Ellie back into her body again, and she rubbed her back.

"Bob Barker," Marc said, "wants you to help control the pet population. Have your pets spayed or neutered," quoting the former hosts closing remarks. He stood up and stretched his back. "I'll give you two some girl time. Rachel, if you're going to be here for a bit, would you mind if I head to the house to grab a few things?"

"Dad?" Ellie jumped in before Rachel could answer. "I don't need a babysitter."

"Forgive me sweetheart, I know you don't. So, Rachel...I guess leave whenever you want to, then." The way he spoke to Rachel came off rather snide. Marc gave his daughter a kiss on the forehead, and smiled at her. He sidestepped Rachel without looking at her and then he walked out of the room.

"Oh no, what's going on with you and dad?" Ellie said.

"What do you mean?"

"What do you mean '*what do you mean*'? I know I'm only eleven, almost twelve you know, but I can tell. Did you and dad have a fight or something?" She gasped. "Is it because of me?"

"No, sweetie of course not."

"Then what is it?"

"It's just grownup stuff Ellie."

Ellie shook her head. "You're just gonna have to work it out then. I haven't seen him this happy since my mom died. Besides, I know the both of you are perfect for each other. He needs you, and you need him, right?"

"Ellie, things don't always work out." As soon as the words came out of Rachel's mouth she regretted them, especially considering Ellie's condition.

"No. Whatever it is that's going on, you need to fix it. I'm not going to be here for him for long."

"Ellie, please don't say that."

"Why not? It's true."

Rachel dropped her head, and then took Ellie's hands into hers. "Ellie, you don't know that."

"It is true. I know it. I've known it my whole life."

"You have to try, sweetie. You can't give up."

"I know. I'll try. I have to for daddy. He worries about me all the time. I'm tired of seeing him worry. I just want him to be happy. The sooner it happens, the better."

"Ellie, please don't." Rachel grabbed her and pulled her little body into hers. "Please don't say that."

Ellie wrapped her arms around Rachel and hugged her. Rachel felt Ellie's warm body against hers, their hearts together, causing tears to run down Rachel's face. She felt Ellie beginning to cry too, and Rachel hugged her tighter.

"That's why I'm so glad I found you," Ellie said. "I know you can make him happy. I just know it."

Ellie pushed Rachel back, and with those wet blue eyes, she locked onto Rachel's and said, "Promise me. Please promise me that you'll try."

Knowing she couldn't speak, all Rachel could do was nod. She pulled sweet Ellie back into her arms once again, wondering if she would have the strength to keep such a promise.

When Rachel left, she walked towards the nurse's station, so she could ask them to check in on Ellie while Marc was gone. But Marc was sitting in the waiting room when she got there. He stood up, as if expecting her.

"I thought you went to pick up some things." Rachel said.

"I haven't left yet. I wanted to talk to you first. Can we get a cup of coffee?"

They walked to the cafeteria and Marc kept his distance from her. Not just physically, but something else too, like he was someone Rachel didn't know as well as she thought she did.

The cafeteria wasn't very crowded, but for some reason, Marc chose a table in the back of the dining area. They sat in silence for a moment while Rachel fixed her coffee.

"Marc, I need to apologize for yesterday. I had no right to—"

"I'm taking Ellie home tomorrow," Marc said, his eyes fixated on his black coffee. He hadn't touched it.

"That's great, Marc. I know she'll be a lot more comfortable at home."

Marc nodded, and leaned back in his chair. He still hadn't looked up at Rachel. "There's something else I need to tell you too."

Rachel felt a flash of heat surface on her skin. She set her cup down.

"I know what happened last week between us was special," he said. "And under any other circumstance, I think we had a real shot at something. I mean that. But, I think it was fragile to begin with. We've both been through a lot, and if it was going to work, it needed a lot of time. Time, isn't something I can spare right now. It's not fair to me and it's not fair to you…and it's not fair to Ellie. Do you understand?"

Rachel nodded. She tried to reach for his hand, but he pulled back.

"I know this might sound selfish, but I want to spend all of my time with Ellie…every second, of every minute, of every day that she has left." Marc stood up from the table, and for the first time since they walked into the cafeteria, he looked her. "I can't do that if I'm trying to love you too. Goodbye Rachel."

Rachel sat at the cafeteria table for a while after Marc left, staring at his coffee cup. Then, for no discernible reason, she stood up and walked out. She walked through the emergency room lobby, paying no attention to the apparent motorcycle accident victim being wheeled in. The receptionist at the entrance of the hospital told her goodbye, and Rachel walked right past her, unaware the she had said anything at all.

The inside of the Jeep steamed with coastal humidity, but she didn't turn on the air. She pulled out of the parking lot, and drove, looking straight ahead, barely aware of the traffic. A traffic light signaled red. She stopped. Then it turned green. She went. A stop sign approached. She stopped.

She didn't care. She couldn't care.

Autopilot.

Finally a subconscious thought penetrated her listless mind. One from another time and from another hospital.

One from Atlanta.

Rachel held John's hand, his skin so thin and pale, an almost indescribable color. Lifeless. His dying body lay on the bed, and his head propped up ever so slightly on a pillow, facing away from her. His breathing so shallow, she could barely hear it.

The time for hope had long past. The time for goodbyes, gone. Only the intimacy of death remained.

In her mind, she was driving along a road, crossing one of the many waterway bridges near Beaufort, and at the same time, in that hospital room in Atlanta. The vision of white gulls flying over the bridge blended with John's dark and bruised feet. The aroma of the salt and sea mixed with the sickly scent of the hospital room. The sound of the heart monitor pulsed with the thud of her tires as they ran over sections of road.

The heat from the steering wheel. The coldness in John's hand.

The bridge railing. John's final breath.

The water below.

Rachel closed her eyes, and tightened her grip on the steering wheel as the heart monitor flatlined. "I'm sorry, John," she cried.

It was time to join her husband.

But then something happened. She heard a rumble under her tires. The same rumble that she heard when she and Marc had gone to the baseball game. The same one she heard on the way to Mallory's Hardware, and when she went into town with Cynthia.

She opened her eyes and realized she was on the drawbridge, on the road to Hunting Island. Suddenly, her lungs stung from the heat inside the Jeep. Drips of sweat ran down the side of her face. Random thoughts of Marc startled her. Then thoughts of Ellie, her sweet Ellie, flooded into her mind: the girl that wanted to save the sea turtles, the girl that wanted to kiss a boy, the girl that lived life to its fullest and elevated the spirit of everyone around her.

Ellie deserved to live, so much more than Rachel. It seemed so selfish that Rachel almost ended it all so easily, when Ellie didn't have any choice but death.

Life! That's what Rachel owed to Ellie. Ellie deserved to live forever.

Immortal.

Rachel pressed the Jeep's gas pedal to the floor, upset she didn't think of it sooner.

CHAPTER THIRTEEN

RACHEL WILLERS SECLUDED HERSELF in the Fleetwood for several weeks. The only time she came out was to walk Riley or to take a quick walk to the camp store to pick up some more frozen dinners. She stopped having nightmares, and she'd given up running altogether. The only time she'd been to the beach at all was a single instance when she really just needed to clear her mind, to allow herself to continue her work on the computer.

Every couple of days, Beverly would stop by to check on her, and they'd chat for a while. She'd tell Rachel what she knew about Ellie's worsening condition. Rachel learned that her hair had completely fallen out from the first two doses of chemo, and that they'd given up chemotherapy altogether after eight treatments. The cancer was just too strong, and Ellie's little body could no longer handle the medicine. They decided to focus on quality of life for the little time she had left.

When the Fourth of July came, Rachel heard a knock on her door. Figuring it was Beverly with an update, she yelled out from the dinette. "Come in!"

Rachel heard the door creak open and someone walk in, but her mind was still working away on the computer in front of her. A few seconds went by before she looked up.

"Marc!" she said, standing up immediately. She put her hands over her mouth, expecting the worst.

"No, no…it's okay," Marc said.

Rachel sat down and took in a couple of deep breaths, staring at Marc. His eyes looked tired and red. The expression on his face looked like a man that had been to war. He didn't even stand up straight.

"How is she?" Rachel said.

Marc walked to the dinette, pausing for a second, looking at the table before taking a seat. "Tired," he said. "She sleeps a lot. The last few days, she hasn't felt that good either. I think the medicine is a mixed blessing. It does mask the pain, but it nauseates her at the same time. She's at Beverly's right now. "

"She's here?"

"Yeah. I told her that we could stay home to watch the fireworks from the back porch. There's a park about a mile away that has a pretty good show. We used to watch all the time from there when Carrie was alive." Marc's smile weakened just a bit, but perked back up quickly. "But Ellie said she wanted to be with you."

"I would've been glad to come to your house, Marc."

"I know. That's what I told her, but then she said she wanted to be on the beach with Aunt Beverly and Uncle Charles, too. Honestly, I think she wanted me to see you again."

Those words tore at Rachel's heart. She thought about the promise she made to Ellie, and considering what Marc had said the last time she saw him, she probably couldn't keep it. One of Marc's hands rested on the table, and Rachel almost reached out for it, but stopped short of making her muscles move. "How are you, Marc?" she said, instead.

Marc swallowed hard and looked out the window. The sun was just starting to sink. "Okay, I guess. I have good days and bad days." For a second or two he didn't say anything. He looked back down at the table. "You know, we always knew this could happen. She went into remission three times before, and that makes you think…you know, that eventually… Well, nothing can prepare you for it." Then he looked up at Rachel. "I know you know that."

"I miss you, Marc." She didn't think about saying it, it just came out.

Marc didn't react to her comment. "You want to go see Ellie? I know she wants to see you."

When Rachel walked inside the Winnebago, she saw Ellie sitting on the couch next to Beverly. She was covered in an old avocado colored blanket, no doubt one of Beverly's relics. Ellie's hair and eyebrows were completely gone. Her complexion, once so white and pure, had turned a pale brownish-yellow. It was a color Rachel was familiar with, but she just wasn't ready to see it on an eleven-year-old girl. It was obvious Ellie didn't have a lot of time left.

"Rachel!" Ellie said. Her voice sounded thin and weak. She pulled her hands out from underneath the blanket and held them out towards Rachel.

Rachel started crying before she even reached her. She knelt down and took Ellie's frail body into her arms and gently hugged her. She could hardly feel Ellie squeezing back.

"I've missed you!" Ellie said.

"I've missed you too, sweetheart. How are you feeling?"

"Pretty good." Ellie glanced up to her for a second, frowning. Then her smile came back and she said, "I'm a lot better now that I'm here with you. Can I see Riley too?"

"Sure, anything you want."

Marc took a couple of steps towards them. "We'll try to see Riley on the way to the beach, okay honey?" He turned towards Rachel. "Is that okay?"

Rachel nodded.

Ellie's eyes, still so blue—about the only thing that looked natural on her body—looked up at Rachel. "I have a surprise for you," Ellie said, "but I don't have it with me. I'll have to give it to you…later, okay?"

Rachel swallowed hard, trying to keep her composure. "Sure," she said, wiping her eyes. "I have a surprise for you too."

"You do?!"

Rachel nodded, somehow able to keep from crying again. "But it's not ready, yet." Ellie's face turned to disappointment, and she dropped her head. "It almost is," Rachel said quickly, but Ellie didn't respond. "Ellie?" Rachel waited until Ellie looked up at her before continuing. "Promise me…promise me you'll wait until I can show it to you, okay?"

Ellie nodded and smiled.

When the sun started to go down, Marc and Rachel helped Ellie to the Fleetwood to go visit Riley, with Beverly and Charles walking close behind them. "Riley is such a good dog," Ellie said, as they approached the camper. "I miss him a lot."

Riley must've missed her too, because right after Ellie said that, he started barking inside the Fleetwood. Marc helped Ellie sit down in a camp chair next to the picnic table, and when Rachel opened the door to the camper, Riley ran out almost as fast as she'd ever seen him run.

"Riley!" Ellie called out as best as she could. Riley turned and found her, then ran and sat down right in front of her. He placed his big yellow noggin in the middle of her lap. Ellie placed her cheek on top of his head. She rubbed him. "I'm gonna miss you, boy,"

Rachel crossed her arms, and then pulled her hand up to her mouth to prevent herself from crying out loud. She looked around, and everyone else had done the same, especially Charles, who had gigantic tears streaming down his face.

As the sun set, they all walked to the beach. It took quite a while to walk from the Fleetwood to the beach because Ellie had to take such small steps and had refused to let her father carry her. She leaned on both Marc and Rachel as they walked. Earlier, Charles had put blankets down on the sand so that everyone could sit or lie down and watch the fireworks.

As they went to sit down, Ellie moved over to Rachel's other side, putting Marc and Rachel next to each other. Marc looked over at his daughter with a curious eye. "You don't want to sit next to your old man?"

"What?" Ellie said, sort of bashfully. "I just want to sit next to Aunt Beverly, that's all." She tried to hide a grin but couldn't.

Ellie and Rachel lay on the blanket as the fireworks started. Rachel turned and stared at Ellie, finding it impossible to look away. Ellie watched the fireworks so intently, and Rachel was taken aback by the thought that Ellie would never see this again. As the huge bursting blossoms of red, green, blue and yellow exploded in the sky above them, she felt Ellie reach for her hand. Rachel looked up and watched the fireworks with her, and suddenly, everything seemed right in the world...if only for a few moments.

A week later, Rachel ran over to Beverly's camper. It was late, but she knew there might not be much time left. It couldn't wait until morning. She rapped on her door several times.

"Beverly! It's Rachel! Open up!"

The lights from inside the camper turned on, and Charles opened the door. "Rachel?" he said, looking down at his watch. "Is everything okay?"

"Yes, everything's fine," she said. "Can you wake Beverly up? I need to speak to her."

"She's not here. She's at Marc's house." Charles frowned, and he hung his head down. "It might happen tonight."

Rachel ignored the grim look on his face. "Do you have a printer?" she said.

"Well, no," Charles replied. "I mean yes...we have one in the office, but it's late and..."

"No, we can't wait. I need it now. You remember the surprise I had for Ellie?"

"Surprise? I didn't think you really had her a surprise, I thought you were trying to keep her spirits up."

"No, I have one! It's done. It's finally done." Rachel raised the memory card up in the air. "Now...I just need you to print it!"

Charles had given Rachel some quick directions to Marc's house, and she'd found it with relative ease. She shut off the poor Jeep's engine, which had whirred quite heavily to get there.

She walked up to the front door and quickly knocked. She started to knock again, but Beverly opened the door.

"Rachel?" She looked down at her watch? "Darlin', it's almost midnight. Is everything okay?"

"It's finished!" Rachel said.

"What's finished?"

Rachel lifted the manuscript in the air, displaying the title for Beverly to see. Immediately, Beverly started to weep. She let Rachel in and pointed towards Ellie's bedroom.

Rachel quietly closed the bedroom door behind her, and from where she stood, she couldn't see Ellie's bed. The curtains were drawn, and the only source of light came from a small, smiley face lamp that sat on her nightstand.

As she walked in, she saw Marc sitting in a chair next to his daughter. He was cupping Ellie's hand with both of his, rubbing his thumb in a circular motion over the top. Rachel stopped, and tears formed in her eyes as she placed her fingers on her lips. For a moment, she stood there, trying to convince herself this was all just a bad dream.

Ellie was lying on the bed, her head propped up on a pillow. Her eyes were closed and her mouth hung slightly opened. Her lips were chapped and cracked. She looked a hundred years old.

Marc turned his head around, and Rachel saw his crippled eyes. He got up and held her, and softly began to cry in her arms. After a moment, he pulled away and walked out of the room, leaving her alone with Ellie.

Rachel sat down next to the bed. Ellie's thin body lay motionless, and the only sounds Rachel heard were the pulsing heart monitor and Ellie's labored and steady breathing. Rachel couldn't help but realize the similarities between the way Ellie looked and John's last days: her eye sockets, sunken and dark; her nose, thin and much too large for her face; her skin, dark and bruised in places.

She placed Ellie's hand in hers and massaged her loose and thin skin. After a few moments, as if by magic, Ellie slowly opened up her eyes.

In a barely audible voice, Ellie spoke. "Hey."

"Hey sweetheart," Rachel said, trying not to look sad.

Ellie looked so tired, her eyes opened for a moment then closed for another. Her breathing labored on with a gurgling sound. After a few moments, Ellie seemed to come back around, and then she swallowed a few times, trying to say something. "My surprise?" she finally managed to utter.

Rachel lifted the manuscript, her arm shaking like she was holding the weight of the world in her hand. Ellie opened one of her eyes and looked at Rachel, smiling as best as she could. "I wrote it for you," Rachel said. Ellie moved her head slightly, and Rachel could barely tell she was nodding. Then a tear streamed from Ellie's eye as it closed, dripping onto the bed.

Rachel cleared her throat, and with everything she could muster, she softly began to read *The Unchained Melody of a Flying Girl.*

As Rachel read, Ellie fell in and out of sleep. When the first chapter ended, Rachel looked at Ellie and started crying. "It's okay," she heard Ellie say. Rachel looked up, but Ellie's eyes were still closed. And then, in what was almost an inaudible voice, Ellie spoke to her one final time. "Don't ever stop reading."

When Rachel finished the second chapter, Ellie had fallen completely asleep. Rachel gently put the pages of the manuscript back in order, and placed it on the nightstand beside her bed.

Rachel stood up from her chair and walked over to Ellie's window. She pulled back the curtains, and gazed outside. It was such a beautiful night. The nearly full moon spilled in and onto Ellie's face. Rachel walked over to the bed, and stood, watching the barely discernible rise and fall of her chest. Rachel knelt over Ellie's fading body and kissed her softly on the cheek.

"Goodbye my sweet angel."

When Rachel walked to the den, Marc was sitting in a chair, wide awake, and staring at the wall. As she passed him by, she placed her hand on his shoulder, unsure if this would be the last time she'd ever see him again. He didn't respond. She took a few steps towards the front door.

"Rachel?" Marc said, as she reached the door, "Do you want to stay?"

When John had died, Rachel was right there beside him as he took his last breath. Through it all, from the heartbreak of finding out he had cancer, to watching him wither away to literally nothing— looking back now, she actually cherished that final moment, in that it was the last thing they would ever share together. With that in her mind, knowing what it had meant to her, and knowing what it will mean to Marc, she declined. Rachel opened the door and walked out.

In the early morning hours, and with her father by her side holding her hand, the wish that she had told Rachel about that day on the beach, came true: Ellie Sanders, having never kissed a boy, got her wings.

CHAPTER FOURTEEN

A NEW DAWN EMERGED. "Okay legs," Rachel said, stretching on the beach next to Riley. "Let's do this." The sun, still just below the horizon, painted its glowing red light upon the eastern sky. She looked up and down the shore, considering each direction. Choosing south, she took her first steps, the first in several weeks, and began her jog.

Immediately, her legs took issue with the exercise. Even though she'd lost a few pounds, she felt heavy and lethargic as she ran. Soon, she started to pant, same as Riley. It'd been a long time for him, too.

But after a few minutes, she hit her stride and her body responded well, almost as if she hadn't missed a single day. She knew she'd pay for it later, and probably feel sore as hell in the morning, but for now it felt good to expand and contract her chest, to feel the warm morning air brush against her cheeks, and to feel in control. Besides, today would be the last time she'd see this beach, maybe forever.

The last couple of days, she researched several campsites near the Gulf of Mexico. The camping season was still in full swing, so it was difficult to find a site, but luckily, due to a last minute cancellation, a spot opened up at a campground on Port Saint Joe Peninsula in Florida. She'd only be able to stay for a couple of weeks, and have to find another campground pretty soon, but at least it was someplace not here. Best of all, it was somewhere she and John had never camped before. First thing tomorrow morning, she was pulling out. She already had a couple of ideas for another book and looked forward to a fresh start.

Still, it was going to be hard saying goodbye to Hunting Island. It was the first place she and John started camping, and really, it changed the direction of their lives forever. She missed John in so many ways, and absolutely knew she would never get over losing him.

But Marc had proved to Rachel that it was possible to move on. She wasn't sure if it was love, but she had to admit there were moments when she felt truly happy being with him. She wondered, and even hoped, that he felt the same way. She was hopeful that the small part she'd played in his life would enable Marc to find love again, even if it might be years down the road. Not that he would ever recover, but it might take that long to come to terms with the loss of Ellie.

Rachel's heart ached thinking of Ellie. From that first moment she saw those inspiring blue eyes, she knew there was something very special about that young girl. Ellie saw beauty in things that others would never see—could never see—or even understand, and at such a young age, too. Perhaps it was the loss of her mother, or always living a life of cancer, knowing that every experience in life should be cherished, because she knew there would be so few opportunities to experience them. But Rachel liked to believe Ellie was born that way, innately seeing the beauty of the world—cancer or not.

And that was the one thing Rachel couldn't reconcile. Why Ellie? Why take someone as good-natured, with such an infectious spirit, with so much to offer the world? It just didn't make any sense. Rachel always heard there was a reason for everything, and yes, she was certainly inspired by Ellie to write the book, but that seems like such a poor reason.

Rachel passed the lighthouse, and the sun now hovered over the horizon, its early morning heat indicated a blistering July day. Rachel could feel her legs and lungs starting to rebel, so she decided it would be a short run. Besides, that way she could take her time getting everything packed, and she wanted a chance to say goodbye to Beverly and Charles.

As she turned around to go back, the lighthouse came into her view once more. Something deep in her soul ached as she looked at it. What was it about that stupid lighthouse, anyway? She wasn't going to miss it one bit. It had been a while since the dreams, but she knew the lighthouse had somehow haunted her ever since she arrived.

She looked away from it and decided there was no point in worrying about it now. Today was her last day on the island and the last thing she wanted to do was to spend it trying to figure out the significance of a few tons of old metal from the Civil War.

After a shower, Rachel fixed herself a cup of coffee, and decided to spend a couple of hours under the awning reading. She knew she had to pack, but really, there wasn't a whole lot to do. Most everything was already inside the camper, and the few items that remained outside would only take about thirty minutes to put away. Later, she'd go find Beverly and Charles and tell them goodbye.

But Rachel didn't have to go find Beverly, because about an hour into her reading, she heard a thud coming from behind her.

"Wow, this thing is heavy," Beverly said.

Rachel spun around in her chair. Sitting on top of the picnic table sat a black guitar case. Rachel gasped at the sight of it.

"I thought it was an acoustic guitar?" Beverly said. She walked around the table to a chair next to Rachel and plopped down in it, setting a bag down beside her. "Aren't they supposed to be hollow? Anyway, Marc said for me to give this back to you."

Rachel didn't respond. She sat there, almost in a daze.

"Rachel?" Beverly said. "Are you okay?"

"I'm fine," Rachel replied. "I guess I'm a little nervous about driving tomorrow."

"I don't blame you one bit, honey. I drove our camper only one time." Rachel knew a story was coming, and honestly, she could use one.

"Charles had to drive the truck because he was pulling a new boat he bought, and there was no way in hell I was going to do that, so he talked me into driving the camper. 'It's only the expressway, Bev' he said. 'There's no turns or anything.' And I guess he was right. It wasn't bad. I stayed in my lane and let the world pass me by. But then, we came up on an accident and had to get off the expressway...in Atlanta."

Rachel gasped and covered her mouth, trying not to laugh. She knew exactly what it was like to drive in Atlanta. Being laid out like a wagon wheel instead of city blocks, it could take a while to find a suitable detour.

"Well," Beverly continued, "we took the exit and before I knew it, I was cussin' like a sailor, trying to find a place to turn that big ass camper around, or even find a right turn I could make. There was no way I was going to hit a lamppost or something. So, I just kept going straight until I found a big parking lot. I pulled in and shut her off. Luckily for me, it was right in front of the Hilton. I checked in, and told Charles there was no way in hell I'd ever drive that damn camper again. Poor Charles. He drove all the way back to Beaufort by himself with his precious little boat, then flew back to Atlanta to get me and the camper…after I'd had a manicure and pedicure that is."

Rachel and Beverly laughed. "I sure am gonna miss you two guys," Rachel said.

"Oh, we're just two old goats, honey," Beverly swatted her hand, southern lady like. The diamonds in her tennis bracelet caught some sunlight, reflecting into Rachel's eyes. "Don't waste your time missing us."

"No…I think I will waste my time," Rachel said, smiling.

"I'm going to miss you too, honey. Now Charles, he might not say it, but you'll just have to know he does."

"I know," Rachel said.

"I told him to help you get your car all hooked up tomorrow morning."

"Beverly, he doesn't have to do that."

"Oh, yes he does! Besides, it'll be his way of saying goodbye."

Rachel nodded, then sat back in her chair and wondered if she should ask about Marc. Beverly hadn't mentioned him at all, and since she hadn't gotten up to leave, Rachel knew she had to ask.

"How's Marc?"

"Devastated."

Rachel nodded. Maybe she shouldn't have asked after all. Of course he's devastated.

"But, he's a Sanders," Beverly said. "It's going to take a while, but he'll eventually recover."

The two of them looked out over the ocean in front of them. Such a beautiful day. Hot, but beautiful. A few of the campers had already headed out to the beach.

"He's gone, you know."

"Gone?" Rachel looked surprised. "Where?"

"Well, I don't know, honey. He only said he needed some time. Said he might be gone for a couple of months, but that he'd be in touch."

Rachel understood. It's exactly what she had done after John died. It's just that it took her over two years to finally do it.

"Beverly?"

"Yes, honey."

"When you hear from him again, please tell him I'm sorry…about everything."

"Why don't you tell him that yourself?"

Rachel thought about it for a second. She didn't want to cause him any more pain. In a way, there was a part of her that loved him, even if it was only for their brief time together. But she knew he deserved better: someone more selfless, without baggage, someone that could truly devote herself to him. She was sure there was a wonderful, deserving woman out there for him somewhere.

"Well, honey, time for me to make my rounds." Beverly said, standing up. "Oh, I almost forgot." She reached down, and picked up the bag she brought with her and gave it to Rachel. "Just something for your trip tomorrow."

"Beverly, you shouldn't have."

"Don't get excited. It's nothing fancy. Just some fruit, and snacks and stuff. There's also a few milk bones in there for Riley. I had one last bottle of red wine in the camper so I tossed it in there for you. You know, to celebrate with when you get to wherever you're going."

"Beverly, I don't want to take your last bottle."

"Now honey, you know I'm a gin drinker!"

They both laughed and gave each other a hug, each trying to keep from crying, and they vowed to keep in touch. Beverly said she'd let her know when she and Charles moved on to host at another campground, and told Rachel she'd always be welcome wherever they were at...even if she had to kick some southern ass to do it.

By mid-afternoon, Rachel had everything all packed up and ready to go...everything except for the guitar case that still sat on the picnic table outside. Every time she thought about stowing it, something else more important came up instead. But soon, she found herself checking things she knew she'd already packed up.

"Oh, this is so stupid," she said to Riley, who was lying in the middle of the camper, asleep. By willpower brought on by absurdity, Rachel marched to the door, went outside, picked up the guitar case by the handle, marched back in and placed it on the dinette table.

She looked around the camper, thinking about what was left to do. Secure the food in the refrigerator: check. Put away the three picture frames: check. Make sure all the drawers were pushed in and locked: check. Look in the bag Beverly had given to her: *not check!*

She opened up the bag, and found milk bones for Riley, two apples, a bag of pecans, one grapefruit, a bag of Twizzlers, and half an apple pie. The bottle of wine was angled to the side, and she pulled it out a bit to see the label. Yep. Cabernet Sauvignon. As she went to put the bottle back, something else caught her eye in the bottom of the bag. She took everything out and pulled out a copy of *Time Magazine*, dated several years ago.

Adorning the cover was some politician she didn't recognize, white haired and wearing glasses. He had his index finger placed over his mouth, pressing against his lips. The classic symbol for hush. Typical.

She flipped through the pages, glossing over a few of the articles, when one caught her eye—*The Lost City of the Incas*. Rachel remembered when Marc said Machu Picchu had been one of his favorite assignments. She looked at the breathtaking photos of the ruins that sat high on a mountain ridge overlooking a valley. On the last page of the article was a picture of Marc holding his camera. He looked so young and thin, and his hair was a little longer.

Closing the magazine, she recalled that Marc wanted to take Ellie there one day, maybe even all three of them. Ellie would never get to see that place, nor spend another day with her father. So unfair.

Rachel stared again at the guitar case, and after a minute, she got up and calmly walked to it. As she opened it, the first thing she noticed were that the strings were well worn. And just like the day she had met Ellie for the first time, when she had opened the guitar and realized that John had been the last one to play it, she knew that Ellie had played it last. Rachel reached in and pulled the guitar out of its case. She walked back to the couch and sat down and placed it over her knee.

At first, all she did was lay her left hand over the strings, and a couple of off sounding notes sounded. Softly, she began strumming the chords to the song she knew Ellie had last played. Rachel closed her eyes and whispered the words.

Rachel remembered how Ellie had asked her to sing it on that first day. She'd been too embarrassed to sing at the time, but now, more than anything, she wished she had. She wished she had sung it loudly, and with as much vivacity and feeling as Ellie did everything in her life.

The sound of the guitar filled the Fleetwood, and Rachel thought she could feel Ellie's soul resonate with hers. Maybe if she played long enough, Ellie would come back, and in the morning, she'd surprise her as Rachel drank her coffee. She'd smile from ear to ear, asking questions about life, talking to her about boys, flying girls, and sea turtles.

But she knew it couldn't happen.

As she let the last chord ring out, Rachel closed her eyes, and she placed her cheek on top of the guitar, and cried. If there was a heaven, she knew Ellie Sanders would be there, and maybe she'd tell her mom about this woman she met at Hunting Island who helped her out for a while. And even though it was only for a short time, Ellie had given Rachel the gift of motherhood, something no man could ever do.

"Thank you, Ellie," she whispered.

And then a tear fell from Rachel's face and dripped down the back of the guitar. She pulled herself away from it and went to wipe the wood dry, and that's when she saw it.

Ellie's surprise.

On the back of John's guitar, beautifully detailed in pastels, was a painting of Rachel and Ellie walking hand in hand along the beach with Riley. Above them, two seabirds flew next to the rising sun, and painted almost transparently on Ellie's back, were a pair of white wings.

At the bottom, Ellie signed it:

—Your Angel

Sometime after Rachel went to sleep that night, she had the dream again. It began like it always had with someone banging on her door. She raced to it as fast as she could to try and catch John this time, or at least see what direction he went. When she opened the door, she caught a glimpse of someone walking away into the thick fog.

"John!" she yelled.

The person stopped and turned around, looking at her with big, sapphire eyes. She smiled at Rachel and waved. But the next instant she turned and ran towards the ocean.

"Ellie wait!" Rachel jumped down and ran after her. Darkness filled her vision, and she slammed into branches and stumps. She reached out with her hands, feeling for the trees, but still, they scratched her arms and stomach, and the underbrush sliced into her shins and thighs. She didn't care. She ran as fast as she could in the woods, stepping on pinecones and rocks, nothing slowing her down.

Rachel finally reached the ocean, and she ran south, frantically searching for her. "Ellie!" she screamed. But, all she heard was the sound of rolling thunder in the distance. "Ellie! Where are you?" she yelled again.

Rachel heard a giggle echo from behind her. She whirled around and saw Ellie. Ellie waved, and then started walking north, away from Rachel.

"Wait! You're going the wrong way." Rachel ran after her. "Ellie, please! Come back!" But Ellie ran too, and soon she slipped away into the thick fog. Rachel tripped over some driftwood that had washed up on shore, but she jumped back up as fast as she could and kept running until she reached the very tip of the island. She called out into the night, but the thunder, now closer, overpowered her voice.

Rain started to come down, and the lightning flashed across the sky. It was then that she saw Ellie standing in the water. "Ellie, wait!" But Ellie didn't. She started swimming out to sea.

Rachel rushed to the water, and then ran through the waves until she had to swim. Another bolt of lightning struck, and soon, the rain poured, pounding Rachel's back as she battled over the waves, taking in mouthful after mouthful of salty seawater. "Ellie!" she screamed, but the thunder was so loud and the wind so strong, Rachel couldn't hear the sound of her own voice.

Rachel's arms pounded into the ocean, and she swam as fast as she could, but she started to tire. The muscles in her legs burned with every kick, and the saltwater stung her skin where the woods had cut her open. Rachel slowed as she rose and fell with the waves.

But then the thunder boomed, and lightning stuck which such ferocity, it lit up the entire sky. That's when Rachel saw the lighthouse in the ocean…and Ellie was swimming right for it!

Rachel used every muscle she had in her body to swim, the waves, now larger and stronger, rocked her body as they came crashing over her. Finally, she reached the rocky base of the lighthouse, exhausted. The sea tried with all of her might to knock her down as she climbed.

Rachel reached the top of the rocks and ran to the lighthouse, but there was no sign of Ellie. She darted around the base, searching for an entrance. On the opposite side, she found a door, but it was locked. She pounded on it, trying to get it to open, but it wouldn't. She took a few steps back, then slammed into it, trying to break the door open, but it wouldn't budge.

The waves began to crash on the top of the rocks, as Rachel kept slamming into the door, time and time again, unable to open it. Another wave crashed over her head, nearly sweeping her out to sea.

Then she looked out over the ocean and saw an enormous wave coming that would surely carry her with it. She took a few steps back and turned her head, watching the approaching wave. Just when it was almost to her, she ran as fast as she could towards the lighthouse door. The thunder clapped and the lightning struck as she smashed into the door with every ounce of energy she had left in her body. At that very instant, the wave crashed down on top of her, bursting through the door, sweeping her inside with a rush of seawater.

The water instantly receded, flowing out through the lighthouse door, and the thunder and the lightning stopped. Rachel stood and coughed, ejecting seawater from her lungs.

"Ellie!" she yelled out. Her voice echoed inside the lighthouse, but no one answered. "John! Ellie! Where are you?"

She walked to the base of the spiral staircase that led up to the lantern room, the railing rusted, and the wooden planks rotted. Wondering if it would support her, she took a few steps, and the boards creaked and moaned under her weight. Her thighs and calves burned with each step, and the cuts along her legs stung as the salty water began to evaporate from her skin.

Exhausted, she crawled up the last remaining steps, finally reaching the lantern room. Breathing so hard she was almost wheezing, she stood up and placed her hands on her knees, catching her breath.

"John," she called out, her voice barely able to call out. "Ellie!" She stood up and looked around for them in the lantern room. "Please say something. Anything."

She opened the door to the platform that circled the lantern room and walked outside, searching. Seeing no one, she started to cry as she circled the lantern room for a second time. She took the rusted railing into her hand, looking out over the ocean, about to scream out, when she heard a thud.

"John!" she cried out. "Is that you? Ellie?"

The lighthouse lantern came on, shooting its light out into the night, brightening the fog, illuminating the platform that surrounded the lantern room. Out of the darkness above, a single sheet of paper floated down and landed next to Rachel's feet. It looked wadded up like it had been thrown away, and then smoothed out by someone. Rachel picked it up and saw that it was a letter, dated the day she returned from the Willers' farm. She began to read.

Dear Rachel,

Words cannot explain how deeply sorry I am for what has happened. As I write this, I realize how wrong I had been to withhold Ellie's illness from you. Though I cannot change the past, and I now know that I will never be able to share your heart with John, I want you to know that I am forever grateful, not only for our time together, but for the love you gave to Ellie. It has meant the world to her.

I know that we only spent a few days together, and though I realize such a short amount of time could be considered insignificant for some, especially considering true love as you have known, for me, they will be days I will always remember.

But what still amazes me, and something I don't think I will never completely understand, is how natural it was for me to share my feelings with you. Not even with Carrie, whom I once thought was the love of my life, have I felt so secure around. I fear I will never find such easiness again.

Tomorrow, I will be taking Ellie home so that I can spend our final days together as father and daughter. There is no question in my mind that I will be lost when Ellie dies, as she has surely been my lifeblood. I know it sounds selfish, but I want to spend every minute that she has left with her. I know you'll understand.

Rachel, I am truly sorry that I have failed you. I hope you can find it in your heart to forgive me someday. It was never my intention to hurt you. My only hope is that perhaps my shortcomings are part of a bigger plan to help you find the life that you lost when John died. So it is that I must let you move on, but know that there will always be a part of me that will never let you go.

Love always,
Marc

After Rachel finished reading the letter, the wind picked up and pulled it from her. The letter hovered over her as she watched it crumple, as if by Marc's own hands, and then ascended into the darkness above.

The lighthouse lantern began to dim until only the darkness and the sound of the waves remained. Rachel turned around and walked through the door to the lantern room. John and Ellie stood at the top of the spiral staircase, holding hands. John smiled at Rachel, then waved goodbye as he and Ellie descended.

"It's a pretty sight isn't it?"

It took a second for Rachel to realize she'd heard a voice and then another second or two to realize it was meant for her.

"The lighthouse," Charles said, pointing to it. It stood about fifty feet away from the bench where Rachel sat. The orange rays of the morning sun glistened off the calm water and lit up the bottom of it. The lighthouse almost looked like it was on fire.

"I suppose," Rachel said, unenthusiastically, not looking up to the lighthouse at all.

Charles sat down next to her. "Beverly wanted me to get your Jeep hooked up. When I couldn't find you at camp, I thought you might be here." He reached down and gave Riley a good petting for a minute or two.

"Did you know," Charles said, "that the Confederate Army blew up that lighthouse during the Civil War?"

She shook her head. She wasn't really in the mood for a story right now.

"Yep," he continued. "They did it to try and stop the Union fleet from approaching during the Battle of Port Royal. Apparently, the fleet was caught up in a terrible storm on their way down the coast, so the Confederates decided to take down the lighthouse to try and hinder them further. It didn't work out too well though, because the Union Navy easily defeated them. After the war, the lighthouse was rebuilt using several iron sections that could be unbolted in case they ever had to take it down or move it. I suppose they learned their lesson."

"Do you know what you're going to do?" Charles asked.

She thought she had. But then last night's dream happened. She had to admit to herself it was a pretty incredible dream. If she believed in them, as if dreams were a message, like some sort of window into the soul, then it would be obvious what to do. But it wasn't. She also knew this entire trip had been so emotional. Every bit of her dream could've been conjured up, some figment or illusion that her mind created. She came here to the lighthouse this morning to see if she could somehow connect the dots.

"I don't know what I'm going to do," Rachel said. "I thought I knew…but now?" She looked up to the lighthouse. "I just don't know." Charles nodded, as if he could help her. He couldn't.

"Well," he slapped his knees with his hands like he always does when he was done with a conversation. "When you get ready, come find me and we'll get that Jeep of yours hooked up."

"Thank you, Charles."

"You're welcome." Charles turned around and took a few steps towards the beach before stopping. "You know, they *did* end up moving it." He pointed up to the lighthouse. "Just before the turn of the century. It's about a mile and a half away from where it used to be. I guess it was a good thing they built it in sections the way they did."

Rachel nodded, but the look on Charles' face indicated that he sensed her mind was elsewhere. "Anyhow, I'll see you later."

"Charles?" Rachel asked quietly, a couple of minutes after he left.

She got up from the bench and looked around, but he wasn't there. "Charles!" she yelled. She grabbed Riley's leash and ran towards the beach, back towards the campsite. She saw him up ahead, walking along the shore, and she ran faster after him. Riley had a hard time trying to keep up.

"Charles!" she screamed again, but Charles couldn't hear her because of the wind coming off the ocean. When she and Riley got closer she yelled again. "Charles!"

Charles spun around, startled. "Yes, Rachel. What is it?"

"Where did it used to be?" Rachel said, her voice winded and frantic.

"Huh? Where did *what* used to be?"

"The lighthouse. Where was it before it was moved?"

"Oh…originally, it was built on the north point of the island. Why?"

"Do you know why they moved it?"

"Well," he said, thinking, "if I remember correctly, it was because the tide kept creeping closer and closer to it. The island was actually getting smaller, so they had to move it. If they hadn't of, the lighthouse would be a few hundred feet out in the ocean by now, just beyond the sandbar. What's this about?"

Rachel looked back to the lighthouse. Then, she gazed over Charles' shoulder, looking north along the shore and out towards the ocean. Things were starting to add up. That's why she couldn't find the lighthouse previously in her dreams. All along, she was searching for it in the wrong place. She was searching where it stands today, instead of the original location.

But she didn't know the lighthouse was originally built on the north point of the island, much less the fact that it had been moved, so how could she have dreamed about Ellie leading her to it? After all, it was only a dream—a desperate illusion that she conjured up in her mind because that's what she wanted to believe. She *wanted* to believe that Ellie helped her find the lighthouse. She *wanted* to believe that Marc had written that letter, that he cared deeply for her. But it wasn't real. It was a dream.

Just then, Rachel felt Riley tug at the leash in her left hand as he started walking. Over the ocean she saw two seabirds flying above the rising sun.

Rachel gasped, and placed her right hand over her mouth. She realized the beautiful scene looked just like the pastel picture Ellie had painted on the back of John's guitar—only Ellie was missing. She remembered how she signed it.

—*Your Angel.*

"Will you do me a favor?" Rachel asked. "Will you watch after Riley for me?" She handed Charles the leash and he took it. Riley barked as Rachel started for the campsite. "His food is in the camper. I'll leave it unlocked. Thank you, Charles!"

By the time Charles had a chance to respond, Rachel was at a full sprint.

CHAPTER FIFTEEN

FORTY-EIGHT HOURS LATER, the wheels of the airplane came to a halt, and Rachel stepped out on the tarmac—somewhere near Machu Picchu, Peru.

EPILOGUE

THE FLEETWOOD'S DOOR OPENED, and a breeze from an early April morning spilled in, mixing with air that had been trapped inside the camper since last autumn. Rachel turned on the lights and walked across the tile floor where a wine glass had once shattered into pieces, and she passed the dinette table where fresh cut flowers had once rustled from the breath of the sea. When she reached the bedroom, she sat on the edge of the bed and opened the top drawer of the nightstand, pulling out a frame.

Rachel looked at the picture of John, and for a moment, she could feel him gazing into her eyes from inside the photograph. She touched the glass with her fingers, tracing the outline of his face. She smiled at him, realizing that she'd been able to keep her promise.

"I love you, John," she said. "I will always love you."

She placed the frame on the nightstand, and then walked to the closet and opened the door. In the very back, sat a simple looking cardboard box that had been there since the very beginning of her trip to Hunting Island last summer. She sighed, then reached in and pulled it out.

Rachel closed the door to the Fleetwood, and the lights from the Jeep lit up her body as she walked in front of it to the passenger side. She got in, and placed the cardboard box on the floorboard behind her, next to another, similar looking box. Riley was sitting on the backseat, and Rachel gave him a quick pet. She looked up at Marc and smiled, then nodded. Marc put the Jeep in gear, and pulled out of his driveway.

The parking lot to the lighthouse was completely abandoned. Marc had worked it out with the park manager to open up early for them, in exchange for a quick photo shoot on the beach with his family.

When Marc, Rachel and Riley reached the top of the lighthouse, the sun was just starting to come up, and for a few moments, they gazed out over the water, taking in the spectacular view.

John Willers and Ellie Sanders never knew one another, but their miracle had brought Rachel and Marc together. Their ashes spilled out from the top of the lighthouse on Hunting Island, and their bodies were forever mixed when Mother Nature's breath swept them up in her clutches and carried them out to sea.

Marc came up behind Rachel, and he put his arms around her. Rachel placed her hands over the top of his, and leaned back against him. As they looked out over the ocean, with the sun's golden rays emanating from behind the clouds that floated along the horizon, they were given the grandest miracle of all.

The baby kicked.

About The Author

http://trippblunschi.com
http://twitter.com/trippblunschi
http://facebook.com/authorTrippBlunschi

Thanks for reading *Hunting For Light.*

If you enjoyed the book, please take a few moments to rate or review it at your favorite literary web site that provides such a service.